'A superb debut… fascinating. The writer has obviously been somewhere or something in the spy business.'

MARCEL BERLINS,
The Times Crime Book of the Month

'Superb: an adventure from London to Lebanon to Syria and the desperate struggle for survival in the face of war and betrayal. Wolff is a new maestro.'

SIMON SEBAG MONTEFIORE,
Evening Standard, Best Books of 2018

'A real original… trembles with realistic detail. I know we'll hear more of him.'

JAMES NAUGHTIE,
BBC Presenter of *Bookclub, Radio Times*

'Best new spy novel by a mile. Don't let this one pass you by if you are a fan of intelligent, complex spy thrillers.'

PAUL BURKE,
NB Magazine, Top Noir Novels of 2018

'Wolff writes masterfully about the badlands of Beirut, suggesting that he knows what he is talking about – plots and counterplots, secret agents, ISIS, Hezbollah, the CIA and our own secret services.'

Literary Review

James Wolff grew up in the Middle East and now lives in London. He has worked for the British government for over ten years. His first novel, *Beside the Syrian Sea*, was published in 2018.

HOW TO BETRAY YOUR COUNTRY

James Wolff

BITTER LEMON PRESS
LONDON

BITTER LEMON PRESS

First published in the United Kingdom in 2021 by
Bitter Lemon Press, 47 Wilmington Square, London WC1X OET

www.bitterlemonpress.com

Extracts on p. 15 from *Tender Is the Night*, by F. Scott Fitzgerald (first published
in *Scribner's Magazine* in four issues between Jan. and Apr. 1934).

p. 224, quote from *The File* by Timothy Garton Ash (1997, Flamingo Books)
© Timothy Garton Ash 1997.

A CIP record for this book is available from the British Library.

ISBN 978–1–913394–51-6
EBook ISBN USC 978–1–913394–52-3
EBook ISBN RoW 978-1-913394-53-0

Typeset by Tetragon, London
Printed and bound in Great Britain by CPI Group (UK) Ltd Croydon, CRO 4YY

For L.
Without whose belief, patience and encouragement
this would never have been written.

PART ONE

Money

INKWELL/129

TOP SECRET

FOIA EXEMPT

FROM: Gatekeeping
TO: Private Office
SUBJECT: Re: Urgent request for INKWELL update
DATE: 28 September 2016

1. You asked to be kept informed about this most sensitive of matters.

2. Events beyond our control brought Operation INKWELL to a sudden and violent conclusion this afternoon. We are doing what we can to restrict knowledge of the case within the Service, but the sight of an officer washing blood off his face in the toilets and trying to re-set a broken nose was unusual enough to have triggered the rumour mill. We must be realistic: staff will be talking. INKWELL has attracted considerable attention because of the regrettable characterization of the perpetrator as some sort of Robin Hood figure. There will no doubt be those advising you

to issue an office-wide bulletin downplaying the incident. My own view is that this would be a waste of time. It is, after all, quite unreasonable to ask a community of spies to accept the official version of things and refrain from further enquiry, even – or perhaps especially – when it is their masters making the request.

3.   Almost four years ago to this day, you set my team the task of identifying the insider responsible for this series of most unusual security breaches, and of collecting sufficient evidence to enable a prosecution. We agreed at the time that the best deterrent to others of a similar mind would be the news that a traitor had been caught and placed behind bars.

4.   It is with regret, now this sorry episode has come to an end, that I can inform you we have been only partially successful. CPS lawyers concluded last week that there is no "smoking gun" in the attached file. Collecting evidence that would stand up in court against an officer with such extensive operational experience proved too much of a challenge, although the CPS does note the existence of a "damning (but ultimately circumstantial) collection of daggers, ropes and candlesticks" within the pages of our INKWELL file.

5.   Despite this, I remain of the firm view that INKWELL has been a model of patient and thorough investigation, and that in August DRUMMOND we have identified a grave threat to the integrity of the British intelligence community. Our strategy of confronting him this afternoon with such a detailed, compelling case is undoubtedly what forced him to accept that the game was up, which in turn

triggered his violent outburst and subsequent dismissal. We may not have got the confession we wanted, and there will be those who continue to argue that other than the Egyptian episode the evidence against him is flawed, but the problem has been dealt with. And there is, I maintain in my old-fashioned way, value in the principle of *keeping things quiet.* I know that in our current incarnation as a counter-terrorism agency we view anything not resulting in a prison sentence as a failure, but the reputational damage ensuing from a prosecution of one of our own officers for multiple breaches of the Official Secrets Act would have been huge. We have avoided that outcome, and for this my staff should be congratulated, not least Lawrence, whom I have sent to St Thomas' A & E to be examined for signs of concussion.

6. There is a wider point here about the insider threat. Over the past year we have been working at full stretch dealing with reverberations from events in Beirut. While we remain some way off understanding the full scale of Jonas WORTH's betrayal, it is surely becoming clear that we must broaden our understanding of what a British traitor might look like in this day and age. Concepts of nationality and loyalty are changing, whether we like it or not. This does not mean that we should take our eye off the traditional threat from states such as Russia and China. They will continue to recruit our officers and steal our secrets. But we must reposition our antennae. Inevitably this will require more staff and more resources, at a time when such things are at a premium.

7.   I attach for your information five key INKWELL documents (report numbers 001, 023, 046, 071 and 128) that span the years 2012 to 2016. These may prove useful as an aide-memoire in your conversations with Whitehall seniors, as they describe the five acts of disobedience and betrayal for which we assess with a high level of confidence August DRUMMOND was responsible. Of course, there may well be others.

8.   Whatever office wags will soon be saying, it is in our view no more than an ironic footnote that WORTH and DRUMMOND were contemporaries at Cambridge.

Charles Remnant
Head of Gatekeeping

2

"You want to keep an eye on your drinking, buddy," said
the man in the seat next to him. "They might call it a
bridge between East and West but these days it's tilting
towards Mecca, if you know what I mean."

Three cups of gin, half a bag of peanuts and two visits
to the toilet to get a better look at the young man four
rows ahead in 34c and August Drummond still hadn't
finished cataloguing everything that was bothering him.
People didn't understand, his neighbour certainly didn't
understand: drinking wasn't *leisure* in this context, drinking was *work*. Drinking was making sense of things, it was
transformation – of details into observations, of random-
ness into patterns. 34c's unfamiliarity with the workings
of an overhead locker, for example, or the old socks and
the new shoes, or the way he took a copy of *Foreign Affairs*
from his bag, peeled off the plastic and raced through
the pages in a matter of minutes, astonished by all those
words. Drinking was alchemy and magic was all around
him. How else could you explain the fact that he was
floating at 35,000 feet?

"Erdogan, now he's your traditional strongman." He
lowered his voice and leaned towards August. "Locks up

journalists, protestors, politicians, even schoolteachers. Make no mistake, he's turning the clock back."

August closed his eyes and imagined the scene: 34c waiting until his mum was watching TV downstairs – a comedy, that way he could hear her laughing, if it was *EastEnders* or *Emmerdale* he wouldn't have a clue until she appeared on the landing. Clothes laid out on the bed, duvet ready to pull down like a shutter if the floorboard creaked. His suit still smelled of vomit from those three months working on nightclub doors but everyone knew the only kind of suit that got stopped at airports was a tracksuit. He'd bought it one size too big, had a whole programme of protein shakes and dawn workouts planned, but the job spat him out ten pounds lighter, what with all the fights, the banter about white boy jihadis, the jokes girls make. He'd use his mum's razor at first light, take the beard off, apply some wax to his new haircut. It'd be a while before it stopped feeling weird putting his hand up and finding nothing there. Lonely Planet, Rough Guide and a second-hand Fodor's from 2007 he bought from a market stall for 50p. Look, what's your problem, the books said, I'm just a tourist. If he'd had the money he would have bought ten, put the matter beyond doubt. I've always wanted to visit the Bosphorus, the Sultan Ahmed Mosque, the thingy Sophia. Built in AD 537, it was originally a Greek Orthodox patriarchal basilica. Beautiful.

"I'm not saying you shouldn't drink, buddy, Istanbul's a party town. I'm just saying you need to be aware of the local customs. I once heard of a fella got chased by a mob for having a couple of Friday beers on the wrong street corner."

August picked up his book and read:

Dick said no American men had any repose, except himself, and they were seeking an example to confront him with. Things looked black for them – not a man had come into the restaurant for ten minutes without raising his hand to his face.

"Live and let live, that's my motto. But they've got a rule for everything, that's the problem, and I mean *everything*: alcohol, pork, women, cartoons – you name it. Who would have thought anyone needed a rule about *cartoons*, for Christ's sake? And heaven help any of us if we cross the line, even if we're not Muslims, even if we didn't know there was a line there in the first place."

A well-dressed American had come in with two women who swooped and fluttered unselfconsciously around a table. Suddenly, he perceived that he was being watched – whereupon his hand rose spasmodically and arranged a phantom bulge in his necktie.

That was it, that was another thing. Deploy in a secret capacity for the first time and you will feel that everyone is watching you. You will see surveillance everywhere; the most innocent of encounters will be freighted with suspicious intent. And if you think everyone is watching you, August thought, you will want to look your best, especially if you are a young man engaged in something you believe to be heroic, and so without knowing it, while those around you are taking advantage of the gloom to loosen their belts and pick their noses, you will adopt the expression you use when wanting to look your best, for Facebook or Tinder – in this case: jaw clenched, brow furrowed, shoulders raised and pushed forward to broaden the trapezius, deltoids and latissimus dorsi. If 34c had been wearing a necktie he'd have been making sure every few minutes that it was just so.

August was fortunate not to have the same problem himself. The impulse to be a hero had stopped on the day of his wife's death, four months earlier, like a frequency jammed by an enemy he didn't know he had but who was suddenly everywhere, armed to the teeth with weapons that made him ache in ways he had never dreamed possible. He refilled his plastic cup. The alcohol might have done its job – he could close the file on 34c, it was no longer his responsibility to worry about such things – but still more transformation was required. That was the problem with alcohol: it didn't know when to stop. In his case it had a long to-do list, filled with items such as grief, regret and anger. It had to turn a tall, bony, broad-shouldered, darkly dishevelled and comprehensively disgraced spy with a slight stoop and hands like shovels into someone prepared to submit calmly to the humiliations of international travel. It had to stop him crying in public.

His neighbour was still talking.

"Don't get me started on Saudi. Men buried up to their waists, women up to their shoulders. Stones gotta be small enough that a couple of them alone won't do the job. Dig yourself out in time, you go free, like the Hunger Games. Those are the rules."

"I can imagine how that'd feel."

"What's that, buddy?"

Other transformations were less desirable: sour breath, loss of appetite, rudeness.

"I'm just saying that I can imagine how it'd feel to be trapped at the waist somewhere I'd give anything to escape from, unable to stop an endless barrage of trivial but deadly —"

"Hey. I don't know what... Stewardess spotted you drinking from your duty-free, that's all I'm trying to say. I've seen people taken to one side at the other end for not much more than that. A friendly warning. Sorry to trouble you."

And then the guilt. He hated other people because he hated himself, or so the grief counsellor had said. Was it as simple as that? Another thing to depress him, the idea that his feelings about the world were nothing more than his feelings about himself, written across the sky.

"That came out wrong," he said, offering his hand. "My name's August. Truth is I can't get by with the booze they give you on aeroplanes, I swear they water it down. Would you like some? Come on, I insist. You keep an eye out for the stewardess and I'll... There we go. Sounds like we'll both need something to fortify us, with all those barbarians crowding the gates of Constantinople."

"I'm not saying... Whoa, steady on there, buddy. Got anything to mix with this?"

"It's expensive stuff, you don't need a mixer. Look here, it's flavoured with liquorice, almonds, grains of —"

"Uh, okay —"

"Tell me," said August, "it sounds like you know this part of the world pretty well."

"I should do, I spend enough time here. Austria to Azerbaijan and everything in between."

"Is there even a country between those two?"

"Are you joking? Hungary, Romania, let's see, Bulgaria —"

"Oh, I thought you meant alphabetically."

"What? No, no, on a map."

"My money's on ambassador, something like that."

"Agricultural equipment, regional sales manager for the second largest firm in the US. Yourself?"

It was the first time he'd been asked that question since being fired just eight weeks earlier. Civil servant? That certainly didn't apply any more. Between jobs, unemployed, on a career break? Former spy under investigation for breaches of the Official Secrets Act?

He watched 34c stand up four rows ahead to check for the third time that his rucksack was still in the overhead locker.

"Me?" he said. "Executive recruitment."

With that, having decided that 34c wasn't his responsibility, August was suddenly working again, thinking about collection, about agents, about deniability, about risk. He was imagining the operation going wrong, as he'd been trained to do, and watching from 35,000 feet the subsequent investigation running its course like a river, and building a dam here and weakening the banks there so the water would run off into unimportant fields. Espionage was a complete system, that was its chief advantage to someone in his position – someone looking for distraction. It required minimum input; he could do it without thinking. It was like one of those vacuum cleaners that works its own way discreetly around a room, taking its time and keeping things tidy, powered by the belief that this way is good and that way is bad, as universal a principle as one of those plugs that will fit any socket.

And he had been good at it, too, before it all went wrong in such spectacular fashion: gifted with tenacity, imagination, natural authority and a gently eccentric manner that put people at their ease. If it is true that most people are defined by a number of "facts" that orbit them like vague moons, like space junk, the ones that circled August, truthfully or otherwise, were as follows: that he found it impossible to sit at his desk for any period of time without removing his shoes and socks; that the bump halfway down his long nose had been acquired during a short but reasonably successful amateur career in the boxing ring; that he had once been formally reprimanded for using what was described in the official record as "language unbecoming a representative of Her Majesty's Government" towards a senior CIA agent; that he'd had a mysteriously aristocratic upbringing, as evidenced by a surprisingly shabby collection of Savile Row suits, the ability to speak Romansh and attendance at a long succession of boarding schools; and that you didn't want to find yourself sharing a crowded lift with him, as he was

19

oblivious to the idea that conversation in public spaces should be limited to the blandly impersonal. More than once a colleague had got out a floor early to avoid a looming question or confession.

All that had changed on the day his wife died. Suddenly *that* was the only thing people knew about him – that and the fact he should be avoided where possible, because of behaviour described in a steadily increasing stream of emails to the personnel department as "taciturn, tearful and prickly", "wilfully reckless to the point of seeking out risk" and "utterly fucking oblivious even to the *idea* of a management chain".

He had written his own reference and used a clean email address for the Istanbul job, to avoid giving his former employers the opportunity to block his application. Not that he would have been too disappointed if it came to nothing. It was hard to imagine a more dead-end role than the one waiting for him on the third floor of a building in Cihangir. Give it a week and he suspected his new boss would find it hard to imagine a more deadbeat employee.

"Executive recruitment?" asked his neighbour. "And what – your firm won't fly you business either?" His brown hair was combed in straight lines like a freshly ploughed field. "Fucking cutbacks. With your height too. What are you, six three, six four? Cheap bastards."

"It's a point of principle with me," said August. "Downsizing, you should try it. Last year I had an epiphany, sold my BMW, the cottage in the country, gave twenty Italian suits to my local charity shop."

"The result being that you don't look like any executive I've ever seen. What, did you sell your washing machine too?"

"One of the perks of being the boss is that no one can tell you what to do."

"*You're* the boss? No offence but you look a bit … what are you, thirty-five? Forty? I thought business prodigies were into yoga, tofu, that kind of thing. Not drinking neat gin from a bag hidden under the seat."

"I only drink when I fly. I'd be a bag of nerves otherwise."

"Okay, it's like that."

"I've got two days of back-to-back interviews followed by an overnight to New York. And perhaps the most difficult client I've ever seen."

"My home town. You recruiting for this client?"

"In theory, yes. In reality, nobody's good enough. Plenty of interested parties, given the crazy bonus structure. They're offering upwards of – well, it's a good package. They keep on saying they're looking for someone a little different. What does that mean, though, that's my question."

"Someone from outside the sector is my guess."

"Who knows."

"Okay, Mister Recruiter, you've got me interested. Tell me more."

"What? Oh, I see. Listen, no offence, but it's a few levels above agriculture salesman."

"Regional sales manager."

"Let me top up your medicine there while Nurse Ratched is out of sight."

"I'm good, thanks. What's the company?"

"Come on, hold your cup still."

"American or European?"

"Can't say, it's all very hush-hush, they're still clearing out dead wood."

"What sector, then?"

"Your firm probably makes a machine for clearing out dead wood, am I right?"

"Finance?"

"No, and it's not farming either, don't worry, your job's safe."

"Industrial?"

August sighed. "Could be."

"If they're paying top dollar it's got to be either —"

"I'm not going to confirm any names."

"That sector's not a million miles from agriculture. As I tell my team, end of the day it's all about men, money, materials and machines."

"Or plants, pitchforks and pesticides in your case."

"You're kidding, right?"

"Tractors then."

"Our bestselling combine starts at half a million, buddy, and I closed on six of them last quarter. Have you heard the saying 'sell snow to the Eskimos'?"

"What? No. I like it, though."

"That's me all over."

"Come on, let's stop talking business and make a toast. To a successful —"

"I mean it, I'll send you my numbers. You on LinkedIn?"

August thought: now's as good a time as any. Quicker and considerably rougher round the edges than he would have liked, but over the years he'd seen too many opportunities missed by people waiting for a perfect opening that never came. Besides, he had to dodge the LinkedIn question somehow.

"I'll tell you what," he said. "See that young guy with gel in his hair? Four rows ahead of us?"

"What? Listen, I've got —"

"In seat 34c. Sell him … this." He picked up his paperback. "Instead of sending me your numbers, show me how good you are. You can't give it away; I want at least ten dollars. Now, this is the important bit. See if you can find out in the process where he's going and what he's doing there. You must be good at reading people in your line of work. He doesn't look like a tourist, does he, in that cheap suit, but he's got all those books stacked up. So what's his story?"

"I'm not going —"

"If it makes it easier, imagine he's an Eskimo."

It was only as his neighbour was lowering himself into 34b with a wink in August's direction and a loud comment about how the view was better from this side of the plane that he suddenly remembered the book had been a gift. Martha had even written an inscription inside the front cover, just one year ago, on the occasion of his fortieth birthday. What else did he have with her writing on it? He had burned all the letters, all the cards, in a bonfire that made his eyes water for days afterwards, the smoke clinging to him like grief. Two parks police had appeared from nowhere and chased him as far as Battersea Bridge. He wished he'd burned the book too – that he'd burned everything. Her clothes filled three bin bags. He tried to leave but found himself sitting at a bus stop outside the charity shop for the rest of the day, watching through the window as other women bought pieces of her. He even followed one of them home, the one who bought her pea-green winter coat, and on the worst nights he was ready outside her house long before her morning walk to Clapham Common Tube station, the change at Stockwell, the Earl Grey with skimmed milk from Starbucks and the arrival at work at nine on the dot. Some evenings there were work drinks or a date. He even saw off a mugger once, snapping his wrist and throwing him into a rose bush while she clutched the coat around her and ran off in tears down the street. That night his house felt emptier than ever.

"Piece of cake, buddy."

"What's that?" August said, rubbing his face. He couldn't swear he hadn't fallen asleep.

"The book, he bought the book."

"What did he say?"

"I told you, he said yes. Ten US dollars for a rare first edition complete with an inscription from the author's wife."

"With a what?"

"Talk about making lemonade. There's some handwritten thing on the first page that makes no sense at all so I improvised —"

"Hang on, let's start at the beginning. What's his name?" asked August.

"Joe or John or something like that."

"Why's he wearing a suit?"

"I don't know, I was trying to sell him a book, remember?"

"Where's he going?"

"Istanbul would be my guess, Sherlock. Listen, I started telling him how Turkey's changed, all the years I've been going there. He comes across pretty nervous, must be the flying thing, like you. He's a tourist – I could hardly shut him up about the places he's going to visit: the Blue Mosque, Topkapı, the spice bazaar. He's from Trafalgar Square in London. Is that good enough? Now listen to this." He leaned towards August and lowered his voice. "I told him the book was a gift from the writer's crazy wife, what was her name, Zorba, Zelda, something like that. Anyway, I spun him a story about her last night in the asylum before she topped herself. Puts the value of the book *through the roof*. His lucky day, though, because I need cash for a cab. You should have heard me, I've got her stuck in the tower of this castle, thunder and lightning outside, she uses a bed sheet to fashion a noose —"

"Okay, I think I've got it."

"Then the rafter breaks but it's too late, she's writhing in agony as the staff rush in —"

"I get the picture."

"They can't bring her back, they search for a suicide note but the only thing they find is this crazy inscription about —"

"Jesus Christ," said August, "I'll give you ten dollars to stop talking too, how about that?"

"Hey, what's your fucking problem?" His neighbour pulled back sharply from their conspiratorial huddle. There was a sudden, audible hush. All around them faces appeared in the gaps between seats like rows of pale fruit in a slot machine. "This was your idea, remember? Don't look at me like that, what, you want to go back to sleep, you want to go back to your *gin*? What am I doing this for if you're just snoozing? Who drinks neat gin anyway?" Even 34c was watching them now. "You want some free advice, you're such a fucking success story, run a comb through your hair, have a shave, have a *shower* for Christ's sake. You know what one of those is?"

On the plus side, had he still been in government service, August would have had to heap praise upon his agent, however talentless and unproductive he'd been. He would have had to apologize and empathize and agree that no one could have done a better job. He would have had to consider a substantial pay-off to keep him quiet.

"Tell you what, buddy," he said, turning away and closing his eyes with a sigh. "You keep the ten dollars and we'll call it quits."

Perhaps there were some benefits to being on the outside after all.

You couldn't call it sleep, what came next. Six cups of gin and his mind was nothing like the map on the screen in front of him, each thought like a country with a name and a border and his mind a pixelated plane, crossing neatly and in the straightest possible line from one to the next. Instead he roamed over a dark and illogical landscape: the songs Martha liked to sing, the last words she had said to him, the way 34c had started four films but not watched more than twelve minutes of any of them. Converts were among the fiercest people August had known – if that's what 34c was. Often it took so much momentum to propel themselves through the thicketed objections of others and over the line that they ended up further than they had ever expected, in a place they had never imagined.

August felt some sympathy with this. In his own way he was a recent convert too. He would have been the first to admit that by that point the unsurfaced road of grief had done its bit to judder loose the nuts and bolts that held him together. But while walking an anti-surveillance route on his way to meet an agent in Green Park, six weeks after her death, ten weeks before he boarded the flight to Istanbul, he saw the same man – late thirties, short brown hair, athletic build, grey business suit – behind him on no less than three separate occasions.

Things weren't quite the same after that, and not just because of what he went on to do. It wasn't that the man in the grey suit had been following him. Rather, August realized that he had seen him three times because they caught the same early train to work from the same exclusive neighbourhood, because they drank the same expensive coffee, because they favoured the same well-maintained streets, because they made the same small choices about when to cross and how fast to walk and when to stop and look at something in a shop window that had caught their eye. It was a poor anti-surveillance route, that's what the tradecraft instructors would have told him – and with some justification. Wrong time of day for that part of town, not enough stops. Your route should be able to defeat pure coincidence, which is exactly what this was. But all August could think about was that in a city of ten million people he was living in a town of thousands, one that might cover every geographical corner of the city but was as separate from it and the people who lived there as it was possible to be. It wasn't political, this epiphany. It wasn't about rich and poor or black and white. It wasn't about class. It was an understanding that despite everything he had done, so much of his life still ran like a factory machine along grooves worn into the air around him by routine and conditioning. It was a conversion to the belief that he wouldn't be free until he smashed everything around him to pieces.

The plane banked and tipped August out of his thoughts. Four rows ahead, 34c began his preparations. He stood up to open the overhead locker and August saw him take a small piece of paper from a pocket of his rucksack, glance at it and then feign a cough in order to put it into his mouth and swallow it. As the wheels hit the runway he covered his face with his hands and moved his lips as though in prayer.

It was all for nothing. Two men in cheap suits stood at the end of the gangway, watching the passengers enter the terminal. August saw the confusion in their eyes, and it registered for the first time that he and 34c were the same height and build, with the same dark hair, even if they were a good ten years apart in age. The two men examined a piece of paper and settled on 34c, following him closely, more concerned with control than discretion. As they turned a corner another three policemen standing to one side looked up and started walking in their direction. At that point even 34c realized what was going to happen. He stopped to tie his shoelace and made a sudden dash for a nearby bathroom door. The two men following him were slowed by the passengers streaming past. When they came out one of them was carrying 34c's rucksack and the other one was holding him by the elbow. There was a red mark on his face and he looked as though he might cry.

August watched the group disappear through a narrow grey door in the corner of the arrival hall. He had to be quick – the bathroom wouldn't stay empty for long. Inside, six cubicles, cisterns behind wall panels, no signs of interference. Anything flushed away would be long gone by now. A padlocked storage cupboard. The ceiling panels were too high to push loose without a broom or a mop handle, even standing on a toilet seat. The bin was a slot in the far wall. He rolled up his sleeve and pushed down through damp bundled paper towels until his fingers touched something. He was surprised – he hadn't expected this. Did he really want it back, along with whatever trouble it was about to get him into?

He waited until he was on the train into the city. The inscription from his wife was still there. And on page 26, newly written in the margin, "Clive Albert Scrivener", on page 173, "Feriköy cemetery, Abide-i Hürriyet Cd.", and on page 210, "b. 1930".

August was working again.

3

It was crazy, what he was planning to do. Whatever he might have told himself, August hadn't *really* stopped to consider the possibility that 34c had been released, or allowed to make a phone call, or persuaded to talk, or that the reason he had been picked up in the first place was that the police knew all along exactly what he was planning to do. His attempt to conceal the name and address of the cemetery in the margins of the book must surely mean something was supposed to happen there, something he wanted to keep secret from the Turkish authorities. And it wouldn't take an expert to point out that the people still on the side of Islamic State in 2016 weren't doctors and engineers and teachers – the early nation builders. They were the ones who had seen the Jordanian pilot, the Yazidi slave markets and the balaclava, and they had thought: yes. It was crazy from every angle. But August, who intended to deal with his grief by throwing himself down every rabbit hole he passed, thought: it's just a dead letter box. How much trouble can you get into with a dead letter box?

The problem was that he was still drunk. He had sobered up a bit by having three cups of coffee at the airport, by eating a cheese sandwich on the train, by not drinking any more gin. He sat on a narrow bed in the two-star Hotel Turkish Delight, a towel wrapped around his waist, his room higher than it was long or wide, like a matchbox tipped onto its end. It looked as though he was made of rib and muscle and shadow. Far above him a dusty bulb swayed, casting barely enough light for him to study the map of Istanbul spread out on the faded black and white floor tiles. He found Feriköy cemetery in the neighbourhood of Şişli and looked for the nearest metro station. It would be safer than taking a bus, given that he was unfamiliar with routes and prices. There should be nothing that linked him to this journey, nothing that stood out – no phone, no bank card, no interaction with a city employee who might later remember a tall foreigner with a stoop who slurred his words and didn't understand the coins in his pocket. He dressed in dark colours, ran a comb through his hair and slipped on the stairs on his way down to the lobby. All that free advice on the plane about drinking and here he was going out drunk. At least gin didn't smell.

A dozen or so cats watched as he emerged unsteadily. His hotel, its once-grand facade the colour of dried mustard, was by some measure the most dilapidated building in a narrow street taken over by coffee bars, fashion boutiques and a costume shop promoting a discount on superheroes. The door slammed shut and a shower of fine grit settled on his shoulders. The rusted scaffolding over the entrance, he understood, was not there to facilitate repairs so much as to catch pieces of falling masonry.

He set off through a series of steep alleyways, on cobbles glazed by rain. Parked cars and vans were tucked in tight along the edges, allowing him the opportunity to step out and see whether anyone was following him. He stood for a while to watch a solitary man working patiently on a piece of furniture in the depths of a dimly lit workshop. As he approached Taksim Square the streets filled with evening shoppers and people returning home. He found a Turkish newspaper on a bench and put it under his arm. Before long he was lost in crowds of commuters and allowed himself to be gently swept along in the direction of the metro. In the train carriage he pulled his woollen hat low and avoided eye contact with other passengers. It was two stops north to Şişli-Mecidiyeköy. He could have walked, but he knew that surveillance teams hated metros at rush hour, and this was an opportunity to take his first deep breath of Istanbul in full flow. From there he doubled back and walked for twenty minutes to the cemetery. He stopped once to buy water, hoping to clear his head, and then at a bus stop, just after rounding a corner, where he consulted the timetable and waited to see if anyone came after him.

The black metal gate was locked from the inside, but he was able to push his arm through the bars to slide the bolt open. August walked quickly into the cemetery in case anyone had seen him. He had no idea how to find the right gravestone. Pale crosses floated in the gloom around him at different angles, as though falling at different speeds. There were trees everywhere he turned, and the ground was uneven. A loudspeaker crackled and a nearby mosque began the call to prayer, and within seconds three or four others had joined in, each one the echo of its neighbour.

August stopped at a noticeboard and read that the cemetery had been a gift to the Protestant powers of the day, and that graves were laid out according to nationality. "Clive Scrivener" certainly sounded more English than Swedish or Dutch. He followed a stone path around the high external wall at a calm and unhurried pace, stopping every now and then to look at a grave and listen intently, and once he knelt down to brush away the plants obscuring a date. He had seen some terrible dead letter boxes in his time – in toilets cleaned hourly by staff who would immediately notice anything different, in the flower beds of a busy London park, in a museum filled with cameras and closed at the weekend. But whoever had selected this one had given the matter some thought. It wasn't just that he was being sent to the English section of an international cemetery – something that would need very little explanation if he was challenged – rather it was that in a busy city this was one of the few places almost guaranteed to be empty. It was somewhere a person could pause for a few minutes, or pull up the weeds that crowded a headstone, or plant a flower or two. Communicating an exact location would be as simple as passing on a locker number in a train station.

It took a while to find it. Second row down from the east wall, IN LOVING MEMORY OF CLIVE ALBERT SCRIVENER, 3RD ENGINEER, WHO DIED AT SEA, 1845–1872. The date was wrong, but the name was a match. August walked the adjoining rows one more time to see if there was a similar name, but ended up in the same place. The stone itself was grey, knee-high, leaning backwards, the earth around it filled with weeds. A crack ran along one edge of the base.

He looked around, stepped off the path and knelt down. The surrounding earth had not been visibly disturbed. Some of the weeds were thick and high enough to conceal an item from anyone walking past. He explored the crack with his fingertips, he ran his hands over the earth, he even shuffled backwards to widen his search. There was nothing there. Had he made a mistake? *Clive Albert Scrivener, b. 1930*, according to the paperback. Why was the date different? There had been plenty of time on the plane for 34c to get it right, and the sort of person who checked on his bag in the overhead locker that many times would have made sure he copied it down correctly. August looked around for rubbish – a chocolate bar wrapper, a cigarette packet – that might conceal a small item. It came to him suddenly. What if it wasn't a mistake? 34c had been cleverer than he had thought. 1930 wasn't a date: it was a time. 34c hadn't planned to collect a message – he was meeting someone. August looked at his watch.

"What are you doing?"

He hadn't even heard the sound of footsteps. He started to turn around.

"Keep looking forward," the man said. His voice was deep and quiet and uninterruptible. And then: "Remember what we discussed."

All that time spent admiring the choice of location and August hadn't stopped to consider there might be a vantage point from which someone could watch the grave.

"I expected you more than thirty minutes ago." The man's accent was Arab but his English was perfect, as though he had lived there at some point. "Your flight was not delayed. So tell me, why are you late?"

August didn't know what to do. He didn't know 34c's name, where he was from, what languages he spoke, whether he had an accent. He couldn't claim to be in the cemetery by chance – the man would have seen the way he had stepped off the path and searched the ground around the gravestone.

"You look ... different," the man said. "Thinner. Older."

August thought quickly. He was either there because he was 34c or because he had taken 34c's place.

"Answer me."

"I haven't been eating." It was the only possible choice. Say as little as possible, he thought, keep your voice low and quiet. "Because of the stress." All those sibilants, it made him sound drunk. And then, in case they had agreed to use a code: "My head's all over the place. I haven't slept for three days, I can't remember whether I'm coming or going."

The man considered his answer in silence. Uninterruptible, unhurriable – August couldn't stop his mind reaching for observations, such as that this was a man profoundly accustomed to being in control.

"You did not follow my instructions," said the man. His voice was louder, as though he had taken a step forward.

"What?"

"Clean-shaven, I said. Shave your beard on the day you travel. What you did, shaving several days ago, it tells everyone you are going somewhere."

"I told people I was getting hassled by the police. Listen, akhi —"

"Have you forgotten this also? No Islamic language. Not with me, not with anyone. You are an ordinary tourist."

"Okay, yeah. Look, I'll shave first chance I get."

"Who shaves on the first day of their holiday? You must learn to think about these things. And your clothes. Dress like a tourist, this is what I said. Put a camera around your neck, carry a guidebook in your hand. If the sun is shining, wear shorts. Why do you have a Turkish newspaper with you? Do you speak Turkish?"

"I found it on the metro."

"This is not a game. If I give you an order, you must obey it without question. I have been doing this for a long time. The only reason I am still alive is because I do not make mistakes. You checked into the hotel?"

"It didn't feel right," he said. "The receptionist was asking lots of questions." A silence. "She wanted to take a copy of my passport," he added.

"This is normal. So where are you staying?"

"I haven't found anywhere yet."

"And your bag?"

"I left it somewhere."

"You left it somewhere? You are being very vague. Where?"

If this had been a training exercise, thought August, right now would have been the moment to put his hand up and admit that he had learned a valuable lesson about preparation.

"Well?"

He had to break the pattern of question and answer. He made a series of fast assumptions: that 34c was an IS recruit, that IS recruits came from difficult backgrounds, that people from difficult backgrounds were sometimes unpredictable. They had tempers, they said the wrong things. For the most part, before leaving for Syria, they had struggled to make a success of life. They hadn't progressed through a series of issues like footholds on a rock face – anti-colonialism, the problem of Palestine, the limits of peaceful demonstration, American atrocities in Iraq – to emerge clear-eyed at the logical summit of extremism. Driving vehicles into crowds and throwing gay people from buildings didn't emerge at the end of an argument that began with the desire for justice. It emerged at the end of an argument that began with an argument – about how everything was shit, about how life was unfair.

"Well what?" August said, raising his voice. "Why all these questions? What's my bag got to do with anything? I'm here just like you said, I've taken big risks travelling, I haven't slept for three days and I want to know what's happening next. What's it matter where my bag is?"

By the time he heard a noise – gravel, a twig, the sound of breathing – the man must have covered half the distance between them. August started to move. A dark shape appeared in the corner of his eye, closer than he would have thought possible, and from nowhere a hand took hold of his neck and forced his head back towards the gravestone. His fingers splayed in the dirt. He felt around for a stone, for a stick, for anything. The man's hand was cold and enormously strong. The only thing August could hear was the wind, searching the trees for something it had lost. He didn't care what happened. This wouldn't be the worst place to die. There had been moments over the past few months when the idea had seemed almost desirable. Here there were trees, there was grass. At dawn there would be birdsong. No doubt there would be those who found it ironic that a traitor should come all this way only to end up in a corner of a foreign field where the dead were laid out according to nationality, as though a sign reading "England" or "Denmark" or "France" meant anything to the people lying all around him. He wondered what her grave was like. He'd never even been to see it.

"Come on," he said. "Get it over with."

It was a long time before the man spoke.

"I have money and a phone for you," he said. He took his hand from August's neck. "Check the phone at least two times a day, morning and evening. Not from your hotel, go somewhere busy. You will not use it for anything else. Is that clear?"

"What about the thing I'm here for?" August said. At the bottom of one rabbit hole and he started looking for another. "Don't make me sit around waiting for —"

"It will be a few days, no more than that," the man said softly. It sounded as though he was smiling. "Until then, remember what you are: a British tourist in Istanbul. You have no religious affiliation, you are not political, you do not possess any strong opinions. Explore new places, learn new things. Take a ferry ride on the Bosphorus. Have you heard of Atatürk, of Mimar Sinan, of Suleiman the Magnificent? There is a place in the Grand Bazaar where they make excellent coffee, where you can sit in peace and listen to workmen tapping at brass ornaments two streets away. See if you can find it. Discover the best borek and tell me where it is made. Remember to check the phone. You will hear from us when we are ready."

A few steps, first on gravel and then on soft earth. When August turned around he saw that a mobile phone and five hundred lire had been placed on the other side of the path.

4

INKWELL/001

TOP SECRET

FOIA EXEMPT

SUBJECT: Operation INKWELL

DATE: 1 October 2012

1.   The purpose of this Note For File is to record the opening of Operation INKWELL. The operation will be run by the Gatekeeping team, and its objective will be to identify the member of staff responsible for the leak described below.

2.   On 30 September 2012 a Sunday newspaper published an article under the headline "Terror Sheikh in Prostitute Love Triangle" that claimed Islamist cleric Abu YAHYA Al Biritani @ Nigel WILLIAMS (METAL CUSHION of Operation FOSSILDOM) was a regular client of two Walthamstow-based prostitutes. The article included quotations from "a top-secret phone call" between the cleric and one of the prostitutes that had allegedly been handed to the paper by "a government insider".

3.   The newspaper's website contains a link to a 22-second excerpt of the phone call. We have confirmed it is genuine. The excerpt contains a brief negotiation over the price of a particular sex act and general discussion about the scheduling of the appointment. As the total call duration was 7 minutes and 16 seconds, much of which was taken up with conversation of a sexually explicit nature, we assess that the "government insider" is likely to have only given the newspaper the 22-second excerpt, as we can see no reason why the editor would have refrained from using some of the more colourful passages.

4.   METAL CUSHION has been a priority SOI for investigators for the past three years, and remains a highly effective radicalizer of young and vulnerable men in the south-east.

5.   We can assume that knowledge of the recording was widespread within the intelligence agencies and counterterrorism police because of its sensational nature. In recent years, high-profile investigations such as ELVEDEN have highlighted the unofficial relationships that exist between some police officers and journalists – relationships that, while dwindling in number, remain a cause of serious concern to this team. However, preliminary enquiries indicate that although a written transcript of the call may have been shared widely with police partners, only those within this building have access to the recording itself. For this reason, we are treating it as an internal breach and will investigate accordingly under the name Operation INKWELL.

6.   We are focusing our early efforts on creating a list of those staff members with the technical access required

to obtain a recording of the call. We have also begun to review vetting files for any mention of this subject, such as an expression of frustration at the way that METAL CUSHION has been able to get away with his radical-izing activities for years, or for any instance of an officer reporting a colleague making unauthorized contact with a journalist. Warrantry to allow further investigation of the journalist in question is currently with the Home Secretary.

7. One final note on motivation. There are aspects of this leak that raise questions. Why did the "government insider" choose to provide a recording rather than a written tran-script, given that this has put them at greater risk of being identified? If they provided this material for financial gain, why did they only hand over a partial excerpt of the call? Why did they not include the most sensational segments? We remain open-minded about these questions. We also remain open-minded about the possibility that this is a leak of a non-traditional nature, and that the motivation of the officer in question was a desire to harm the reputation of METAL CUSHION and degrade his ability to radicalize impressionable young men rather than a straightforward wish to make money.

5

August couldn't remember much about his new employer. He couldn't even remember what the company was called, other than that it was something to do with chess. Castle Communications? Knight Strategies? Bishop was too obviously Christian, king and queen a little old-fashioned, pawn out of the question for a number of reasons. When he finally turned up at the address he'd been given, one day after arriving in Istanbul, there wasn't a sign outside the building as he'd hoped, just a walk up three flights of what appeared to be a run-down residential block to a reinforced door opened by buzzer after a wait of several minutes, and inside a four-bedroom apartment, the furniture pushed into corners and covered with plastic sheeting. Nobody was waiting for him. In one room three Syrian men were talking loudly about a video they were watching on a laptop, and in another a man was shouting in Turkish into a mobile phone. Wires hung from the ceilings and a puddle of grey water sat in the middle of the floor.

"Can I help you?"

A young man wearing a cream-coloured linen suit and a pair of dirty white running shoes stood in a doorway off to one side.

"I'm August. It's my first day."

"William." He offered a delicate hand. He was in his early thirties, with thinning shoulder-length hair so blonde it was almost white. "Beatrice is on a call with London. Wasn't she expecting you … earlier?"

"Really?" said August. Three hours earlier, to be exact, but he had either slept through his alarm or forgotten to set it. After he had woken up and realized how late it was, it had still taken him over an hour to get out of bed, and even then the only real reason for moving was to get away from room 18 in the Hotel Turkish Delight. At one point between three and four in the morning he had sat upright in bed and considered going down to the reception desk to complain about the cockroaches or the rattling window or the thin mattress and demand to be moved. Not that any of those things bothered him in the slightest. He just didn't think they would take him seriously if he complained about a ghost. He couldn't blame them. And it wasn't as though he had seen anything, or heard any inexplicable noises. It was just that everywhere he went she was both there and not there, a presence and an absence, and he didn't know any other way to describe that.

"Beatrice is more than a little annoyed, I won't lie," William was saying. "Brace yourself for a telling-off. She said the mobile number you gave her wasn't working. She even had me call your hotel to see if you'd checked in." Which explained the loud knocking at his door that morning, not that August had paid it much attention. "I don't know if there's anything for you to do until she's free. Beatrice likes to be the one to set the scene – you know, manage people's first impressions. She'll want to make sure you understand that all of this" – he held up his hands to take in the unpainted walls, the wires and the puddle – "is evidence of a company moving fast and breaking things. A PR woman to the ends of her fingers and toes. Do you know what you're going to be doing?"

I don't even know what the company's called, August almost said, stopped only by the mention of PR. He had to start thinking about such things – he had applied for the job, after all, and there would be little sense in getting fired on day one.

"Not a clue," August said. "Beatrice is the boss then, is that right? My phone interview must have been with her."

Three o'clock in the afternoon, four weeks earlier, an autumn London downpour outside. August had been sitting in his dressing gown and thinking about a drink when the phone rang. He had forgotten about the interview, arranged during a brief period of engagement with the outside world that had also seen him speak to his parents, do his laundry, take out the rubbish and discover that he was days away from having his electricity cut off. He thought about letting it ring. Once he heard who it was he thought about telling Beatrice that he didn't know anything about distribution channel evaluation, or that he was emotionally incapable of holding down a job, or that he'd made up so many aspects of his application that it was basically worthless. None of those things would have made any difference, he suspected. "A job like this will look great on your CV," she had said almost immediately, her desperation audible down the line. "Managing budgets, significant stakeholder interaction, the opportunity to really make your mark. And if you want to return to government at a later stage, well, the embassy here is our principal customer, involved on a weekly basis and keen as mustard on the work we're doing. You could easily go back in but at a significantly higher level." I very much doubt *that*, thought August. He wondered how much trouble the company was in to be this short of staff. "The private sector would bite your arm off too," Beatrice added quickly, in case she'd misjudged her pitch. "Not many people in strategic comms have such a unique opportunity to experience the digital front line. I like to describe our little frontier outfit as a sort of press office for the moderate opposition in Syria, that's my shorthand for it – promoting their leaders, highlighting their military successes, showing them to be a force for good. It's all completely above board, funded by the British government's conflict and stability fund. In practice that means videos, military reports, radio broadcasts, news and magazine articles and social media content, all pushed out into the regional and global marketplace. What do you think?" It might have been the only question she'd asked.

William took out a packet of cigarettes. "Did Beatrice explain what we do?" he asked.

"Mmm. Propaganda."

"She doesn't like us using that word."

"I bet she doesn't," said August.

William peered at him. "What … um … what did you do before this?" he asked, lighting his cigarette.

Now that he was in the propaganda business, August thought, he should be able to do a better job than the plain truth, which was that he had been doing a fair amount of sitting, a lot of walking, too much drinking and nowhere near enough sleeping.

"Civil service," he said.

"Ah, got it – another spook. You might know our new contact at the embassy, then, a guy called Larry. A real charmer. Arrived here last week."

Larry? It couldn't be him, unless he had rebranded himself. Even then…

William's phone beeped.

"She's heard us talking," he said. "She wants me to make sure you don't disappear. That happens a lot – people turn up and then they disappear. One chap was arrested, someone else was attacked on the street outside. Plenty of others have just gone home." He lowered his voice. "Beatrice isn't the easiest boss. Let me get you a coffee as an incentive to stay." Stepping carefully around the puddle, he led August into the kitchen. "So what brought you out here?"

An easier question to answer. He needed a job. He needed money. He needed to do something that reduced the time available for sitting, walking and drinking, something that made him hungry enough to eat and tired enough to sleep. The last time he had slept for more than three hours in one stretch had been in an Antwerp hotel, four months earlier, at the end of a long day of discussions with a twenty-four-year-old dual British–Belgian national who had returned from Syria after seeing his best friend executed by IS for desertion. It was a day that had also seen August's wife knocked off her bicycle at a busy junction near King's Cross and pulled under the wheels of a ten-wheel lorry carrying a delivery of lilies from Aalsmeer. Not that August had known anything about it until the following morning. Hospital staff had called a number for his office they had found on her phone, but the switchboard operator, accustomed to fending off callers asking vague questions about what kind of office it was and who worked there, hung up before they could grasp what had happened.

He didn't want to see anyone after that. He stopped answering the doorbell, ignored calls from his colleagues, dealt with his parents by letter. He informed the coroner's office that he wouldn't attend the inquest and then slipped into the back row a few minutes after it had started. By that point he was already familiar with the facts of the case. He had read the police report, spoken at length with the doctors who had operated on her and stood at the junction near King's Cross every morning for a week, for at least an hour each time, watching the rush hour traffic roar and stutter. His job had taught him that information on its own was of little value, since so much of it turned out to consist of theories, allegations, promises, rumours, speculation or lies. He wanted context, not information. He wanted the driver.

The man was tearful as he gave his testimony, describing a journey from Hull, a six o'clock start, the fifteen-minute stop at Wetherby services, his route through London and the way the cyclist had appeared from nowhere, slipping on the wet road and disappearing from sight somewhere between the third and fourth axles. It was like someone had flashed a torch in his side mirror, he said, a burst of yellow jacket that tugged his head to the right and then suddenly was gone. He didn't know what was happening until a pedestrian started screaming.

Afterwards August saw the driver on the pavement across the road, smoking a cigarette and talking on his phone. He was only metres away when the man laughed. He didn't stop to consider that he might have been laughing at something funny his child had said, or out of relief that it was all over. So much for wanting context. Within a week August had flown to Leipzig. The driver had been taken off the road by his company after the accident and given a temporary position in the sales office. Using a different name, August called from a payphone and made an appointment, saying that he represented a large UK manufacturer and would appreciate a discreet chat to explore whether the German company could provide a cheaper service than their local rivals. In his hotel would be preferable, to avoid the risk of being seen visiting their office. He had learned by then that the driver had an old conviction for assault and three arrests for domestic battery, that he was fifty-eight, left-handed, ten kilos overweight and kept a hammer in the glove compartment of his Skoda, which was in the garage after having all its tyres slashed late one night. August chose a hotel not far from the small apartment the man shared with his elderly mother, in the expectation he would walk home from their early evening meeting through a nearby park.

The man was uncomfortable, apologetic about his faltering English and ill-suited to his new role as salesman. He couldn't understand why this client had asked for him by name. A workman set about replacing a broken window and a cold wind quickly emptied the lobby of other guests. He sat there in his coat, wondering what to make of this shabby Englishman, so unlike other people he had met in the haulage business and with little interest in the subject beyond a few cursory questions about routes and costs. Even when he got his figures mixed up the Englishman didn't seem to mind at all. He just stared in that way he had, his large hands gripping his knees and his eyes watering in the icy wind that rushed in through the broken glass. Winter in Germany can be brutal if you're not used to it, he thought. And the English are so soft.

"August?" said William. "Everything all right?"

"What's that?"

"I was just wondering what made you come out here."

"Oh, a chance to be on the digital front line," he said, pulling himself together. "Who wouldn't want to work for … here." He really needed to find out what the company was called before it became a problem. "If Beatrice is the boss then the company's name must have been her idea – I'm still trying to decide whether I like it or not."

"It's not everyone's cup of tea. At least it's not called something strategies."

"What do you think?"

William shrugged. "I worked for a company called FGM Solutions once."

"This one strikes me as a difficult name for non-English speakers to pronounce."

"What?"

All right, he was running out of ideas. One last try.

"Beatrice used a good analogy about the digital space being like a chessboard where all the pieces move however they want."

"And I thought I'd heard all her shit analogies."

"Is that where the name comes from?" asked August.

"How so?"

"The chess thing."

"What chess thing?"

A woman appeared at the kitchen door. She was in her late forties, short and plump and wearing a pair of oversized spectacles with red plastic frames. Her short blonde hair was cut into the shape of a helmet.

"Walk with me, August," she said, smiling broadly. She arranged a purple silk scarf around her neck. "I'm heading out to a meeting, but five minutes will have to be better than nothing." She turned to William, her smile still in place. "Please check your emails. There's a small crisis of your own making to be dealt with before you go home."

She led August out of the apartment into the hallway, closed the reinforced door and lowered her voice. "I didn't want to do this in front of William, but I checked my emails and it *was* nine o'clock you were supposed to be here. You know that, don't you?" August started to reply but she cut him off: "Ssh, my turn to talk." He wondered when his turn had come and gone. She walked down the stairs, speaking loudly over her shoulder. "It's important that I set the scene for you, August, make sure we're on the same page from day one." Her heels clattered on the stone steps. "The key message is this: I want you to feel good about being here. These are very exciting times. There are opportunities appearing at an incredible rate and it's my job to make sure that we identify, seize and exploit those opportunities. There is also a lot of money floating around, a hell of a lot – it's what happens when governments want to do something but don't have a clue what that something should be. And who can blame them? Islamic State is collapsing, the Kurds are seizing territory, the opposition is splintered and Assad looks like he'll be here until long after we're all gone. It's difficult for anyone to find answers in all of that. Are you following me?"

"Literally and figuratively," August said.

Beatrice threw a puzzled glance over her shoulder. "Good. Where was I? Yes, enormous implications for our national security but no obvious military solutions. What does that mean? It means that it's up to us to establish a digital toehold in Syria that will give the government the ability to expand back into the strategic space as and when the opportunity arises. Now, for us to get into pole position in this very competitive bunfight it's going to take aggression, imagination and determination. What it's *not* going to take is turning up three hours late or having a day off to visit museums. Don't look at the wires and the puddles and come to the conclusion that you can get away with behaviour like that here, August. Don't come to the conclusion that we're not a deadly serious outfit. Mark my words, the surest sign of a company in its death throes is freshly painted walls, fancy artwork and a long-term contract with a landlord. What you see here, on the other hand, is a company moving fast and breaking things. Bottom of our priority list is making ugly stuff look pretty for the sake of it."

"And I thought you were in PR," said August. "Isn't that all about making ugly stuff look pretty for —"

"There's a danger that we might get off on the wrong foot," said Beatrice. She turned to face him as they reached the last stair, her smile gone. "I want to like you, August, I really do. And your application was very impressive. But there's something not quite right in the air. So let's write today off, how about that? A freebie, on me. Go back to your hotel, find someone to iron your shirt, have a shave, get a good night's sleep and we'll start over at nine on the dot in the morning with a brand-new attitude. We'll pretend this conversation never happened. Is that accept-able? Any questions?"

"Just one," said August. "Since we'll be starting from scratch in the morning. What's the company called?"

6

August found a local bar, sat at a corner table with a view of the door and quickly drank three glasses of beer. He took his time over the three after that. The only other customer was a tourist smoking a hookah in the doorway. He made a precise adjustment to the coals and drew deeply on the pipe, making the water bubble, as though he was conducting a science experiment and had inserted himself into the process. August checked his phone. He wanted the man from the cemetery to call. He was dimly aware that the course of action he was considering was not sensible, just as someone waking at night might be dimly aware of a shadow in the doorway – in this case a shadow with a voice but no discernible edge, a shadow that bristled with competence, purpose and violent energy. The sensible thing would have been to call the embassy and hand over responsibility to them. Let them identify him, let them establish what he was up to and how to stop him. But distraction from grief was August's only objective, and momentum the sole principle guiding his decisions – he was like a stone skimming across a body of water, willing himself to keep going, aware that the moment he stopped moving he would begin to sink. If anything, he wanted to go faster.

The phone rang just before seven o'clock.

"You are alone?"

That voice again, deep, calm and transmitting on a frequency all its own.

"Yes."

"You slept last night?" the man asked.

"A few hours."

"In a hotel."

"It'll do for now."

"Which one?"

"I don't think I should say on the phone. You know, in case someone's listening."

A brief pause as the man absorbed August's refusal to answer the question. He had constructed the barest of legends. He had no real information about 34c to work with, and so he had taken elements from those IS recruits he had met in the course of his career, particularly those who were converts, and decided that in his case there had been problems with his parents and run-ins with the police, that there had been drink at one point and drugs at another, that he was impatient, didn't appreciate being asked questions and lost his temper more quickly than anyone around him liked. Being awkward was the key to survival. It would allow him the freedom to refuse to answer questions or follow instructions. Just as importantly, it would make him look less like a spy. What kind of spy was argumentative and contrary and always spoiling for a fight?

"What did you do today?" the man asked.

"Just looking at stuff really."

"Where did you eat?"

The basic tool of the interrogator, asking questions that required a precise answer.

"I found a McDonald's," he said. "By a metro station, Sultan something."

"Sultan Ahmed. You did not want to try Turkish food?"

"I don't like kebabs."

"You are in the wrong country."

"Am I?" He sighed loudly. "You tell me. I didn't think I was here for the food."

August was in a hurry; he had to keep pressing. He might have put questions of personal risk – of kidnapping, of injury, of death – to one side, but he couldn't ignore the possibility that something might happen to bring all this to a sudden end. That was what concerned him most. MIT was a competent intelligence agency; they would have sources, they would have SIGINT. It was only a matter of time before they realized something was going on, and when they did, they would put a stop to it immediately. August had to move things forward before that happened. It was also possible he had misunderstood the situation. Over the years he had encountered plenty of hustlers looking to spin a few threadbare details into something that glittered, and there were any number of people who had tied up agency time with talk of dirty bombs and red mercury that came to nothing. The trade in secret information attracted more than its share of charlatans and liars. The man at the end of the phone might belong in that category, or he might be a fantasist, or a facilitator whose network had been degraded to the point where it no longer functioned. August didn't want to consider these possibilities. If any of them were true, all he would have left was a job he didn't want, a hotel room he couldn't sleep in and a paperback he couldn't bring himself to open. The thought was intolerable.

"If you prefer Syrian food," the man was saying, "there is a restaurant —"

"Can we talk about what's going to happen next?" August said. "I'm ready to get moving. All that time thinking about getting here and now my head's like a can that's been shaken up."

"— a restaurant in the Grand Bazaar. All the food there comes from the city of Gaziantep, near the border, so it is a mixture of Turkish and Syrian cooking. Now tell me – Topkapi, Hagia Sophia, Sultan Ahmed, this is what everyone does on their first day in Istanbul. Which one did you visit?"

"Who cares? What are we talking about this for?"

"I understand your frustration, but you need to be patient. These things take time —"

"I haven't got time," August said, raising his voice. "I've come all this way... If you can't help me, I'll go somewhere else."

"Where will you go?" The man chuckled. "Everything is under control, everything is progressing correctly. You cannot hurry this. If you act too quickly it will lead to mistakes and then —"

"I don't care, do you understand? I'm not sitting around visiting museums and eating kebabs while you get your act together. We both know what I came here for. Now tell me what's going to happen next or that's it, I'll disappear."

The driver of a delivery truck leaned out of his window, less than twenty metres from where August was sitting, to wave his arm and shout at the car in front. There was a burst of horns like the beginning of a scale. When the noise finally died down August realized the man on the phone was laughing.

"I did not realize you were so ... excitable," he said finally. "Like a child. It is funny how a person can seem different when you speak with them directly. We had an agreement, you are correct. You come here and we arrange your immediate travel across the border. We have done this hundreds of times for other visitors. So why am I asking you to wait? I did not intend to discuss this with you at such an early stage, and especially not on the phone. But the truth is that something has happened – an opportunity, let us call it that, an opportunity that will never appear again, an opportunity that one way or another we are determined to seize. I am trying to decide whether you are the right person for the task – this is the reason for the delay. I admire your passion, this is true, but it will not be enough on its own. It will be very difficult. It will demand courage and skill and intelligence, but if everything goes according to plan it will make a big difference to the success of our ... our company. Do you understand what I mean?"

"Whatever it is," August said, "I'll do it."

"You do not want to know more?"

"Of course I do. But you'll tell me at the right time."

"One minute you are impatient, the next minute you say you can wait. I am not sure what to make of you."

"Can we meet —"

"Be quiet and listen. You must understand that when you cross the line into this world, into my world, everything changes. The rules that you have followed all your life do not exist here.

"Let me teach you a simple history lesson. The janissary bows his head before the vizier, the vizier bows his head before the sultan and the sultan bows his head before Allah, no one else. The janissary was a young man from the Christian West, hundreds of years ago, who became first of all a Muslim and then an elite soldier in the Ottoman army. He left behind his family and embraced a life of discipline and war and service. It is strange, don't you think, that the best soldiers, the soldiers the sultan trusted with his life, were the ones who came from Europe, from the heartland of his enemies? They say he loved them so much that he would come to the barracks dressed in their uniform to receive his pay alongside them. In battle they would fight with the passion and ferocity of a hundred soldiers.

"Now close your eyes. Feel the rough wooden handle of an axe, feel its weight, run your finger along the blade. Listen to the battle cry of your brothers all around you. When you swing your arm the axe flashes suddenly in the sunlight and the sand around your feet turns dark with the blood of your enemy. Can you imagine anything more beautiful?"

He was quiet. August wondered if he was still there. He pressed the phone against his ear.

"My friend, you have come home." The man's voice was soft and distant as though he was walking away. "You are among your people. Do you understand this? You do not need to be angry with me. I love you. We all love you. But you must be patient and you must be disciplined. Like the janissary you must obey your vizier. Everything else will follow from this. Check the phone tomorrow and make sure you are not followed to your hotel. Is this clear? Good. Now go."

7

FILE EXCERPT FROM INVESTIGATION INTO AUGUST DRUMMOND

INKWELL/023

TOP SECRET
FOIA EXEMPT

SUBJECT: Possible second INKWELL incident
DATE: 11 October 2013

1.   Lawrence – see below. Do we think this might be something
      of concern to the Gatekeeping team? It's the transcript
      of a call that took place yesterday between the Russian
      foreign ministry and their embassy in London. It's been
      a full year since the cleric/prostitute tabloid recording
      leak, and we've been talking about closing the investi-
      gation in the absence of any other possible INKWELL
      incidents during that time. But there's something in this
      that strikes a familiar note to me – of an unidentified
      person trying to set things right, trying to deliver an
      unorthodox kind of justice. If this is one of our officers
      taking independent and unauthorized action against a
      Russian diplomat in London, we've got a real problem

on our hands. Have a look and let's discuss when you've got a few minutes.

Charles

BEGINS

— Caller introduces himself as Arkady IVANOV from the "ministry" in Moscow. He congratulates Sergei POPOV on his promotion to Second Secretary. He says he is calling to discuss the increase in POPOV's diplomatic allowances. Brief conversation about whether housing allowance will be affected and the weather in London.

— POPOV interrupts to say that he recognizes IVANOV's voice. He recalls meeting IVANOV previously at MISHKA's house. [By context a former colleague.] Conversation about MISHKA and his recent health problems.

— POPOV says that his wife will be happy about the new allowance because London is so expensive. He says she isn't at all happy about the circumstances of his promotion because of the rumours in the embassy about VASILIYEV [by context Mikhail VASILIYEV, former Second Sec.].

— IVANOV says that VASILIYEV arrived back in Moscow last week and is storming around all the ministries telling everyone that he was set up by the British special services. VASILIYEV is calling the ambassador an "idiot" for falling into "their" trap and sending him home. IVANOV says that whatever the circumstances it is very foolish to make such comments about an ambassador. He asks POPOV what really happened.

— POPOV says that the embassy mechanic found a bag of [literal] "gay sex drugs" hidden in the tyre well of VASILIYEV's car. Laughter. POPOV says the ambassador terminated VASILIYEV's posting the next day. More laughter.

— POPOV says that he heard from ALEXEI [possibly Alexei GRIGORIN, Assistant Naval Attaché] that according to VASILIYEV he had driven to an evening meeting outside London the day before and that when he came out of the hotel a "beautiful young woman" stopped him to ask for directions. VASILIYEV didn't think it was odd until he got back to his car and found that the front window had been smashed and a small amount of money taken from the glove compartment. The next day he took the car to the embassy mechanic to have the window repaired. VASILIYEV said to ALEXEI that the woman was trying to delay him and that "your guys" should track her down. When ALEXEI asked how on earth they should do that, VASILIYEV said that she was wearing a green coat. Prolonged laughter.

— POPOV says that between the two of them it's better that VASILIYEV is gone. He says that VASILIYEV was stopped three times last month by the British police for driving while drunk. One time he was going "over seventy" and almost hit a child. POPOV said "he" would have been arrested if he hadn't been protected by diplomatic immunity.

— IVANOV says that whether the accusation is true or not VASILIYEV's career is over. He said he has heard "they" might send "him" to Cyprus or Australia.

— General discussion about the merits of Cyprus and Australia and the different allowances connected to each posting. POPOV asks IVANOV to let him know when the current Second Secretary in Washington is thinking of leaving.

ENDS

8

Youssef was the last candidate on the list. He was wearing a dirty white shirt under a brown tweed jacket, and his red tie, which reached to the middle of his small belly, was patterned with images of the *Playboy* bunny.

"I apologize for my tardiness," he said, offering a hand that trembled. A scar marked the inside of his wrist. "Unavoidable traffic circumstances."

August had already interviewed six other candidates, all of whom had been professional, enthusiastic and credible. Some had experience of media work, others had degrees in business administration from Syrian universities. One of them, a forty-six-year-old former bank manager from Aleppo, had managed similar projects at a rival American-owned company for two years, and was only leaving because of what she described in her excellent English as "a wish to broaden her exposure to the European client base". Three of the six were older than August.

In a long and rambling conversation about his duties, Beatrice had asked him to be the "centre forward" on a "bold and ambitious" project to set up an "opposition media centre", which she insisted on referring to as "the hive". Her vision was that a core management team would continue to run the company from the current office but that much of the media work – recording video and audio material for broadcast, managing Twitter and Facebook accounts, training new and existing staff, producing written copy for regional publications – would relocate to a new, larger site in a cheaper neighbourhood. The early part of the process had been depressingly bureaucratic. According to Beatrice, the funding had been approved in principle by the embassy but needed tidying up on paper, and so August's first few days in the office had been spent producing a draft budget, a feasibility study and an impact assessment. It had left him feeling close to despair, all of it – the tedium of the paperwork, Beatrice's demands for a progress update every few hours, the way the candidates all saw the opposition as a new economic sector capable of providing them with a secure, long-term career.

"Welcome to Endgame Consulting," said August, picking up a CV from the pile in front of him. "Shall I explain what we're looking for?"

Youssef nodded vigorously and adjusted his tie. He was in his late thirties, with pale-brown eyes, stiff upright black hair and a neatly trimmed beard. He might have been considered handsome, but there was something about his long neck and the gaps that appeared between his teeth when he smiled which had the effect of knocking that perception off by a few degrees.

"We're looking for a project manager," August said. "What that means, in this case, is someone to set up a new media centre. It's a pretty big task. We'll need to choose a suitable location, negotiate with the landlord, get the necessary building and decoration work done, source technical equipment and coordinate the logistics of moving people in. Does that all make sense?" Reading from the notes Beatrice had given him, he added: "The successful candidate must demonstrate an understanding of the technical aspects of setting up a recording studio as well as a proven track record of meeting deadlines, managing a budget, working as part of a team and over-coming obstacles."

"Yes, I can do all of these things," said Youssef.

"It says on your CV that you were an English teacher in a school."

"Ah, this is the wrong CV. I have a better one."

"What do you mean?" asked August.

"More suitable for this position."

"A man after my own heart. So what did you do?"

"My job was project manager."

"That's handy. So you weren't a teacher?"

"No."

"Can you tell me about the project manager job you did?"

"Well, it was a very busy job." He paused to see whether this would be enough. "Very, very busy. With lots of respon-sibility. A staff of many people, perhaps twenty or thirty or possibly many more. My goodness, they admired me very much." Youssef leaned back in his chair and chuckled to buy himself some time, a panicked look in his pale eyes. He ran a trembling hand over his threadbare beard. "I started early each morning with a positive mental atti-tude, took no more than ten minutes for my lunch, and

I would work late in the evening, sometimes until six o'clock. Tireless. There was plenty of visiting locations, choosing, logistics, technical equipment, decoration – all these things you mentioned. In particular I am very good at decoration."

"What was the project?"

"The project?"

"What were you doing all that work for?"

"For a very successful company."

"That's good to hear. But what was the project, what specifically were you working on?"

"Many, many things. Big projects, small projects." He swung his hands together and apart as though playing an accordion. "All of them successful."

"Any experience of film in all that successful work?"

"My goodness. Extensive."

"Such as?" August asked.

"Action, thrillers, detective. These are my favourites."

"What I mean is, have you made any films?"

Beatrice appeared in the doorway. Ignoring Youssef, who had leaped to his feet and extended his hand, she said, "Larry has just called to say he's on his way in to discuss the proposal for the hive. He must have flown in from Ankara this morning. He tells me you two know each other. Why didn't you mention that? It could be useful to us that you're an old friend of his."

So Larry *was* Lawrence. August shrugged. "I'm not sure I'd use those words to describe our relationship."

"We might have to make this one of your objectives. It's Larry's job to advise his seniors on whether to renew our contract, so having the inside track could be very valuable indeed. Don't pull a face, August. All sorts of people become friends overseas who wouldn't go within a hundred metres of each other back home."

"I can't imagine he'd be particularly keen on the idea."

"Well, that just goes to show how wrong you can be. He was surprised to hear that you're out here but said he's looking forward to catching up. He's probably a bit lonely. Is he single too? Get in there before he finds a girlfriend on the diplomatic circuit. Two young bachelors on the prowl. I'll even let you expense it, as long as you deliver results."

Youssef finally withdrew his hand. Beatrice looked him up and down and frowned slightly when she saw the *Playboy* pattern on his tie. Turning to August, she said, "You can probably cut this one short. No point wasting anyone's time. Do you want to pop into my office in, shall we say, ten minutes? Play it smart – nice to see you, Larry, you're looking well, let's go out for a drink. That sort of thing. Don't let me down."

She closed the door. Youssef took a packet of cigarettes from the side pocket of his tweed jacket. "Do you mind if I have one before I go?" he asked. "It has been a very long day."

"Fine with me," August said.

They both sat down.

"I guess she's not a fan of *Playboy*."

"What do you mean?"

"Your tie."

Youssef looked confused. "What about my tie?"

"I don't have a problem with it. In fact, I've written in my notes, 'evidence of a non-extremist mindset'."

Youssef lit his cigarette and inhaled deeply. He looked thoughtful. "Why don't you like Larry?" he asked.

Putting the evidence to one side (a broken nose, three cracked ribs and a dislocated left shoulder), August would have said it was the other way around, that Lawrence didn't like him. It had been an unexpected end to the disciplinary hearing. Just nine weeks earlier but already it felt like a lifetime ago. August had been content enough to sit through the case against him, despite the theatricality of Lawrence's style and the number of inaccuracies. After all, the verdict had never been in doubt – there was no way they could keep him on, despite the patchiness of the evidence. In fact it had struck him as appropriate, given the nature of most intelligence, that the final word on his career should be such a confounding mixture of fact and fiction, with some of the most significant elements omitted entirely.

The thing that triggered the fight hadn't really been Lawrence's repeated and unnecessary references to his wife's death, if something that lasted fewer than ten seconds and was that one-sided could be called a fight. The first time it was a "recent distressing incident", the second time it was a "terrible accident". What had brought the meeting to an abrupt end was Lawrence's use of her name. "If only Martha was able to see —" he started to say, and August realized he didn't want to hear the end of the sentence, it was as simple as that, and Lawrence's chair was suddenly toppling backwards, blood delicately speckling the white wall next to him, and his ribs popped with a dull cracking sound, and August was scrambling for his throat when an arm circled his neck from behind, pulling him back. He didn't mind too much. He was already feeling much better.

For a while after that there was talk of an assault charge, but it came to nothing. All it would have taken to make the whole thing go away was a suggestion from an appropriately senior officer that making a fuss might damage both the office's reputation and – more importantly – Lawrence's prospects for promotion, and who would want that? Better to let it quieten down and allow the bruises to heal, get that high-profile overseas job you've had your eye on, try some liaison work for a change, maybe even run an agent or two. Everyone knows it wasn't your fault, and there's no way August will darken our door again.

If only overseas hadn't turned out to be Turkey.

"To tell you the truth," August said, "I didn't always dislike him. For a while we were friends. Of sorts."

"Maybe it is time to forgive him."

"You could be right. The reason for us falling out was ... unusual."

"Do you think there are any jobs at the embassy? Driver, security guard, interpreter? Anything except cleaner. I can start today."

"All you'll need is five minutes to produce a new CV," said August, and immediately regretted it.

But Youssef smiled broadly, showing off the gaps between his teeth. "For those jobs I have one prepared already. To be honest, I never heard of 'project manager' before. Is this really a job?" He pinched the end of his half-smoked cigarette, replaced it in the packet and stood up. "Thank you, Mr August," he said, holding out his hand. "It was very pleasant to meet you."

August was still trying to work out why Lawrence had said he was looking forward to seeing him, why he hadn't simply told Beatrice that August had been fired from government for gross misconduct. There was no way she'd keep him on once she heard that, given that the embassy was her most important client. Was Lawrence planning some kind of showdown so he could watch August being fired for a second time? No doubt he would find that satisfying. But August had come all this way to leave that behind, or so he had thought. The last thing he wanted was another confrontation.

"We haven't finished the interview yet," he said, standing up. "Tell you what, I wouldn't mind a cigarette myself. Shall we take this up to the roof? That way we won't set off an alarm."

Youssef followed him up three flights of stairs to a metal door with a bolt but no padlock. The empty blue sky was a rebuke to the cluttered city. Cranes jostled around them like the frames of half-built minarets, and red-tiled roofs fell away sharply down to the water's edge. They looked across the Bosphorus towards the Asian side of Istanbul.

"That is where I came from," Youssef said. "And that is where I am going," he added, turning his face towards Europe.

They leaned against a low wall and smoked in silence. An old satellite dish hanging by a single cable squeaked and tapped against the building opposite. It was rusted in dappled brown patches like cowhide.

"Aren't you going to ask me another question?" said Youssef finally.

"I can if you want."

"If *I* want?"

"All right, why don't you tell me about a time you've successfully overcome an obstacle."

"Wait, I do not understand. Why are we here? It is still possible to get the job?"

"It's Beatrice's opinion that counts, that's the problem. She didn't seem convinced you were the right fit. I don't want you to get your hopes up. If it was up to me I'd give you the job on the spot. Why don't you treat this as practice for your next interview? There are plenty of other companies out there. If you're patient I'm sure something suitable will come along."

"If I am *patient*?"

"Look, if it's any consolation, this seems like a pretty rubbish company to me. I'm only sticking around because I haven't got anywhere else to go. You're not missing —"

"I have been to maybe fifty interviews and I have three more people to speak to this afternoon." He looked across the water to the old city. "My goodness. Overcoming an obstacle? Everything is an obstacle. My goodness. Escaping from Syria? Can I use this as an example? Can I talk about the things that Daesh do, can I talk about staying calm when you see men in masks on the road, can I talk about not knowing what to do when they beat your brother in front of you, can I talk about running out of medicine for my daughter, can I talk about the noise in her throat when she has been crying for five hours?"

He took a final drag on his cigarette and stubbed it out against the wall. He looked close to tears. They were both quiet.

"It all depends," August said finally. He handed Youssef another cigarette. "You'd have to make it sound a bit more impressive. I mean, in the course of all that, did you demonstrate the ability to work as part of a team? Did you put in place measures to assess your progress and adapt your approach where necessary?"

"Do you know what wasta is?" said Youssef. "It is when you get a job because you know the right person. This is the Syrian way. At least with wasta you get a job in the end. Maybe it is not the best job in the world but at least it is a job." He looked at his watch and put the cigarette August had given him into his own packet. "One thing before I go." He looked around, took a step towards August and lowered his voice to a whisper. "Two young bachelors in Istanbul, this is what the woman said. Expense account. You will definitely need girls. Any kind, I can get them all – black, brown, white, young, old." He counted them out on the fingers of one hand. "As many as you want. If you want to go to clubs to watch women dancing, I will take you there, I will make sure nobody steals from you. I can get you very cheap whisky and vodka. Very cheap and very high quality. Marijuana, this is also easy. Cocaine too. Even —"

August put his hand up to stop him. The sound of voices was coming from the stairwell.

"This is Mr Larry?" asked Youssef.

"I'm afraid so. I didn't think they'd find us up here."

"I understand. You do not wish to see him." Youssef looked around the rooftop. "Over there," he whispered, pointing at a water tank on the other side.

Beatrice was speaking. "It's such a stroke of luck, Larry, you two knowing each other. August was thrilled to hear you've been posted out here." It sounded as though they were almost at the top of the stairs. "I can't imagine what he's doing up here."

There was just enough space between the water tank and the edge of the roof for August to stand. He heard Youssef call out, "Miss Beatrice, have I said your name right? What a pleasure to see you again."

"What the hell are you doing up here?" she said. "Where's August?"

"I am afraid he has left for an urgent meeting," said Youssef.

"What do you mean? What meeting?"

"Oh, well, a very important meeting. I do not know any more. With his bank, I think. My goodness. Very urgent indeed. He hurried out in a great rush."

"For Christ's sake. I'm sorry about this, Larry, I really am. What a waste of your time." A murmur or two, nothing August could make out. Then, much louder, "Will you get off this rooftop, please? It's private property."

The two English voices disappeared into the stairwell. A few seconds passed and Youssef called out, "Mr Larry? Mr Larry?" There was the sound of hurried footsteps across the roof. "Mr Larry? My name is Youssef, sir." His raised voice echoed down the stairwell. "Mr August told me many fond things about you. Do you happen to know if there are any jobs at the embassy? Sir? Can you hear me? I can do anything, security guard, driver. Anything except cleaning. Sir? Sir? Shall I send you my CV?"

9

"This is unfortunate," said the vizier, as August had come to think of the man at the other end of the phone. It had rung just before midnight. "We cannot afford mistakes. My information was clear: he will arrive at the address at ten o'clock in the morning, possibly dressed in the same grey suit and black shoes he has been wearing since he arrived, and he will leave approximately one hour later. Fifty years old, short grey hair, glasses with a black frame. He carries a leather briefcase everywhere he goes."

The address had been left for August in the cemetery, printed by hand on a piece of paper hidden inside a crumpled cigarette packet. The vizier had been adamant: no names, no addresses, no numbers to be discussed on the phone. Anything specific to be communicated in writing. He had been able to explain, however, that the objective was to identify where the man was staying. "We need to know this immediately. You are a European, he will not suspect that someone like you would follow him." The only thing they knew for certain was the time of the appointment at the five-storey building in the neighbourhood of Otogar. August wondered if an IS sympathizer worked there and had passed the information to them.

But then the man hadn't turned up and August was having to defend himself.

"I swear he wasn't there. Can you tell me any more about him?" he asked. "Where's he from?"

"How will this information help you to follow him? All you need is a description. It is possible his meeting was delayed, but you must make allowances for such things in your planning. We have talked before about your impatience."

"I waited for ages. I'm telling you, he wasn't there. One hundred per cent. I even checked inside."

"What do you mean? I told you to stay outside the building. What if someone challenged you? I cannot tolerate disobedience. In a few days this opportunity will be gone, and if we fail I will be held responsible."

August was certain he hadn't missed the man. He could be sure about this because of the seven people who had left the building during the time he had been sitting in a café across the road: four had been women, two had been men in their twenties and the seventh had been a builder carrying a ladder. At 11.30, despite strict instructions to keep his distance, August had gone inside to confirm there wasn't a second exit at the back. One reason for this was that it looked disobedient, impulsive, reckless – it looked like something 34c might have done. It definitely didn't look like something a professional would have done, given the uncertain circumstances, and he was at pains to demonstrate that he wasn't a professional. In the real world, a sense of caution was the most important quality a spy could possess – more important than flair or bravery, more important even than being successful. Reckless spies lasted as long as reckless astronauts. Secrecy was the artificial air that they breathed; it was what kept them alive.

"I should have listened to those people who told me you are not suitable for this task," said the vizier. "You are inexperienced, you are impulsive, you do not follow orders."

The lobby of the building had been empty apart from a single computer on a desk, open at the website of a Turkish celebrity magazine, and a mottled green plant in the corner that slumped like a wounded soldier against a cracked bamboo pole. August headed for the stairs. On the first floor, at either end of a landing, were two doors. Engraved on a brass plaque was the outline of an aeroplane next to the Turkish flag. On the second floor were two more doors in the same position. One of them was reinforced with a metal frame and had an intercom system with an expensive camera. He heard a voice inside and continued upwards, making a note of the information on the company nameplates as he went. August considered the crude assumptions forming in his mind: that his target was a businessman, given his age and the description of a suit and a briefcase; that he was linked, possibly as a client, to one of the companies operating out of the building; that he was based outside Turkey, since he was only here for a limited period of time; and that he was in some way an enemy of IS, whatever that meant. It wasn't much to go on.

He saw his target two days later. This time August had been left a note in the cemetery informing him that the appointment was at three in the afternoon. The man emerged from the same building, blinking in the sunlight, after exactly one hour, his leather briefcase clasped tightly in his right hand. He adjusted his glasses, smoothed his fluttering grey hair into place and set off in the direction of the nearest metro station. August knew how difficult surveillance could be even for a full team. For one person on their own, it was close to impossible. He stayed on the other side of the street and kept to a distance of thirty metres, setting his pace by the swinging brown briefcase that ticked like a metronome at the edge of his vision.

It wasn't until they reached the station that it became clear the man was carrying out some form of crude anti-surveillance. Did he know, then, that someone might be following him? At the bottom of the escalator he stopped to tie his shoelace, watching to see who came afterwards, and then slowed his pace to wander into a small arcade. He picked which shops to enter at random and found himself lost and out of place in the aisles of a toyshop and then, several minutes later, a shoe shop, with a bored assistant hovering at his side. He stole nervous glances out of the window while trying on a pair of orange trainers and then fled, clutching the briefcase to his chest. He let two trains go past and crossed to the opposite platform at the last minute to catch one heading in a different direction.

All the while August added to his list of assumptions. That the man didn't speak Turkish, because of the way he didn't even glance at a rack of local newspapers, because of the way those people he spoke to tilted their heads and leaned in, puzzled expressions on their faces. That he had been given some rudimentary training in anti-surveillance techniques but was not a professional, because of the way that nothing he did was fluid or instinctive as it is with the best operators, who understand that the art of making the unnatural look natural is to create a series of tiny narratives to explain their otherwise curious behaviour. That he was uncomfortable and believed himself to be in danger, because of the way he touched his glasses, his hair, his fingernails. His eyes, darting first one way and then the other, seemed to fiddle with the world around him, like a child who can't sit still. On the train he took a file from his briefcase and made careful annotations with a pencil kept in the inside pocket of his crumpled grey suit. When his phone rang he hurried to get rid of the person at the other end, but not before August had caught the edges of three or four words that might have been either Dari or Farsi.

They got off after four stops. The area around the station was grey and dirty; there were no foreigners to be seen. A group of teenagers sitting on a wall shouted at August. One of them threw a glass bottle in his direction and they all laughed when it hit a stray dog.

The man walked directly to a small industrial park less than a mile away. He appeared to have given up on his anti-surveillance drills: he passed up several obvious opportunities to see if he was being followed. He hurried through a black metal fence and disappeared inside a low grey warehouse immediately on the left. August couldn't stand outside to see what would happen next – there was no street furniture, no cover to explain someone waiting.

He had either to go into the industrial park or to return to the station in the hope he could pick up the target later in the day. The sensible option would be to withdraw; there was no need to take unnecessary risks.

But August felt very differently. He wanted to push every encounter as far as it could go – to rattle every door handle and window latch in the hope he might be able to snatch a handful of experience and trade it for a moment's distraction. Without stopping to think he walked through the gates and past the warehouse, turning right and out of sight at the end.

He didn't know what he was looking for, other than that he had to find out what the grey warehouse was used for. He passed a vehicle workshop, its metal shutter half-open and a radio playing pop music far inside. Further along, two men were loading a van with water-stained cardboard boxes. Uncollected rubbish huddled in doorways. There was a sign in Turkish outside the last building before the road, and the window was clean enough in places for him to see a desk and chair, two filing cabinets and a long trestle table. There were dozens of keys hanging on a wooden board in the corner and three cigarette butts in the ashtray on the desk. When he opened the door he could smell that one of them had been recently put out. It might be a management office of some kind, he thought, because of its location, because of the keys. There were no papers on the desk. He tried the drawers and found a file of what looked like invoices or receipts, along with boxes of uncut keys and a broken torch. A sudden gust of wind slammed the door shut and on the back he saw a map, held in place by two nails of different sizes. He recognized the route he had walked, and the different units, and he saw the word "mekanik" written in pencil inside a small box. Other words he didn't recognize or understand. He was still studying the map when the door opened, forcing him backwards, and two men stepped into the office.

They looked around to see what had been stolen. The first man was short and broad; thick white stubble squeezed like garlic from the square press of his chin. The man behind him looked the more thoughtful of the pair. He adjusted his glasses and extended a thin, tentative hand over his friend's shoulder and into the charged atmosphere of the room, as though testing the temperature of bathwater. It didn't make sense, he knew that, what they could see in front of them – it didn't make sense at all. And he wanted to slow things down before it all got out of hand. He wanted to say to his friend: this isn't what you think. All right, the man's unshaven, he's junkie-thin, he's got dead eyes. He doesn't look worried, that's for sure, which means he's probably done this sort of thing before. And the desk drawers are wide open, and units on the estate have been robbed three times in the last month, which we're getting blamed for, and he's got absolutely no reason to be in here on his own. But that coat's not cheap. And I can see from here there are no keys missing. And he might be dark, but he's definitely not one of those thieving Syrian rats. And look, if you were going to do something you should have done it by now, because he's already moved his feet like he knows what he's doing, and his arms are as long as broom handles, and —

But it all happened too quickly. The first man lowered his head and lifted his fists and charged forward. There was an audible crack and he stumbled backwards with a hand pressed to his nose as though dragging himself into an alleyway. Then the stranger in the long coat wasn't there any more. What was there, the man in the doorway could see now that he had a moment to breathe, now that he was able to adjust his glasses, was the new toolbox they'd just bought last week, and the mobile phone charging on the table, the one worth a bit of money even with a broken screen, as if any more proof was needed that this hadn't been just another robbery.

10

That evening August sat in a bar and drank half a bottle of raki while he wrote a message for the vizier. There was no way he could pass on any information of genuine value. He couldn't describe the target's crude attempts at anti-surveillance, because 34c wouldn't have knowledge of such things, and he couldn't pass on any intelligence the vizier might find useful – he couldn't give him a single fact that might conceivably help him plan whatever he had in mind. August knew that much, however fiercely he might have craved distraction. He had his limits.

He also had a plan, or so he would have claimed if anyone had asked him. He would have pointed out that he didn't have enough information to take the matter to the embassy, at least not yet, that if he turned up at their door, a disgraced former spy sacked for disobedience, dishonesty, treachery – whichever word they were using – with an implausible story about a man in a cemetery asking him to follow another man, they would have given it no more than a cursory glance and put it to one side. What else could they do? Could he provide a single fact to validate his story? Far better to let things develop, he thought, and inform them once he had something solid. The plot was still very much in the planning stages, and he was well placed to find out more. Besides, he was getting somewhere. The target was Iranian, he knew that much. And the warehouse in the industrial park was used to store chemicals, at least according to the map on the back of the office door. What was that if not progress?

It wasn't until he left the bar that he realized how much he'd drunk. He felt warm, giddy, tearful, off balance. If it hadn't been a short walk to the cemetery, he might have gone back to his hotel to sleep it off. But the vizier had instructed him to leave the note hidden in the crumpled cigarette packet that same night, because the matter was so urgent, and August told himself it wouldn't take more than a few minutes. The cold night air would revive him. It wasn't as though there was anyone around who might see him, and there were plenty of benches inside the cemetery in case he needed to sit down, and if he did weave a little as he walked, well, what was more innocuous than a tipsy tourist out for a late evening stroll?

It took him much longer than expected to find the gravestone. He looked through all his pockets several times before he found the message.

"What is wrong with you? Are you ill?"

The voice was quiet, at least ten paces away. August wheeled around so quickly that he lost his balance and fell over. He got to his feet but didn't know which way to face. He couldn't see anything other than trees.

"What are you doing here?" he asked, more loudly, more abruptly than he would have liked. The surprise in his voice was genuine. "I thought... You told me to leave a note for you."

"I came to collect the note. I expected you would leave it more than an hour ago. But since we are both here, tell me what happened."

August tried to stand still. He took a deep breath of the night air and swallowed away a hiccup.

"He came out like you said from that place and I saw him straightaway. No doubt it was him – the glasses, the briefcase. I stuck with him down to the station, where he killed a little time." He was talking too quickly. He tried to slow down. "I just about made it onto the same train as him too. Last-minute thing, I had to scramble. I'm sure he didn't see me. But we got to this station called Ulanan, Lunalan – something like that. Sounds like a theme park, doesn't it, Luna Land. Ferris wheel, bumper cars. What was I saying? Oh yeah, hang on, I've got it written down. Can I put my hand in my pocket?"

"This is not a robbery," said the vizier. "No one is pointing a gun at you."

"Yeah, sorry, of course."

"Was it Unalan?"

August unfolded the piece of paper. "That's it. Unalan. I lost him there. Rough place, not many foreigners. Some kids threw a bottle at me. I don't know why, but it spooked me a bit. When you think about the things kids said to me back home because of my beard or my clothes." Another hiccup, this one too sudden to do anything about. He cleared his throat noisily to suggest it had been a cough. "Sometimes they threw worse things than a bit of glass

87

too. Most of the time I'd throw it straight back. Sorry, I'm rambling a bit. Anyway, I waited too long and I lost him. I'm sorry. I'm learning all the time, it won't happen again."

"Is it possible that he saw you?"

"What, the man with the briefcase? No chance. He looked like the nerdy type, belongs in an office. Fiddling with his glasses, the whole suit and tie thing. Nervous too. Reminded me of a geography teacher we had at school. We called him all sorts of names, he had a breakdown in the end. I can't remember his… He went into a toyshop so maybe he's got kids. The man with the briefcase, I mean, not the teacher. He didn't have any kids, no wonder, dealing with us lot all day. What else? I bet whatever's in it's important, the way he was hugging it close. Should I try to grab it from him, make it look like a mugging? It wouldn't be too difficult. Take his wallet too, smash him in the nose, make it look real."

The man was quiet for a while. Finally he said, "What is wrong with you?"

August wanted to sit down. He wanted to sit down, he wanted to stop talking, he wanted to have another drink.

"What? Nothing. I mean… Why are you asking that?"

"You have been drinking."

"No, don't be crazy, it's … indigestion. Making me —"

"You are Muslim and you are drunk. How is this possible?"

"Wait a second, it's not like that. I just ate something funny. You're always telling me to try the local food, turns out it's made me a bit wobbly. I just need to go back to my hotel and lie down for a bit."

The sound of a footstep on gravel was like something breaking into hundreds of pieces.

"What's going on?" said August. "Are you —"

"Do not turn around."

Another footstep, louder. His thoughts jostled like a crowd running for the door.

"Wait," August said, "what are you doing? Is this just because —"

"Look in front of you."

What should he say? He could continue to deny it, come up with a better story, put it down to excitement or nerves or even medication. But it was always dangerous to tell an unnecessary lie.

The footsteps were on grass now, getting closer every second.

"I used to have a problem with all that," he said quickly, thinking about who he was supposed to be, who 34c was, and the path he had taken to reach this point. He put his hands in his pockets and relaxed his shoulders. He felt strangely calm. "I know I shouldn't lie to you. But I'm ashamed, I guess. Sometimes when I get stressed… It's hard here, you know, all on my own. I'm not complaining or anything. I know the brothers are with me, like you said. I know they're in a much tougher place. This is a walk in the park compared to what they're doing." The vizier was standing behind him. His presence hummed with hot malevolent energy. "Do what you want to do," August said. "But you don't understand, that's the truth. I don't sleep, I don't eat, it's like something is killing me from the inside. I'm bursting with all of this, ready to go, more excited than I've ever been, and then suddenly I get nervous that I'm going to mess up and let you down, let everyone down, and I… I…"

He didn't have any words left.

"Do you trust me?" the vizier asked, his voice a whisper in August's ear.

"Yeah, well —"

"Close your eyes."

He could feel warm breath on the back of his neck.

"'I was appointed to rule you but I am not the best among you,'" the vizier murmured. There was something sweet and rotten on his breath. "'If you see me acting truly, then follow me. If you see me acting falsely, then advise and guide me.' Do you know these words? Not a single one of us is perfect – not your vizier, not your sultan. We all do things we wish we did not do."

He put his hands lightly on August's shoulders.

"My brother, I want you to stop drinking. Let me explain why this is so important. Once upon a time there was a man. An ordinary man, certainly, like many thousands of others. He worked hard and made his parents very proud. He studied engineering at university and went to work for a company in a foreign country. He was a happy man – he was married, he had two little girls, he was a success. What else could a man wish for? Then his father died and he moved home with his family to look after his mother. He started to work for his government, first of all in the development of techniques to refine crude petroleum, and then as the director of a research laboratory. Much later on, given his experience, he was the obvious person to help his government in the development of certain … capabilities, shall we say, to be used by friends across the region. He could have said no. He could have retired, he could have gone overseas again, he could have become a respected professor at his old university. Instead he left his family behind in Tehran and has been living in Damascus for the last two years, helping the Syrian regime develop chemical weapons to be used against innocent women and children. In those two years, as far as we know, he has never set foot outside the country, but all of a sudden he arrives in Istanbul. Now can you see what an opportunity we have been given? Can you see how important what you are doing is to us? Do you understand why you must stop drinking?"

His arms encircled August in a fierce embrace that contained within it the threat of huge and catastrophic violence.

"This man must die," he whispered, his mouth next to August's ear. And then, so softly that afterwards August couldn't be completely sure he'd heard it right: "And you are going to kill him."

11

They had met on a flight to the Gulf six years earlier, in 2010, just a few months after August had completed his basic training. He had only spoken to her because his trip had been planned at the last minute and he hadn't been given an opportunity to practise his cover story. The job required a cold start, an approach out of the blue, exploiting whatever opportunity for conversation might arise, whether it was a request for directions, a joke over the breakfast buffet or simply the offer of a cigarette outside a bar, and he had been taught the importance of warming up beforehand on unimportant people. The worst thing would be for your first words to the target to be the first words you had exchanged with a stranger all day. And she looked like a challenge – intense, bookish, cocooned in a pea-green woollen coat like someone whose stop was coming up well before everyone else's, her pretty face held delicately between two gleaming beetle-black headphones as though she was practising dictation rather than slowly filling in a crossword puzzle on the folding table in front of her.

He reached over and tapped her newspaper. "Fourteen across might be 'Francis'. First name of American novelist—"

She was able to squeeze a surprising amount of attitude into the simple act of lifting a headphone from her ear.

"You seem to be avoiding fourteen across," he said. "I think it's 'Francis'. Author of *Tender Is the Night*."

"Mmm. Seven letters. It could be 'disturb'."

"Interesting. It doesn't really fit the clue though."

"But it does apply in a more *general* sense, don't you think?" she said, smiling.

"To the occasion, you mean?"

"Or, I don't know, 'disrupt', 'prevent', 'bedevil'."

"If only there was a hyphen," he said. "There are a few four-three combinations that might also work. What are you listening to?"

She sighed, turned away and allowed the headphone to settle back into place over her ear. He couldn't let it end like that. What if his target turned out to be just as difficult? Better to push through the hedgerow of her objections and afterwards pick out the thorns, pull the grass from his hair, than to do it for the first time with his target. After all, she didn't matter. What she thought of him didn't matter one little bit.

He waited until the meal was served. Having watched her eat a tiny pot of crème brûlée and leave the rest, he balanced his dessert on the edge of her tray. She looked at it and raised an eyebrow.

"Two words," he said. "Five-eight."

She looked out of the window while she thought about it.

"'Burnt offering'?" she suggested finally.

"I had in mind 'peace offering', but to be honest, 'burnt offering' is much better."

He talked too much and too quickly in that first conversation, in the hope that she'd find it impossible to return to her headphones once she'd heard about the limp his dachshund had developed, his parents' difficulties with the central heating during their first winter in the Lake District, the demanding schedule of meetings he had ahead of him in his capacity as representative of a small academic publisher based in the Oxfordshire countryside. He told her his name was Tom and she told him her name was Martha. To put her at ease, he intended to mention a girlfriend at the first opportunity, but for some reason the right moment never came up. Together they worked out the last three clues to her crossword. He learned that she had one tattoo she regretted and two she loved. She told him about an argument she'd had with her brother in which he'd slapped her. She explained her work for a charity that campaigned on behalf of detained journalists and showed him pictures of a protest she had helped organize outside the Bakırköy women's prison in Turkey, where a number of writers and activists were being held. It was aeroplanes, it was their fault – they left him giddy. It was an unreal world of cotton wool and pastel blue that made the grounded realities of work and weather seem unimportant. The first sign that something was wrong came when she told him she was travelling to visit a friend. To his surprise, her words landed like a well-thrown javelin, sticking unexpectedly and unignorably into the mud and the dirt of his heart. She resisted his attempts to find out who this friend was.

Afterwards he could remember every word of their conversation. They were indelible, like her tattoos. He regretted all of his, for their clumsiness, and loved all of hers, repeatedly, as he failed to sleep that night in his hotel bed. It was too late for sentiment, he knew that. It was possible, in his line of work, to build a professional relationship on a foundation of lies – that betrayal was painless, that the other side would never find out, that all it would take was one little favour and that would be the end of it. Over time a skilled case officer could gently tap loose the rotten brickwork and replace it with something more robust, and by the time that was done it was usually in the interests of both parties not to draw attention to the changes. Any lingering spores of mistrust could be covered up by a bonus, an expensive dinner, a visit from the chief. But August had built a large and complex lie that could not be repurposed. He had given a different name, he had described a different career, a different background, a different family – he had described a different person. She hadn't really even met *him*, if he was honest. It was obvious. He couldn't see her again.

It was when he finally approached his target, two days later, that he realized she had done something to him that would have to be set right: she had made him bad at his job. She had also made him bad at sleeping and bad at eating, not that that was as important as the rest of it, the thinking, the concentrating, the talking – all things that mattered quite a lot if you wanted to recruit a Palestinian professor in the same small city where the Israelis had very publicly assassinated a Hamas official less than a year earlier. August's objective was to make first contact with the target, establish a reason for them to stay in touch and gently float the seed of an idea that might later grow into a financial opportunity. In the process he should take no risks.

He couldn't imagine a clumsier performance; he was glad his instructors weren't there to watch. It was the first time his target had been alone, and he was leaving early the following morning. There were three empty seats between them at the hotel bar. The professor was in his early sixties, his long bald head shaped like an olive. He wore a pair of tortoiseshell glasses low on his nose to read the magazine in front of him. When loud music and clapping erupted in the lobby, they both turned to see a large wedding party, led by the bride and groom, streaming through the doors. The professor sighed, folded his magazine and looked for the bartender.

"Rather him than me," said August quickly. This might be his only chance. He knew his target had been married twice, was currently single and had recently spent what savings he had on his youngest daughter's university fees. "The bigger the wedding, the quicker the divorce – that's my theory. From the looks of it, they won't last the year." He kept his eyes on the bartender, who smiled and shook his head as though August had ordered a cocktail he didn't know how to make. There was no reaction from the professor.

Now that he had started, August had little choice but to keep going. He wouldn't be able to manufacture another chance encounter without it looking decidedly odd. "One more, please," he said, pushing his glass forward. "This brings back bad memories," he said, waving towards the wedding party in the lobby. "The worst thing about two publishers getting divorced is dividing up the books. It took us longer to sort that out than it did the house and the car." No reaction from the target, but at least the bartender offered something. "We are closing in ten minutes," he said, placing the drink on a coaster. "That's fine," August said. "I've got a meeting at the university in the morning, so an early night is no bad thing."

And that should have been it. A positively under-whelming performance; it turned out he had played all his good shots and run his legs into the ground on the practice court with Martha. These things often didn't work, he knew that, because the target was in a bad mood or suspicious or hard of hearing or had spent all day with other people and just wanted five minutes of peace and quiet. It was also true that August had come across as the worst kind of barroom bore, wanting to complain about marriage and other people's happi-ness to anyone who'd listen. There was a lesson to be learned there. But it was over. And nothing incriminat-ing had happened, that was the most important thing, nothing that could be pinned down or reported back, just a coincidence or two in a snatch of overheard chat between a bored, talkative foreigner and a bartender, as was undoubtedly happening at that very moment in hotels all around the world. They could try again in a month or two, in a different city and a different setting, ideally with an officer who wasn't beginning to suspect he had fallen in love for the first time just two days earlier.

Then he saw that the man's magazine was open to an article about Egyptian prisons, and he thought: Martha might be interested in that. Before he knew what he was doing he said, "What magazine are you reading?"

The professor turned on his stool towards August, flipped the pages over to show him the cover and began talking about General Sisi and his regime, and asking whether August had visited Egypt, and how long he would be in Dubai for, and what was the name again of that publisher he represented? He suggested they squeeze in one more drink before the bar closed. His manner was relaxed and friendly, and he showed an interest in August's reflections on his visit to Jerusalem several years earlier before talking about his own fondness for English bitter and the Royal Family.

"I drove my first wife crazy," he said, "dragging her around Windsor Castle and Buckingham Palace. A country like yours, Tom, that is able to tell itself stories of its courage and its importance over the centuries, is a lucky country indeed. Your kings and queens, your battles, your writers and universities and scientists – most of the world does not have this luxury. Most of the world tells itself stories of humiliation."

A white dove flew into the bar and rushed anxiously into one corner and then the other, looking for a way out. Two waiters entered in pursuit, waving their arms in an attempt to steer it back towards the lobby.

"My first wedding was just as noisy as this," said the

professor. One of the waiters was holding a cushion aloft and waving it to startle the bird out of its corner. "I am afraid this is the Arab way."

"You wouldn't get this at a royal wedding."

"I come from a small village in the West Bank near Kafr Kanna, which is where some people say Jesus turned water into wine. You see, even in those days the party was important. You are not married yourself?"

Perhaps he hadn't even heard August's blunt, clumsily cast hooks whistling around his head just a few minutes earlier. It was easy for professionals to fall into the habit of assuming everyone was as paranoid and riddled with ulterior motives as they were. They talked for a while about marriage and divorce, and August gently steered the conversation around to an anthology on Palestinian literature he was hoping to commission in the near future.

However much he might have been off his game, he quickly realized that something wasn't quite right. It was hard to identify what it was. But he had been trained to control the balance of energies needed to get a conversation off the ground while not being too direct or obvious, and he could tell when someone else had their hand on those same dials and levers. The man knew what was happening, that was his conclusion. It might have been August's clumsy opening gambit, or that he was showing too much interest, or even that the man had once been pitched in another hotel bar by a rival agency. But it was not necessarily a bad thing. There came a point in every recruitment where you had to ease the subject into an understanding of what an intelligence relationship would require of them, and if the man was ripe for the approach, as his file suggested he was, his early acquiescence might save them a lot of time.

"Your little publishing house, Tom," the professor said with a smile. "People tell you their stories and you do … what?"

"We make sure we understand the material properly, that's the first thing," said August. "In some cases we might need a clarification or two. But that's the author's work done. Of course, we honour the contract we have signed and make sure they are looked after, that they can enjoy a long and rewarding career. That's in both our interests. But I don't want to make it sound too … dry. We're passionate about the material, that's why we do this. It's very much a vocation, both for us and our authors." He took a sip of his drink. A band struck up in the ballroom across the lobby. "Perhaps you'd be interested in contributing something small yourself one day. That's the best way to understand how it all works."

The man chuckled. "Oh, I think I understand how it works. Where I come from there are plenty of publishers. Some of them are famously … what's the right word? Yes, famously *aggressive*."

"You might find us more accommodating."

"But this is one of the stories that you tell yourselves, no? The mild-mannered Englishman. In truth you are as aggressive as anyone, whether you care to admit it or not. You have read Orwell?"

"We're only aggressive when it comes to protecting our authors." August turned on his stool to face the professor, leaned in and lowered his voice. "To be honest, I don't really see us as an exclusively British company. That might have been the case in the past. But there are lots of important voices out there, voices that aren't speaking in English, voices that aren't being heard – at the national level, sure, but also at the European level, at the international level. It's less about the country these days and more about the values. My job is to make sure that your ideas go directly to the most important readers in the world."

"Bravo, bravo – so seductive!" He patted August on the shoulder, pulled away and beamed. "I can tell you are a good publisher. But it remains *your* book until the very end. You choose the title, you choose the cover. If it is an anthology you surround it with voices saying many different things. You write the introduction and – this is most important of all – you write the conclusion. Never mind the unreliable narrator, this is more a case of the unreliable editor."

"If your chapter is good enough, the readers will recognize that. As your editor I'll be able to guide you in the right direction. And bestsellers can do very well indeed. To give you an idea, we'd be willing —"

"Please, let me stop you there. It is late, I am old, and the music from the wedding is beginning to give me a headache." He signalled to the barman that he wanted to pay for both of their drinks. "And I want to make my escape before you offer me an advance, Tom, and I have to say no, and then things become awkward between us."

"There's really no need to go. You might have misunderstood what I am proposing."

"It is entirely possible. Metaphors are such a minefield, would you not agree?"

"Can I give you my card?" asked August. "I'd very much like to stay in touch."

The professor smiled and said, "Even better, Tom, I will give *you* something, entirely free of charge, for your next anthology. I will tell you a story that you are free to edit as you wish and share with your colleagues.

"Do you remember I told you that I come from a small village in the West Bank? My great-great-grandfather was a lemon farmer, and he passed the land down to his son, who passed it down to my grandfather and then to my father. All of my childhood memories are of this place.

"A long time before I was born, my grandfather was shot dead among his lemon trees. The man who shot him was an English soldier searching for a boy who had thrown stones at a jeep. It was an accident, really. The soldier was running across the uneven ground in the darkness and his rifle was not secure. He tripped and fell over and somehow he fired his weapon. My grandfather was helping him chase the boy because he admired the British very much and because boys who throw stones at jeeps are the same boys who steal lemons. When he saw what had happened, the English soldier threw his rifle away – this is what he was punished for later on, not for shooting an innocent man – and ran to my grandfather to try to stop the bleeding. After the funeral this soldier came to see my grandmother every week. He was heartbroken. She would shout at him and chase him from our land with a stick but still he came back the next week. Sometimes he would bring chocolate or cigarettes and leave them at the gate. It caused him many problems, this behaviour of his. He wasn't promoted, he didn't want to carry his gun, his colleagues didn't trust him. I think he was sent home early. My grandmother received a letter from him in July 1949. By this time he was married with a small baby and working as a gardener and teaching himself Arabic in the village library every Saturday.

"Now what was a man like this – kind, gentle, thought-ful – doing in a foreign country he did not understand, chasing a boy across uneven ground in the darkness with a rifle in his hands? What was he doing there? Do you have an answer, Tom? Why does a good man find himself doing such bad things when he puts on his country's uniform? I do not know the answer to this. I do not know if the soldier ever found out the answer to this. I can only tell you what I think, which is that I never had the opportunity to meet my grandfather, and this makes me very sad, because from everything I heard he was a kind and honourable man."

He put his magazine back in his jacket pocket.

"I have enjoyed having a drink with you, Tom," he said. "My only advice, as an old man to a young man, is that you should think carefully before putting on your country's uniform."

He checked that he had his room key, patted August twice on the shoulder, and walked out of the bar.

Over the long night that followed, during which every-thing bled together – August chasing Martha through a moonlit lemon grove, her stone-filled pockets rattling like a convict's chains – the idea came to him with the full force of nocturnal logic that somehow she was the only alternative to a life lived in uniform. He hadn't even been conscious of wearing one before that point. In his first days in the job everything had been so overwhelming that he hadn't noticed the scratching and chafing of new cloth, and now he was startled to discover that in places his skin had already grown so tough that it was hard to distinguish it from the uniform. Things that would have horrified him once now seemed commonplace. He floundered on the life raft of his vast hotel bed. It was all her fault. She had thrown a stone and shattered his windscreen. She had made him drive into a ditch.

He saw her again exactly one week later, back in London. It hadn't been difficult to find her office. After an hour he was on his second newspaper and his third cup of tea. His hair was neatly combed and he was wearing a dark-blue suit and his favourite red knitted tie. He used the time to work out the answers to the crossword but didn't fill them in, and he imagined scenes in which he would have the opportunity later on to impress her with his sharp mind, or make her laugh at the clever jokes he pulled out of nowhere, like a knotted string of silk handkerchiefs from a magician's sleeve. It was the most important piece of operational work he had ever planned. But then she stepped onto the busy street, wrapped in her pea-green coat and looking more beautiful than he remembered.

She turned when he called out her name.

"Five letters," he said.

"What?"

"It's a crossword clue. Five letters."

"I'm sorry, I don't —"

"No, *I'm* sorry, it's just a lame joke." Christ, what was he thinking? "We met last week on —"

"Come on, Tom, give me a clue at least."

"Oh, a popular greeting."

"Ah, okay, *hello* to you too." She smiled. "I'm not sure this is a viable long-term form of communication," she said. "What are you doing here?"

He had a plan. He always had a plan. That this was a coincidence, that he had just come from a meeting around the corner, that they should grab a coffee sometime so he could begin the impossible process of dismantling the edifice of his lies. It would take a while but there was no rush.

But instead of any of that, he surprised himself by saying, "I wanted to see you again."

"Well." She looked hard at him. "I'm not sure if that's charming or creepy. I've got a meeting in half an hour on the other side of the park. Do you want to walk with me? We'll be in public the whole time, in case you come down on the side of creepy."

Beneath a cathedral ceiling of winter trees he told her everything. He told her about growing up overseas, about the boarding schools, about the fights, about how a lonely little boy had learned that getting expelled was one way of forcing his parents to come back from abroad. He told her he was a spy and explained what that really meant. It was an unforgivable breach. His employers would have withdrawn his security clearance on the spot had they known. High above them a slice of lemon moon bobbed in the sky.

"Why are you telling me all this?" she asked.

"I don't know. I want to buy you a coffee."

"You must take your coffee seriously. This is the most intense preamble to a first date I can remember."

And, later on: "I don't much like the sound of what you do."

"I understand," he said. "I'm not sure I like it myself."

"Please don't lie to me again. Is there anything else?"

He realized he hadn't told her his name.

"I'll call you Gus," she said.

"No one calls me that."

"It'll be your new alias. Is that what you call it? Just for us."

Everything afterwards happened so quickly. They were inseparable within weeks and engaged within months. And then a German lorry took a corner too fast, and now August was like a pincushion, stuck with a thousand needles of grief and regret and anger, and it was dark, and he was running across uneven ground, and somewhere a gun was about to go off.

12

FILE EXCERPT FROM INVESTIGATION INTO AUGUST DRUMMOND

INKWELL/046

TOP SECRET

FOIA EXEMPT

FROM: Data
TO: Gatekeeping
SUBJECT: Possible new INKWELL incident
DATE: 31 October 2014

Charles,

Your presentation on Op INKWELL and the insider threat at last week's SMG conference was much appreciated. It was also very timely, as we've just uncovered something decidedly peculiar that may or may not be a new piece of the puzzle. I hesitate to go any further than that in my assessment – I recall that the two incidents you're looking at under INKWELL are very different from each other (apart from the fact that they both took place at the beginning of October, albeit one year apart, and they share a possible "Robin Hood" motivation), making it difficult to judge whether the same individual is responsible for them both. You may soon conclude that the information below only serves to muddy the waters further.

In the course of our routine monthly review of the office's communication data holdings, one of my analysts has found an alert created on 1 October this year by persons unknown using open-source software that appears to trigger some sort of warning system. In short, when the mobile phone of individual A comes within one mile of the residence of individual B, our systems have been programmed to send a text message to an unregistered pay-as-you-go mobile (located somewhere in the area of Waterloo station) that in turn sends another text message to the mobile of individual B. The message that individual B receives states: "Be careful. Curtis is on his way to your house right now. From a friend." This alert has been triggered on three occasions in the past month.

We've done a bit of digging. It turns out that individual B is a long-standing female Iranian agent and that individual A is her British ex-boyfriend, about whom she has made numerous complaints of stalking and harassment over the last year. The handlers have spoken to the agent and she says that she had assumed the text messages came from someone close to her ex-boyfriend who was trying to warn her. It didn't occur to her that the wording was identical each time. On all three occasions she was able to leave her house before he arrived.

As I said, it's a peculiar one. Putting to one side the "Robin Hood" angle (forgive me – I know you hate people using this term and I've used it twice), the incident obviously involves a monumental breach of the law and will have to be reported to the Data Commissioner at the first opportunity.

The Intelligence and Security Committee will no doubt wish to be informed as well, but I'll leave that to Private Office to take forward.

The individual responsible might have taken steps to disguise their involvement, but it's clear there will be opportunities for your team to make investigative headway. The number of people with access to the administrative account is between 25 and 30 (assuming the culprit didn't steal someone else's credentials), the pay-as-you-go mobile in Waterloo may yield fingerprints (if you manage to find it), and of course knowledge about the agent's problems with her ex-boyfriend will have been tightly held.

I'll leave it there, with best wishes for a swift and bloodless hunt.

Margaret

13

"There's a Syrian man called Youssef here to see you."

"William, darling – I said no interruptions."

"Not you, Beatrice. He wants August."

"What? He's busy."

"It won't take a minute," August said. "I'll get rid of him."

He was grateful for a reason to leave. The meeting, which had started two hours earlier and was ostensibly a review of his first week in the job, had begun with Beatrice's views on the importance of professionalism ("you're rarely here on time, you wander around in a daze, you disappear for *hours*"), moved on to August's budget proposal for the hive ("way, *way* under the amount HMG would be prepared to spend on something so bold and ambitious") and finally settled into a comfortable, well-worn groove that weaved its way through the motivational flagpoles of art, history and the destiny of man ("not since Napoleon brought the printing press to Egypt has the region stood on the threshold of such monumental change").

Beatrice had talked without drawing breath for much of the meeting. She possessed absolute faith in the idea that the judicious use of strategic communications could pat the world into a better shape. "This job, it's like sailing a boat," she said. "There will always be a million and one practical tasks to be done but you have to remain just as focused on the smallest change in the wind, in the tremors of the ocean. You have to find it in you to wonder where all the seagulls have gone. And sometimes you will be toppled into the sea, that's the nature of the game, but you have to fight your way to the surface with, with —"

"With an ancient Greek amphora in each hand."

"What?"

"Nothing, I was just —"

"Come on, what do you mean?"

"A bit Russian, isn't it?" said August, rubbing his head. "You've lost me."

"Sorry, nothing. Go on."

"What are you talking about?"

"Using social media to destabilize another government."

"What?"

"Nothing, nothing. I'm rambling. You were talking about the sea."

August didn't know what he was doing. He had no interest in an argument. It was his wedding anniversary. He had made a considerable effort the night before to obliterate the occasion by drinking enough to render him chaotically distracted by pain on the day itself, each gin and whisky and beer like an explosive charge primed to go off at a different hour the following day. By his calculations he'd be fine until nightfall, at which point he'd start to feel better. All he had to do was keep his mouth shut.

Beatrice shook her head. Her stiff helmet of blonde hair barely moved. "I can't tell if you're being serious," she said. "This is about access to the facts, August, this is about producing an honest and unbiased informational flow to combat the other side's disinformation and lies. We're taking power away from a tyrannical regime and placing it in the outstretched hands of ordinary people who are hungry for truth. That's the beauty of the new media landscape, that anyone can —"

"Okay, okay, I see your point."

"Good. Shall we get back to the plan for the hive? Did you speak to the property agent about a viewing tomorrow?"

August longed for his bed. At least they were off philosophy and back to practical matters. It wasn't as though he disapproved of what the British government was doing. In a way he even admired it. States that thrived were those that focused ruthlessly on their own interests, that entered into alliances on pragmatic rather than sentimental grounds, that didn't care about their neighbours beyond wanting to make sure any trouble stayed on the other side of the border. Emotion was too unstable an ingredient to introduce into such matters. Emotion led to weakness, emotion led to defeat; it would be like giving a beautiful spy a job in the minister's office. It was obvious what would follow from that: one or two minor lapses in security, a new and dangerously casual attitude towards classified material. The unwanted sound of laughter disrupting the quiet industry of civil servants. Long-standing policies would turn out to have been amended in the small hours to allow room for compromise. The only response to such a disaster was a purge. Weed out sympathizers, interrogate anyone who looked guilty, remove all evidence that the spy had ever set foot in the building. Even an old paperback tossed into a corner, even a pea-green coat hanging on the back of a door.

Youssef was slumped in a chair, his red *Playboy* tie dividing into two meandering streams just below the baggy knot.

"There's nothing I can do for you," August said.

Youssef spent a second or two overcoming the exhaustion evident in his bloodshot eyes before leaping to his feet with huge sudden energy. "My friend, my old friend," he said, rushing forward with his trembling hand extended. His small belly pushed proudly against his shirt. When he smiled his cheeks filled and stretched his beard so that it appeared threadbare. "How are you? You look very well. My goodness."

August couldn't have looked worse. He was unshaven and his crumpled shirt had worked its way loose of his trousers. In that sense they were a good match. Youssef's collar was rimmed with dirt and he smelled of sweat and tobacco.

"There aren't any jobs at the moment," said August. If he could get rid of Youssef quickly there would be time to escape to the roof for some fresh air. "The best thing would be to call back in a few weeks."

"No, no – I did not come here to discuss employment." Youssef laughed awkwardly. "I was passing through the neighbourhood and I thought to myself: I wonder how my friend is on this fine day." He paused expectantly, but when August didn't respond he hurried forward attentively with his words. "Was I very helpful last time, did I save your bacon? It was my pleasure to do you a big favour, helping you to hide. We did not have the opportunity to talk afterwards. But in my opinion we worked very well as a team, with you in charge giving me the benefit of your experience, and together we pulled the wool over their eyes."

"I'm sorry it hasn't worked out, Youssef. Beatrice has the last word on hirings – my hands are tied. Now I've really got —"

"There is no need to apologize, my friend. I was pleased to meet Miss Beatrice, as well as Mr Larry from the embassy. No positions vacant at present, unfortunately, but we established a connection and I believe he will remember me fondly if we have the good fortune to meet again. Now, speaking of good fortune, I have a few of your favourite cigarettes here." He took a crumpled packet from his pocket and shook a couple loose. "Shall we go to our usual meeting place upstairs and enjoy the sunshine on this fine day?"

Even from a couple of metres away August could see that the cigarettes were a cheap local brand that had been placed into a different packet.

"I don't have time for this," he said, fighting a wave of nausea. He took Youssef by the arm and turned him towards the door more roughly than he intended. "There's nothing I can do to help you —"

"Help *me*? Do not say this, my friend." A flash of anger and then a broad smile. Youssef gently shook his arm loose. "Have I asked for your help? My goodness. If any-thing, I wish to help *you*." He leaned in and lowered his voice. "Bachelors about town, this is what Miss Beatrice said. I have made certain arrangements, I have paid certain deposits on your behalf. An evening of execu-tive entertainment for Mr August and Mr Larry, exactly as you were instructed to plan. You can tell her that you prepared everything, it will be our secret. I have spoken to the finest cabarets and reserved VIP seating for two gentlemen, they will prepare cocktails and delicious food while the most beautiful girls in the city dance in front of you. It will be a night like you have never dreamed."

"You're right about that much. Look —"

"A small commission from the club, a small commis-sion from you, that is everything I need. Miss Beatrice said there is an expense account, so I know this will not be a problem."

"It's not going to happen, Youssef."

"As I said, a deposit has been paid on your behalf, exactly as you instructed. You asked about drugs too."

"I didn't say anything about —"

"Cocaine, hashish, even Viagra – anything you want. Look, I brought you a free sample." Youssef took a dusty tissue from his pocket and unfolded it to reveal five grey pills. "For a small price…"

August leaned against the wall and took a deep breath. The last thing he wanted was to become entangled in someone else's need.

"What kind of lady do you prefer?" Youssef asked. "Blonde or brunette?"

He couldn't expect anyone to understand. He didn't know how he would have explained it if someone had asked. Her death had not been an event, a thing that had happened at 3.54 one afternoon and was from that point onwards in the past, retreating by the day, like the ripples that followed a stone thrown carelessly into a puddle by the wheels of a lorry turning too fast. Her death had torn things open. It had stained time. It had disfigured life forever, like a jar of acid across the face.

"My friend?" said Youssef. "Let us agree on a date for —"

"Listen, I can't help you. You've got to leave."

"I am not asking for your help!" shouted Youssef.

Beatrice appeared at the door to her office. "What on earth's going on here?" she said.

"Miss Beatrice," Youssef said, quickly finding his smile. "I am sorry to disturb you in this unforgivable manner. Your employee here is creating chaos. I have come to offer my services —"

"Is this a joke?"

"Not at all. I have excellent qualifications and —"

"We're not hiring."

"Perhaps the walls need painting and —"

"I don't care about the walls. Move fast and break things, that's our motto."

"Terrific, terrific." Youssef looked confused. "What about cleaning up afterwards? Someone must clean up afterwards. Of course I am not a cleaner, but in this case…" He indicated the unpainted walls, the tangle of coloured wire casings thrust from the ceiling like something used to teach children about arteries and veins and muscles. "There is water on the kitchen floor. What about unexpected slippage? What about electricity?" He shook his head. "I will be very happy to come here and make everything shipshape. No, please do not shake your head, I am very happy to do this, please, I am desperate for —"

"Youssef – is that your name?" Beatrice said. "Youssef, we haven't got time for this. There are no jobs and even if there were, frankly, you're not the sort of person we'd give one to. I mean, take a look in the mirror sometime. We have very high standards. August and I have discussed this and we're in complete agreement. Perhaps you should try, I don't know, a restaurant or a construction company. They seem to take on plenty of unskilled workers. Now will you please leave so we can get back to work? Or do I have to call security and have you thrown out?"

Youssef folded the tissue paper around the pills. His hands were shaking and he dropped one on the floor. It bounced three times and skittered towards the puddle spilling out from the kitchen. He hurried to retrieve it and untucked a corner of his shirt to dry it carefully.

"For God's sake," said Beatrice, "is this some sort of fucking joke? Will you hurry up and go?"

Youssef tucked in his shirt and raised his head. There were tears in his eyes. "This is not fair," he said. "This should be fair. I have to… I need…" He looked at August. "I did you a favour, I was kind to you when you needed my help. And in return…" He turned to Beatrice. "He is a mess, his clothes are dirty, he drinks at lunchtime. Why does he get a job?"

"He's got a reference from the British government. One of the best I've ever seen. Have you got one of those?"

August stepped into a corner and threw up into a plant pot. He wiped his mouth on his sleeve. He was fairly sure Beatrice had never read his reference. It said things like "August has demonstrated imagination, diligence and a painstaking attention to detail in his work for the department" and "August is well liked by his peers because of his sympathetic and generous manner." As he had become bored, run out of things to say and begun to doubt he even wanted the job, he wrote things like "A keen golfer, August can often be found among his many friends in the local clubhouse, where his name adorns numerous trophies" and "In his free time, August routinely takes to the wilds of Scandinavia on a dog sled in search of the Northern Lights." He sat in his flat beneath the sugary glow of an energy-efficient light bulb, wrapped in an old dressing gown, wondering if that's what he was too, energy-efficient, rather than listless or lifeless or pallid or dull or any of the other things he felt. "Dynamic and high-impact," he wrote, "August is a rising star, destined to do great things in the service of his country. V. sorry to see him go."

Once the door had closed Beatrice turned to August.

"What on earth does he mean?" she asked. "You don't drink at lunchtime, do you?"

14

August had been there for fifteen minutes when he heard the front door open. By that point he had lost count of all the reasons the house was unsuitable. That it was on the Black Sea coast an hour's drive from the office, that it was in need of serious repair, that it didn't have a phone line, that anything brought in would have to negotiate an overgrown driveway that swung down off the main road through a melee of pines, a set of crumbling stone steps and a front door that was clearly too narrow for the larger pieces of equipment needed to set up a media studio. There wasn't another house in sight. Beatrice would hate it. She had made it clear that her internal mood board, when it came to the hive, was dominated by images of clean desks, crisp shirts, earnest young men huddled around computers, and a swarm of bees to signify the buzz of round-the-clock industry.

But the truth was that August had decided to sign the contract as soon as he had seen it. There was something that appealed to him about the house's dirty wooden exterior, lopsided over four narrow floors with alcoves and balconies and inexplicable rooms like a face swollen after a beating, the sunlight from the water splashing off windowpanes where shutter louvres had gone missing. He had half an idea to move in while it was being refurbished, to swim every morning in waters that in time would wash up on the shores of Odessa and Sebastopol. At least the house was exorbitantly expensive because of its proximity to the sea – it had that in its favour. Beatrice had been clear that the worst crime of all would be to come back with something under budget. And it did have a kitchen and two bathrooms and enough space to accommodate everyone. August could tick those things off his list. It also had a fridge in the top bedroom, an infestation of mice, three broken windows and any number of loose floorboards that depressed like organ pedals to sound an off-key melody of groans, squeals and sighs.

Two floors below him the front door clicked shut.

Turning to the window, August saw the property agent smoking a cigarette in his car, the radio tuned to a distant music station. He went downstairs. Lawrence was leaning against the far wall with his right hand in the trouser pocket of a tailored, dark-grey woollen suit. His wavy fair hair was combed back and he wore his school tie and a pair of expensive-looking round spectacles that gave his thin, handsome face an owlish expression.

"Beatrice said you wanted to see me," he said in a soft voice that still held traces of an Irish childhood. "Something about 'a night on the town'. No doubt it's her idea, not yours, since I imagine you'd rather be hung, drawn and quartered than spend five minutes in a bar with me, but I can see why it might be tricky to explain that to her." He appeared relaxed but spoke a little too quickly for the look of insouciance he was trying to convey, as though rushing to the end of a monologue before he forgot the words. "Between you and me, August, did you know she's applied for our office twice and been turned down both times? No wonder, if this is the general quality of her subterfuge. My guess is she's worried about her contract coming up for renewal and has asked you to find out what HMG is thinking over a few G & Ts. Am I right? It must annoy someone with your experience and ability no end having to answer to a halfwit like her."

Adopt an apologetic tone, be generous with flattery, share a secret, establish a common enemy. All done smoothly enough, thought August. He especially liked the reference to "our" office. It couldn't have been easy to think up a way to open the conversation, given their history. He took a step forward into the room and for the first time Lawrence looked uncertain.

"Now steady on, August," he said quickly. "I'm not here for another fight. In fact, I've asked the chap outside to give us a few minutes because I want to hold my hands up and apologize for what happened in London. I was too" – he sighed and looked around until he found the right word among the cobwebs in a corner of the room – "enthusiastic. I overstepped my brief, I didn't present the evidence impartially, I trampled all over what should have been private territory. It was unforgivable. I have a habit of..." He looked away and chuckled. "I'm still doing it now, I suppose. Talking too much. My mother's always saying that I sound just like my father. He was a criminal barrister in the Four Courts in Dublin – I must have absorbed more of his courtroom manner than I realized. He died last year, I don't know whether you knew that, and I suppose I'm still working all that stuff out, you know, something like that triggers all sorts of thoughts about what kind of a person one wants to be."

Lawrence paused to look out of the window. August had no intention of accepting the apology. It would be like surrendering a piece before it was even clear what game they were playing. There were small indications that Lawrence was nervous about the encounter, that he could be thrown off balance, and August knew he stood a greater chance of finding out what was going on if Lawrence was forced to deviate from his script and improvise. That didn't mean he was sure Lawrence was definitely up to something. Assuming that everyone had an ulterior motive all of the time was one of the side effects of spying for a living, August knew that, along with being suspicious of the smallest coincidence, developing a pragmatic attitude towards the truth and avoiding any new social contact who might ask too many searching questions about the government department you claimed to work for but in truth had not visited for many years. It could also be that Lawrence had simply fallen victim to another common side effect, that of approaching all relationships as though they were something to be handled. Martha had been quick to learn the signs. More than any course she had driven August's skills underground and out of sight where they belonged, teaching him to lose the artificial bonhomie and clumsy empathizing that new case officers tottered around on in the weeks and months after completing their training. "Stop it," she would say, or "Fuck off," or, leaning forward, wringing her hands and earnestly screwing up her face, "I know, I know. It must be so tremendously hard for you. You know that I'm with you every step of the way, don't you? Now, back to that ticking bomb…"

"Anyway, I'm sorry," said Lawrence finally. "I should have listened to wiser heads, counselling me to be a bit less … passionate." When August still didn't say anything, he threw out another line: "Or a bit less of a fucking idiot, that's another way to put it."

"That sounds like the kind of thing Bill might have said." Given Lawrence's native confidence and aggression, August suspected that merely pointing towards a diversion would be enough to send him off his prepared route and into the chicane of a country lane. "I haven't spoken to him since I left. It feels longer than – what is it, a couple of months? Did you know he was my mentor when I first joined the Service? I hope he's all right."

"Bill?" A beat as Lawrence checked the mirrors, adjusted his hands and spun the wheel. "He's very well. He graciously accepted my apology, and gave me some very helpful advice about the world of agents."

Which was contrary to the rumours August had heard, rumours of Lawrence tirelessly pursuing an accusation of harassment in the days after the disciplinary hearing, alleging that Bill's unprofessional language had created the atmosphere of confrontation that had given sanction to August's assault.

"He confided in me over a few drinks that he'll be retiring soon," said Lawrence, warming to his theme. He took off his glasses and wiped them on a handkerchief. "More than a few, if I'm honest. We got through the best part of a bottle of Connemara. I'm sure he wouldn't mind me telling you about his retirement. It'll be a huge blow to the office. He's a legend among the younger generation of officers."

It was true that Bill was serving out his notice, having decided to take early retirement. A non-operational post at a lower grade had been the compromise on offer after the head of personnel had decided there was enough merit in Lawrence's claim to take action. That was what bothered August most: that on the way out he had dragged someone else down with him.

"Mind you, you're on the way to becoming a bit of a legend yourself," Lawrence said hurriedly. He was far from being an idiot – his instincts were sharp enough to realize that in turning off his prepared route he might have clipped an edge on something. "That whole Egypt episode. I'd love to hear your side of the story, if you ever want to talk about it; I'm sure we only scratched the surface. If things were different it'd make a great case study for new recruits, not that I'm suggesting for a moment it would send the right message. But in terms of demonstrating creativity, working with limited resources, planning under pressure, overcoming obstacles, dealing with risk – there's a hell of a lot there people could learn."

It was admirable, from the perspective of a former practitioner, the way Lawrence chose to apply a list of competencies lifted verbatim from the office's HR manual to what had happened in Egypt, throwing them like a net of words over one of the worst examples of disobedience in recent history as though seeking to subdue and domesticate the very act for which they had fired him. August would have to be careful. Lawrence had clearly given this some thought. Or perhaps he simply viewed *everything* in terms of how he would describe it in his next application for promotion. August didn't know which was more likely. He also didn't know what he was supposed to make of the flattery. It was so excessive and inappropriate – he had, after all, lied to his managers, misused official resources, put an agent at risk and threatened Britain's intelligence relationship with Egypt – that he wondered how he could be expected to take it seriously.

"It's a real shame that you're on the outside," Lawrence was saying. "We all feel that. No one is happy about the way things turned out."

The house shifted nervously around them. August watched dust drift along bright diagonals of sunlight like crowds on a bridge. He was in no hurry. Somewhere upstairs a tree rattled against a window.

"I suppose what I'm getting at," said Lawrence, "is that we might be able to find a role for you going forward." He smiled. "What do you think? Would you like to come back?"

It was the last thing August had expected to hear. It made absolutely no sense. Why would they want him back? They had only just got rid of him, and he had no doubt that if they had found enough evidence during the investigation he'd be in prison right now. The only thing of value he could tell them was —

The answer landed with a thud that knocked the air out of his lungs. He struggled to keep his sense of shock under control. They must have found out about 34c, the cemetery, the Iranian scientist: there was no other possibility. They knew what was going on. They knew what was going on and they wanted to stop it. He would do the same in their position – far better to recruit the person already involved in a conspiracy than remove them and insert someone new, with all the risks that carried. It didn't matter how awkward that person might be or how complicated the situation. Dealing with awkward people in complicated situations was what spies were there for.

"As an agent rather than an officer, of course," Lawrence added. "Unfortunately, how shall I put it, that particular bridge has burned down in spectacular style, in a blaze of technicolour glory."

"You've found another way across the river," said August.

"Pardon?"

"A rope swing, perhaps, rather than a bridge."

"That's a good analogy. I know which one sounds more fun, don't you? Listen, agents are the heroes, you know this better than anyone – they are the ones at the coalface, the ones who collect the intelligence. All we do as handlers is fill out the paperwork and take the credit for their good work. I doubt there's a single handler who didn't wish they were an agent instead. You'll have a blast. Look, you're smiling – you know I'm right."

"I'll admit you've taken me by surprise, Lawrence."

"Call me Larry."

"You want *me* to be *your* agent?"

"You're too good to let go."

August laughed. He wanted to find a bar and mark the end of his Istanbul adventure with a drink. And this was definitely the end – there was no way he could continue to pretend to be 34c, not now that Lawrence and his colleagues knew what he was doing, and the last thing he wanted was to stay involved but take his orders from them, and the prospect of turning his back on the whole thing and staying in Istanbul with only Beatrice and her wretched job to occupy his time was intolerable. He'd be on a flight back to London by the end of the week.

"It's a generous offer, Lawrence," he said. "Given everything that's happened. And I want you to know that I don't bear any grudges. But I'm not going to be your agent."

"You haven't heard the offer yet."

August laughed again. It was the funniest thing he'd heard for a long time, the idea that Lawrence would run him as an agent. "Look, I'll tell you whatever you want to know," he said finally, and then he started laughing again. He wiped away the tears. "I'm sorry," he said. "Honestly, I'll answer your questions. I can guess what this is about, and despite what you might think the last thing I want is for them to succeed in what they're planning."

"They? So it's not a solo operation then?"

"What?"

"You see, you've still got the instincts of a spy. We can't let that go to waste, August. You've ended up in the most incredible position, with access to this … conspiracy, there's no other word for it, and —"

"Come on, ask me your questions. I want to go and have a drink."

"Of course I want to hear what you already know. But even more valuable than that would be for you to stay in place and help us find a way to disrupt what's happening. And I'm prepared to make you a very generous offer, August. I'll cover your rent, your flights home, your medical insurance. And five hundred dollars a month on top of that. You could have a very comfortable life here, considering that you're getting a salary from Beatrice as well. And I'll protect you, in case you find yourself in a spot of bother. There's a formidable woman called Elif from the local Service who's breathing down our necks a bit, always wanting to know what we're up to, but I fancy I can get her under control. We can discuss all that later. You said you wanted a drink – why don't you let me treat you to dinner? There's a fancy rooftop bar called 360 Istanbul that everyone's been telling me —"

It hurt, it physically hurt, August found, laughing that hard. Like a rusted old car rolling down a hill, there was friction and spark and clatter, and anyone watching might have wondered if he'd make it to the bottom in one piece, but by the time he finally came to a standstill, a few minutes clear of the hill, he found to his surprise that beneath the rust and dead leaves and bird shit he was still a car. It was as good a feeling as he'd had for a long while.

Lawrence's smile had disappeared.

"What's so funny?" he said, his face turning red.

"I mean … you as an agent handler, Lawrence, and me as your agent. You have to admit it'd be a funny pairing."

"I don't see why."

"Come on, you're not thinking straight."

"I know what I'm doing, August."

"No, you don't. You're out of your depth. It's not your fault, but that's the truth."

"I doubt you'd find it so amusing if you lost your job."

For the second time that day Lawrence had surprised him.

"What do you mean?" August asked.

Lawrence took a step into the middle of the room. "I'm just saying, I doubt you'd find everything so fucking amusing if you found yourself out of a job for the second time this year."

It was quiet, except for the sound of the car radio outside and the distant rustle of water. It was unmistakable what had just happened: the sudden bloom of humiliation, Lawrence's threat charging the air with heat. The last thing anyone wanted was an agent who had been coerced. As a handler, you wanted an agent who was doing it freely and for their own reasons, whether patriotism, ideology, money or even revenge. It didn't much matter if their motive was dishonourable – a grubby banknote was worth the same as a clean one. But a coerced agent was a different thing altogether. August wondered whether he was responsible, whether by humiliating Lawrence first in London and now here he had planted in him a desire for revenge that had quickly outgrown whatever values of respect he had been taught. Perhaps the surprising thing was that more officers weren't like Lawrence. It would always be easier to secure cooperation through coercion than by being clever, persuasive and likeable. No one doubted that in this respect Russian spies had a much easier task than their British counterparts.

"Why would I lose my job?" said August.

"Ah, it's just idle speculation. Hypothetically, though? There's an economic downturn or the war in Syria comes to an end or…" Lawrence shrugged. He was quiet for a moment, as though coming to a decision. "The British government imposes all sorts of regulations on contractors like Beatrice. One of them being that she has to properly vet all her staff, and if she found out that an employee had been in prison or used a fake reference or tweeted something unacceptable she'd be forced to fire them." There it was, a clear suggestion of pressure, doing its best to look innocent like a criminal in a line-up of respectable citizens. "Not that any of that applies in your case, of course," he added. "You're not on Twitter, August, are you? There you go, you're in the clear. I'm merely saying that life is full of uncertainty and anything you can do to give yourself an insurance policy is a good thing, right?"

So that was the offer. Either he accepted it, made a bit of extra money and from this point onwards took his orders from Lawrence, or he would find himself out of a job. It was an easy decision to make; it wasn't Lawrence's fault that he didn't know how much August hated working for Beatrice, that he thought of quitting every day. But something held him back – he wanted to know how

Lawrence had found out about 34c and the vizier, and the only way to do that was to let things play out. It was professional curiosity more than anything else. Had he been careless with his tradecraft – allowing himself to be followed to the cemetery or overheard on the phone – or had the mistake been the vizier's? Or had 34c talked?

Lawrence took out a packet of French cigarettes and lit one. He didn't offer them to August. He didn't need to pretend any more: they both knew what had just happened. August understood that for Lawrence, whether he recognized it within himself or not, his offer of work was fuelled by the urgent need to reassert himself as the dominant party. August had made him look bad – by running rings around him for four years, by cracking his nose open in front of colleagues. He wondered whether he was witnessing the first act in the ruining of an intelligence officer.

"Well, I'm glad we've found ourselves on the same page at last." He crossed the room to stand directly in front of August. "I'm sure it'll take a little time for us both to get used to this new arrangement. And that's fine. Rome wasn't built in a day. To make it easier we can start off with a few little things – errands, you might call them. Low risk, eyes and ears stuff, pass on any gossip you hear around town. While you get used to being on a leash." He breathed out a mouthful of smoke and smiled. "But a friendly warning might be in order. Ah, warning is too strong a word, August. I don't like talking about things like chain of command. We're not in the military after all. I just don't want you to make a mistake and ruin what could be

131

a good thing for both of us because you're still adjusting to this. So let's agree that you'll take things slowly and come to me if you've got any doubts, if anything's worrying you. We can talk it through." Lawrence took another slow mouthful of smoke, letting the silence build. "Remember that I know your style. It got to the point that I was able to spot your fingerprints at a hundred metres. We might not have found enough evidence for a prosecution, but I have no doubt at all you were our Robin Hood. Come on, you can admit it now. My favourite was probably the Russian diplomat, just in terms of amusement value, but for sheer chutzpah it'd have to be the Norwegian thing. I mean, leaking intelligence to a foreign government *inside the building*? Hats off, August. The only question I have is why you did it all, why you ruined what could have been an impressive career. Was someone else involved? Was it a Chinese plan to weaken our defences from within? I imagine you felt like one of those plucky World War II saboteurs, running around with a rucksack full of dynamite trying to put cracks in dams and bring down bridges. For a while we wondered whether you were in it with Jonas Worth. The two of you worked together briefly, didn't you? Now there's a motive I can understand – trying to save his father. I can't imagine what he went through. But you?"

His phone beeped and he took it from his pocket to read a message.

"Good," he said, looking at his watch and smiling. "It's all coming together nicely. Now, how about that dinner? I took the liberty of booking a table for half seven. You a steak man?"

"How did you find out about it?" said August.

"What, your faked job reference?"

"The plot."

"I'll tell you over dinner."

"Tell me now."

"Did you hear all that chain of command stuff a minute ago?" said Lawrence. "Well, this is your chance —"

"I'm curious, I'll admit that. But not enough to sit through a whole dinner with you."

"And if I tell you that you haven't got a choice?"

"Are you sure that's a good idea? With steak knives on the table?"

Lawrence laughed nervously. "Maybe I should book a Chinese restaurant," he said.

"I'd happily kill you with a chopstick."

The colour drained from Lawrence's face and he took a quick step towards the door. "Very funny. The property agent will be coming in any minute now."

"If I buried you out here, they'd never find your body."

Lawrence turned the door handle and the room filled with cold air.

"All right, August, suit yourself. Go back to your shitty hotel and eat a Pot Noodle if that's what you want. Just remember what we've agreed today, and what will happen if you don't play ball. I'll call you tomorrow. Make sure you pick up."

"How did you find out about it?"

"Why do you keep asking that? I don't know exactly – probably by going through the books."

"What books?"

"What's wrong with you, August? You said you knew what this was about." He ground his cigarette into the floor with the heel of an expensive shoe. "Beatrice is stealing money from the British government, plenty of it, and I want you to get us the proof."

It was all August could do not to start laughing again.

15

Lawrence was right, August and Jonas had worked in the same team for just under a year, but August had never felt he'd known him well. He doubted anyone in the office had. It was partly Jonas's shyness, which could be painful to observe and often revealed itself as a formality that kept people at arm's length. It didn't help that he always wore a suit and tie – and in an office that surprised visitors by straining with every sinew towards the casual, as though to compensate for the dreadful seriousness of the challenge it faced. And there was the way he would gather up dozens of files and disappear for hours at a time, only to return knowing everything that was in them – every name and code name, every beat of the intelligence case, even most of the telephone numbers. It made his colleagues mildly uncomfortable.

They had first met long before that. A twenty-three-year-old August had wandered by chance into a meeting of the Cambridge University chess society and taken a chair across from the only person without an opponent. He soon realized why that was the case. August had started playing against adults on the outdoor boards in Manhattan's Washington Square Park at the age of fourteen, during a long summer holiday, and at boarding school he had hustled more than a few fellow students out of their pocket money over wet weekends when there was little else to do. But that first game with Jonas lasted a few seconds under four minutes, and they were able to fit another six games into the hour that remained before the hall was taken over by the Christian Union. By the end of term August was able to keep Jonas at bay for sixteen minutes. They never talked while they played, though, and when he went overseas for Christmas – his parents lived in Hong Kong at the time – August realized he barely knew anything about Jonas, other than that he looked like a young D. H. Lawrence, rode around on an old Raleigh and often forgot to remove his bicycle clips.

After Cambridge it was more than ten years before they saw each other again, in the queue for the office coffee bar, and a game was quickly arranged. It soon became a weekly occurrence. In a corner of the staff canteen, their plates pushed to one side, they would play on a pocket chess set belonging to Jonas, largely indifferent to the conversations that hummed around them, conversations about useless bosses, blocked toilets, inadequate pay and office romances. August's best performance, one month to the day before Jonas's father was kidnapped, resulted in a game lasting an entire lunch break.

There was more to their relationship than that, but not much. On two or three occasions they'd had a drink together in a pub, and on a rainy Sunday in late summer one year August had invited him for lunch with Martha. Most of what he knew about Jonas, he reflected afterwards, he learned during that meal, with no chessboard to act as a surrogate for conversation. Martha somehow understood Jonas from the moment she opened the door, and patiently, gently, lovingly put him at ease, to the point that he talked at length about the books he enjoyed, the countries he wanted to visit, the plans he had to leave government work and return to academia.

It had happened soon afterwards. First a grainy photograph of an old man in an orange jumpsuit, then a crazy ransom demand. Everyone expected Jonas to stop working, but he kept coming into the office, kept attending meetings and writing reports and disappearing for hours on end with as many files as he could carry. August knew something was going on. Others said it was just Jonas's way of dealing with it all, to bury himself in work. It would be odd if there wasn't erratic behaviour, they said, if he didn't look exhausted, if there wasn't the occasional day he turned up late or appeared distracted.

But they hadn't been there when Jonas had taken August into a stairwell and asked him how he should go about recruiting an agent. In theory, he added quickly. It depends, August said: on their character, their circumstances, how much time you have with them. Who is it?

"I don't want to get you involved," Jonas said.

"Don't be silly. I want to be involved."

"Do I have to make them like me first?"

"It helps. But it's not everything. It's more important that they respect you. What do you know about them?"

Jonas had taken his time answering, obviously reluctant to give too much away.

"He's … he's older than me, European. He has a drinking problem. I don't know what information is relevant. He's a priest."

"Is there anything you can do for him? Anything you can offer him? That can be an important part of the conversation."

"I don't know. I can't imagine…"

"Listen, Jonas, think of it as a conversation. A recruitment is just a conversation. You're trying to understand what his motivation to help you might be and then developing those ideas so they become central in his mind. But what's this about? What are you going to do? Let me approach this person for you."

"You'd get into trouble. More trouble than you can imagine."

"Listen, I've never told anyone in the office about this before, and I'm only mentioning it because I know you'll be discreet, but I've done things that would —"

"I know about all that."

It was the last thing August had expected to hear.

"They asked me to look at the INKWELL file," said Jonas. "About a year ago. They wanted me to study the incidents and work out who was responsible. It was all very secretive, I wasn't allowed to take the file out of their room. Don't worry, I told them it was impossible to find out, that whoever it was had covered their tracks." He smiled. "Only one very small mistake. But what I'm talking about doing is completely different. It's in the open. Once it happens there'll be no way of hiding – they'll come for me with everything they've got."

"I don't care about that. Let me —"

"What about Martha? If anything happened to you…"

"What's going to happen to me? Listen, Jonas, I want to help."

"You *are* helping. Just by talking to me about it. Tell me, it sounds so complicated. What do you do if you say the wrong thing?"

"Don't think like that. If it goes in an unexpected direction just find a way to keep the door open to a second conversation, and then one after that. It's like a series of chess moves. You can recover from what might look like a mistake. Not that you'd know, the way you play, I doubt you've ever —"

Above them a door swung open and someone shouted August's name.

"Don't worry, Jonas," he said quietly. "This'll stay between us. But let's talk again very soon. Somewhere away from the office. Tell me everything you know about this guy and together we'll work out a plan."

But he disappeared three days later. No one knew where he'd gone. The message filtered down from on high that he'd been granted an indefinite period of leave to deal with what was described as "a complex set of personal circumstances". There were rumours – that he'd moved home to look after his mother, that he'd done an interview with the BBC to generate publicity for his father's case, that he'd been sectioned under the Mental Health Act. One person said he'd flown to Beirut, another said they'd spotted him dancing like a lunatic at a club in Ibiza. August tried to call him numerous times. When he went round to his flat in east London he spoke to a neighbour who said she hadn't seen him for over a month.

And then out of nowhere came news of the rescue of Jonas's father on the Syrian border. There were reports of four British nationals being killed; their relatives confirmed they were a group of school friends who had left in the back of a lorry to join IS three years earlier. The media speculated endlessly about what had compelled them to take a Western hostage from the relative safety of Raqqa into such uncertain territory. But there was no news of Jonas, in the press or in the office, and before long the received wisdom was that he'd formally resigned to spend time with his parents. Understandable, really. And in some ways he'd never really seemed to enjoy working in the office. Probably better for everyone this way.

August couldn't leave it there. He had approached the director of HR and asked for the address of Jonas's parents. It would be odd not to contact them, he explained. He simply wanted to check that everyone was all right and see if he could help. And he had an item to return. But the director told him that Jonas had been extremely clear with the office that he didn't want to see or hear from anyone as he considered that chapter of his life to be closed. Which might have been the end of it if it hadn't been for his parting comment, which struck August as so excessive and unnecessary that it could only be intended to obscure something else.

"You understand how serious this is, do you?" he said. "Leave the matter well alone. I will personally ensure disciplinary action is taken if you try to contact Jonas or his family."

August caught a train from Charing Cross the next day and walked the half mile from the small country station to the cottage where Jonas's parents lived. It hadn't been difficult to find their address. The flower beds along the front were filled with roses, and ivy trailed up the red brickwork towards the roof. A woman in her seventies answered the door. She started to cry when she heard that August was a friend of her son and the noise brought her husband to the door. He walked with a stick and was bent at the shoulders but there was nothing gentle about the way he looked August in the eye and told him to leave them alone. As the door slammed shut he heard Jonas's mother saying sorry over and over again while her husband comforted her.

He was on the platform waiting for a train back to London when he realized he'd forgotten to give them Jonas's pocket chess set. He sat down on an empty bench and arranged the pieces on the board, trying to remember which opening moves Jonas had favoured. It was a beautiful day, the early morning mist slow to clear, and beyond the railway tracks he could see grey-wreathed hills and above them faint patches of chalky blue sky. Two figures made their way slowly across the hillside, and so profound was August's distress that it was a while before he recognized them. Not really knowing what he was doing or where he was going, he left the station and found himself on a path that led through the churchyard and a fruit orchard before turning sharply and beginning to climb. The imprint of a walking stick was visible where the slope was steep.

They were seated on a wooden bench that looked over the village and the patchwork of surrounding fields. He didn't want to disturb them, despite having followed them, and so he stood foolishly behind a clump of trees, far enough away that he couldn't hear what they were saying, wondering if in his entire career he had ever intruded on someone's privacy as thoroughly, as appallingly, as unforgivably as he was doing at that moment. As they stood up to leave Jonas's father took out a handkerchief and wiped a plaque on the back of the bench.

They descended the hill more slowly than they had climbed it, as though reluctant to leave or carrying an extra burden. August approached the bench and read on the plaque: I FOUND HIM WHOM MY SOUL LOVES. I HELD HIM AND WOULD NOT LET GO.

He stood there for a long time, watching trains come and go while mist rolled across the valley like smoke over a battlefield.

16

FILE EXCERPT FROM INVESTIGATION INTO AUGUST DRUMMOND

INKWELL/071

TOP SECRET
FOIA EXEMPT

SUBJECT: Behavioural Science Unit proposal
DATE: 13 October 2015

1. Following high-level disquiet caused by the latest
    INKWELL incident, and in the absence of any real investi-
    gative progress by the Gatekeeping team towards catching
    the perpetrator, we would like to propose a radical new
    method of identifying the individual responsible.

Update

2. On 23 September 2015 the NSA shared with the UK a
    piece of SIGINT reporting that detailed a British nation-
    al's possible terrorist reconnaissance of a shopping centre
    in Oslo. Despite our request to share this reporting with
    the Norwegian authorities as a matter of urgency, the US

declined, citing the aspirational nature of the attack plan and the sensitive technical access that had generated the reporting.

3. On 2 October a high-level delegation from the Norwegian government was in London for an annual meeting to discuss routine intelligence-sharing procedures. Once the delegation had taken their seats and the meeting was under way, it was discovered that someone had inserted an extra page into the agenda on which was printed a copy of the classified US report. As each attendee had been given their own copy of the agenda, it was not possible to retrieve the US report before it was seen by the majority of delegates.

4. As far as we are aware, this marks the first time that anyone has ever leaked intelligence to representatives of a foreign government inside the building.

Proposal

5. We leave to others an assessment of damage done by this episode to the UK's vital relationship with the US. What concerns us here is its corrosive effect upon staff discipline. Anecdotal evidence suggests that an awareness of INKWELL is widespread among staff, in part because of a widely read and deeply regrettable Behavioural Science Unit assessment that characterized the perpetrator as a "Robin Hood" seeking to help the unfortunate and bring the guilty to justice. This is clearly nonsense. Nonetheless it has found its way into the bloodstream of the office and captured idle imaginations.

6. It is evident that the investigative techniques traditionally used to counter the insider threat have not proved effective in this case. In light of this, we would like to propose something never before tried in the UK but which does have historical precedent.

7. In 1994 the CIA were trying to identify a Russian spy within their ranks. In order to whittle their shortlist of 198 down to a more manageable number, they chose 10 trusted individuals from across the CIA, presented them with the list of 198 suspects and asked them to pick the 5 most likely to be a Russian agent, relying on nothing more than their gut instinct. Astonishingly, the name Aldrich Ames featured on the lists of all 10 officers.

8. The list of INKWELL candidates currently stands at 32 names. Subject to agreement of seniors, and recognizing the privacy issues around sharing the list of suspects with officers not involved in the case, we would like to pursue this same course of action. We have among the British intelligence community some very experienced, intelligent, intuitive and discreet individuals. Allow us to harness their abilities in order to find our traitor.

9. We await a decision from Private Office.

ENDS

17

It had started in 2011, at the end of August's first full year working for the government. On that first occasion it was a lock-up in Walthamstow. His agent produced a key in the first minute of their meeting, threw it excitedly onto the table and explained that he'd been asking around as instructed for somewhere to store a few bikes – notionally stolen, in reality borrowed from a police robbery team – and a Somali guy at the mosque had offered up a corner of his garage in return for fifty quid. What got the agent excited was that the brother wore the rolled-up trousers of the Salafi and was rumoured to hang around with members of Al Muhajiroun.

August was less convinced that this added up to anything significant, and decided that a quick – not to mention off-the-books, unauthorized, unwarranted and thoroughly illegal – search would determine whether it was worth arguing that the office should investigate the matter properly, given the number of high-priority operations running elsewhere. That summer there had been arrests almost every week and staff were working round-the-clock shifts. A drive past the brightly lit row of garages made it clear that without additional resources there was no way of doing it covertly, and so that same evening, after tasking his agent to call the Somali and confirm he was elsewhere, August bought a fluorescent jacket, a torch and a pair of work boots. He filled a clipboard with headed paper printed from the website of a local pest-control company. He expected to be in and out within five minutes. What he didn't expect was to find a box of ball bearings behind a loose brick, or a Tesco bag filled with salt and vinegar crisps, a loaf of white bread, three tins of beans and a bottle of beer. It was only the scratches on the bottle cap that made him lean in more closely, into a smell so pungent that he didn't need to open the bottle to realize it had been refilled with something quite different to beer.

He had no choice but to report his discovery immediately, even though he didn't know what the bottle contained, or who had put it in the bag, or whether there was a plausible reason for its presence. There would be clues in the garage owner's criminal record, if he had one, in his social media accounts, internet browsing history, recent travel and contact with known extremists, all of which the office could assess within minutes. August could do nothing on his own.

But when he went in to file a fabricated report claiming it was the agent who had discovered the items, August found the operations room fizzing with the news that an unidentified male had just entered an east London lock-up at the centre of a day-old, top-of-the-grid investigation into a network of IS sympathizers. There were so many operations running that news of this one had passed him by. He stood at the back of the room, his heart racing, watching looped, grainy footage from a camera of a tall, dark-haired, white male in a fluorescent jacket opening the garage door, pulling it shut behind him and then emerging four minutes later only to disappear down an alleyway and into a neighbouring council estate. It was the key that got them worked up. Whoever he is, the team leader argued, he's part of it, he's got their trust. And we have absolutely no idea who he is.

It was luck that stopped him being identified, fired, possibly even arrested. Half the CCTV cameras in the estate had been smashed, and the covert camera – installed in a rush the night before – had been too far away to capture a good likeness, especially in the dark, especially through the beaded curtain of rain. Whoever the man was, he hadn't used public transport to exit the area. Staff of the utility, property, construction and cleaning companies canvassed by police didn't recognize his picture. An examination of phone data proved inconclusive. None of which meant that the investigative team stopped looking for him. If anything the search intensified, especially when the case went to court and the defendant's lawyers claimed it was the unidentified male who had planted the ball bearings and the bottle, not their client, along with the bundle of copper wiring and alkaline torch batteries the police later found taped to a roof beam. Much was made of the fact that the man with the key was white. The jury took less than an hour to reach a verdict of not guilty. The lawyers made a speech on the steps of the court in which they mentioned Guantánamo Bay and the Birmingham

Six and accused the state of fabricating evidence against vulnerable members of a minority community.

The same lawyers weren't quite so conspicuous two months later when their client was arrested on a bus in possession of three knives and the address of a senior army officer. August spent a long time reflecting on the fact that the man had only been caught because a fellow passenger had called the police hotline to report an African acting funny on the top deck.

He came very close to stopping there. There was no way he could justify what he'd done. He'd only broken the rules to prove to Martha he wasn't an automaton who merely followed orders, that he was capable of making his own decisions even when the price of disobedience was high. From the very beginning of their relationship she'd found it difficult to accept what he did for a living. That deceit was hardwired into it, that it knocked so many lives off course, that it was used to justify cordial relations with such terrible regimes. He said that intelligence was a dirty business but a necessary one, faced with the threat of terrorism and the existence of hostile states like Russia and China. She said the tools spies used were the unimportant lives of others, that they would always find a way to justify the harm they did by pointing to matters of state. When framed in such black-and-white terms, how could the right of an individual to freedom and privacy compete with a country's economic prosperity? He said that the alternative was to wait until an attack had been carried out and then investigate the perpetrators. If you wanted to find out what was going to happen before it happened, you had to be prepared to rummage around in people's lives. She told him that was a shockingly casual way to describe it. She told him to stop pretending it was all about preventing attacks. Everyone accepted that a country needed the ability to do that – but what about secret courts and illegal surveillance and rendition and lethal strikes and torture? What about spies allowing politicians to distort their intelligence to start a war? He called her idealistic and naive. She told him to answer the question. At some point they opened another bottle of wine. He said that if he ever saw anything unethical or illegal he'd shout about it from the rooftops. She asked him to name the last British whistle-blower. In this community that you insist is filled with such good people, she said, who had come forward in recent years to alert the public to bad things? Or had there been no bad things? He said that all this talk of bad things made her sound like an undergraduate. But this is how big organizations work, she said. They encourage individuals to avoid thinking about personal responsibility by claiming that it's the responsibility of the organization as a whole, as if an organization can possibly be responsible for anything. Everyone *thinks* they're blameless, she said – look at the Catholic Church, look at tobacco companies, look at the police and its undercover officers. All of those organizations are filled with decent people who allowed appalling things to happen. For Christ's sake, she said, look at the fact that the unofficial motto of the CIA – the agency that gave the world waterboarding – is a line from John's Gospel. Doesn't that tell you *everything* you need to know about which side of this argument you should be on?

They ran out of wine an hour or two before dawn.

"Do you want me to resign?" he asked, his head resting on her stomach. It surprised him to find the thought didn't bother him. He'd been there less than two years – there were plenty of other things he could do.

"No. Don't be silly, Gus. I don't know. It's just that —"

"I will, you know. You're more important to me than a job. And I don't disagree with —"

"It just feels like…"

"I would take a stand, you know, if…"

They were both quiet for a while.

"It's a complex job." She said it very quietly, to herself more than anything, as a way of working out what she felt. "And your attitude towards it must be equally complex. It can't be straightforward. What you do might be, I don't know, seventy, eighty, ninety per cent good, but there's some pretty awful stuff hiding among those last few per cent."

"Maybe I should only do my job seventy per cent of the time," he said after a while.

"Oh, you're awake."

"Barely. What time is it?"

"Or only put in seventy per cent effort," she said. "It's 5.20."

"Give thirty per cent of my pay to charity."

And a little while later, when they were both very close to falling asleep, she said, "It just seems that you've got to acknowledge it somehow. In how you act."

"What's that?"

"That what you do for a living is not always a straight-forwardly good thing."

"How?"

"I don't know. Be willing to break the rules. Be willing to make your own decisions. Do the right thing, even if it isn't what your superiors want you to do."

"Huh? I would be. I am."

"Are you though?" she asked. "I imagine everyone says that. How do you really know?"

"I suppose there's no way of knowing until it happens."

And that might have been the end of it. He closed his eyes, she closed her eyes. Her breathing slowed and deepened. A few minutes passed before he propped himself up on an elbow and looked at her. "Martha?" he whispered. "Are you awake? I'll show you. I'll do something to show you that I'm willing to break the rules."

The promise slipped out unnoticed like a coin from the pocket of someone getting up to leave. Given the hour, given the amount of wine they had drunk, no one could have blamed him for never thinking of the matter again. But then his agent threw a bunch of keys onto the table and started to describe a lock-up in Walthamstow, and in an instant it all came back.

Things changed after that. Not just because he'd come so close to getting caught or interfered in the legal process with such potentially deadly consequences. If I'm going to break the rules again, he decided, it can't be another gesture simply to show Martha I haven't turned into a company man. If I'm going to break the rules, it must be to correct a state of affairs that is clearly wrong. It must be the right thing to do, regardless of official policy, regardless of regulations. It must seek to redress a wrong that is only allowed to persist for bureaucratic, reputational or political reasons. My actions mustn't harm anyone, at least no one undeserving. It must feel fair. The planning must be precise and painstaking and the execution must be professional in every aspect. The tradecraft must be flawless. I must do it alone, without the help of colleagues, and the blame must never fall on anyone innocent.

He took a deep breath. He wondered whether he was being naive or disloyal, whether he'd have the courage when the time came, whether he'd even find anything that met all his requirements. But the next day he picked up the transcript of an intercepted phone call between a prolific radicalizer and a prostitute, and from that moment nothing would ever be the same again.

18

It was hard not to feel a little uneasy in hotel corridors, August thought. That sense of scurrying confinement, and all those people lurking just out of sight, and the interminable build-up to the encounter with the person approaching, as though you were jousting knights and only one of you could pass unharmed. It was harder still if you were about to do something that could get you arrested.

A middle-aged European man in tennis whites brushed past with a curt nod. August heard a door open and close ten paces behind him.

The vizier had insisted it would be straightforward.

"We have his key. A sister who works there got it for us. No one will question a European in a big hotel like this. Once you are inside the room look for evidence of what he wants to buy, his shopping list, who are his contacts. Maybe we can find the people in Istanbul who are helping him and deal with them afterwards. Leave no sign that you were there. A phone is buried in a blue plastic bag in our usual meeting place. The edge of the bag can be seen above the ground. The room key is in there too. Fill in the hole afterwards and put some leaves and dirt over the top. The phone does not have a SIM card but the camera works and the battery is charged. Take pictures of what you find in the room and then meet me in the usual place tonight at eleven o'clock to hand it back. Do not be late. Is this understood? Good. Wait in the lobby at seven. We have been told he has an engagement elsewhere this evening. Read a newspaper, drink a coffee – like any other guest. I will call you when he leaves."

August was seated in a corner of the lobby at half past six. Just before seven he watched the Iranian emerge from one of the four lifts, dressed in the same grey suit and black shoes he had been wearing the last time. His leather briefcase was clutched to his chest.

The phone rang six minutes later.

"We are following him," the vizier said. "Wait for five minutes and then begin. I will call you if he returns in the direction of the hotel. No mistakes this time."

August took the lift to the eighth floor and walked the corridors until he understood the layout and the CCTV coverage. He climbed one flight of stairs. An elderly Japanese couple were shepherding three young children ahead of them towards the lifts; August stood aside to let them pass. He walked a full circuit to confirm the layout was the same as the floor below. There was a "do not disturb" sign on the door to room 907. He knocked softly, waited for five seconds and then held the key card against the reader. Using the corner of his shirt he turned the handle and suddenly he was inside.

Darkness, silence. He counted down from twenty. Nothing in the key slot on the wall to his right. Once his eyes had adjusted he pushed open the bathroom door to confirm it was empty and stepped into the bedroom to do the same. If this was a trap he wanted whatever was coming next to happen in the dark. He put on a cap and a pair of gloves, set his watch to vibrate in five minutes, turned on the light and began.

The wardrobe first. The safe was locked. The hotel slippers, dressing gown and laundry bag had not been used. Three clean shirts and one pair of black trousers. Enough underwear for a week. There was a room-service receipt on the bedside table for that same day, just three hours earlier: a bowl of pasta, a selection of pastries, sparkling water. A three-day-old Turkish newspaper in the bin by the bed, a crumpled food wrapper, a banana peel, a ticket to Unalan and a pair of socks with a hole in the right toe. The bedcovers were rumpled, but when he pulled them back August saw that the bottom sheet was clean and pulled tight; he wondered whether the man had slept somewhere else, or if the cleaner had been interrupted halfway through making it. Nothing under the pillows or the mattress. On the far bedside table a napkin was tucked under the phone with two Turkish mobile numbers in pencil. There was a receipt on the armchair for a fax sent to an Iranian number from the hotel's business centre that afternoon and a catalogue of cleaning products from a company in Ankara, with something scribbled in Farsi on one of the pages. The bathroom was empty other than a toothbrush and a small tube of toothpaste of the kind handed out by airlines.

His watch vibrated. He took a cotton bud from his pocket, swabbed the toothbrush and placed it in a clean plastic bag. He wrote down the two phone numbers. Making sure everything was as he had found it, he left the room and took the stairs all the way down to the lobby.

It didn't matter that he hadn't taken any photographs. He hadn't even handled the phone the vizier had given him, in case there were fingerprints on it. The truth was he had carried out the search not because the vizier had told him to but because it had given him the opportunity he was looking for to collect intelligence for Lawrence and his colleagues, so that when he told them what was happening they'd be able to corroborate his story and identify the individuals involved. It was time to let them deal with this. August had taken things as far as he could. Even his own, unusually elastic sense of risk was showing signs of fatigue when he thought about what IS planned to do. The situation required the judgement and resources of a professional intelligence agency. They would easily be able to identify the Iranian on the basis of his hotel booking and DNA. And he'd have something else for them by the end of the evening: a description of the vizier.

Before walking to the cemetery, he went back to his hotel and dropped off the things he'd collected, rehearsing the story he planned to tell: that he'd been challenged by a security guard, that he'd realized *he* was the one taking all the risks, that it was outrageous he wasn't trusted enough for a proper, face-to-face conversation with the man who claimed they were on the same side. He'd be emotional, he'd be angry. He'd accuse the vizier of tricking him. One way or another, he'd turn around. He'd make sure he got close enough to see his face. He didn't know what would happen after that. He'd sensed the potential for violence within the man, and for that reason he planned to be ready for anything, to limit himself to one drink in a nearby bar. Halfway through that drink it occurred to him that he could use the fact he'd admitted to a drinking problem to add to the theatre of what he planned to do. Given that this would be their last meeting, it didn't matter what the vizier thought of him any more. And if August appeared drunk, there was a greater chance the vizier would write him off as harmless and walk away, never to see him again. By that point it would be too late. August would have everything he needed to disrupt their plot. And so he settled in to make it look real.

Before he knew it he was drunk again. When he arrived at the cemetery it was after midnight. He fell asleep underneath a lemon tree and dreamed of a hand as heavy and cold as stone lying across his forehead and pressing him down into the earth. When he woke at dawn he saw that someone had gone through his pockets and placed everything in a neat pile, his phone and hotel key and money and a crumpled picture of Martha.

And August understood for the first time that he wasn't in a fit state for any of this, that it had all been a huge mistake, and that the idea he was in control of himself or anything around him was nothing more than an illusion, but it was much too late to turn back.

19

FILE EXCERPT FROM INVESTIGATION INTO AUGUST DRUMMOND

INKWELL/128

TOP SECRET

FOIA EXEMPT

SUBJECT: Transcript of August DRUMMOND disciplinary
hearing

DATE: 28 September 2016

IMOGEN: Is that wretched contraption finally working? Everyone ready? Marvellous. For the purposes of the tape recorder, this is Imogen, Deputy Director for Human Resources and Workforce Planning. We are here this morning to review, consider, challenge and ultimately decide upon the disciplinary case against August DRUMMOND that has been compiled by the Gatekeeping team, represented here today by Lawrence. The panel consists of three senior managers: Bill from CT HUMINT; Daphne from Vetting; and Desmond Naseby, on loan from our friends across the river in SIS because of the international aspects of this case. Susan here will be taking notes in case the tape recorder fails us. Now, you've all had the opportunity to study Lawrence's paper and will ask questions and make comments as we go. My role is to oversee the process and ensure that relevant policies are followed. Any questions at this stage? August, how about you? Marvellous. Now, this part is important. As I've said, it is the responsibility of this panel to decide on the merits of the case. Your role, Lawrence, is not to act as prosecution or defence but simply to describe events in a clear and straightforward manner. While it is certainly true that our threshold for withdrawing an officer's security clearance is much lower than the threshold for criminal liability, it is important that we do not terminate what has been an impressive career by placing undue weight on speculation, however tempting that might be. Is everyone happy with that as a basis for proceeding? Excellent. Then let's begin. Lawrence?

LAWRENCE: Thank you, Imogen. Some background to start us off. WINDMILL POET is an agent of nine years' standing, considered to be established and reliable. A dual British–Egyptian national in his mid-thirties, originally recruited by the police CTU in Manchester to provide eyes-and-ears reporting on mosques in the Rusholme area, where he was living while completing a PhD in Engineering. Not a spectacular career as a reporting agent, chiefly because he didn't have an extremist profile, but he was hard-working and liked by his handlers.

BILL: Any disciplinary concerns noted on his record?

LAWRENCE: None.

BILL: No laziness, no lies, no unauthorized disclosures?

LAWRENCE: Nothing. We took over the case from the police in 2011 when the revolution began in Egypt. August has been his handler since then. In addition to providing CT reporting in the UK, WINDMILL POET had access through family members to a number of key figures in the opposition movement and so was deployed upstream to Egypt on a semi-regular basis.

DAPHNE: Interested in that, are we?

LAWRENCE: The Egyptian opposition? An excellent question, Daphne. No, not really. Certainly not any more. But in the right circumstances an opposition can become a government very quickly. SIS – Desmond, with your vast experience you might be in a better position to comment here – SIS in particular argued that having someone at ground level on day one of a new government in Cairo would have been invaluable. Obviously things didn't turn out that way. But everyone remains of the view that the upstream deployments were a worthwhile investment in WINDMILL POET's utility as an agent on CT as well as political matters. To have camped out in Tahrir Square, to have been charged by stick-wielding regime thugs on horses and camels, well, it's a great story to be able to tell and would have enhanced WINDMILL POET's credibility on the streets of Manchester as much as anywhere else.

DESMOND: As soon as the senators begin to crowd around Caesar you need to decide which one of the treacherous bastards is about to become your new chum. Doesn't matter that Caesar himself was your best friend five minutes earlier.

LAWRENCE: I may steal that analogy for use in the future. Now, WINDMILL POET's wife is central to the matter we are here to discuss. A journalist for an opposition website, she was also a dual national, also an energetic opponent of Mubarak, Morsi and now Sisi. She was arrested in Cairo eight months ago and put in Tora Maximum Security Prison, known more colloquially as "The Scorpion". She wasn't charged with anything, which is not unusual, but clearly came under the general category of political prisoner, regime opponent, that sort of thing. No surprise there, as Egypt is routinely in the top three countries worldwide for locking up journalists, along with Turkey and China. Her situation caused us numerous handling difficulties with WINDMILL POET. Quite understandably, he wanted us to intervene with the Egyptian government to secure his wife's release. Our position throughout was that we were doing everything possible through the FCO and embassy but that as she was an Egyptian national our hands were tied. Any out-of-the-ordinary intervention on our part would have signalled to the Egyptians that WINDMILL POET was an agent, thereby putting him at risk. He found our position difficult to accept, especially as news from inside the prison suggested malnutrition, poor health, beatings and prolonged spells inside what they call discipline cells, essentially a cramped space that causes extreme discomfort. At various points he threatened to go to the papers, make a fuss in the media, that sort of thing, but I'm pleased to say that he stuck with us.

BILL: With us?

LAWRENCE: Yes, Bill. Now if I —

BILL: It's a small point but an important one. The relationship you are describing exists between an agent and a handler, not between an agent and an office of several thousand people.

LAWRENCE: Quite so. An excellent point. Now if —

BILL: And August deserves credit for maintaining that relationship during a very difficult period.

LAWRENCE: He certainly does. In fact, if I may develop your point a little further, Bill, it was this close agent–handler relationship you describe that underpinned the conspiracy they entered into together not long afterwards. The fact they trusted each other is evidence —

BILL: Steady on, Lawrence. Remember that you're not an advocate for either side. The fact that August and WINDMILL POET had a good relationship is evidence that August was doing his job and doing it well, nothing more.

LAWRENCE: My point is merely that the plan they made required great trust – something that was evidently there in spades, as you have helpfully pointed out. But if I may, Bill, I'll bring the story up to date. A few weeks ago we had word from the FCO that WINDMILL POET's wife had been released from prison and placed under house arrest at her family home in Cairo. Her health was reportedly poor. An extremely distressed WINDMILL POET called August three days later to request an urgent meeting. In line with standard practice, August made a note of the call and agreed with his

163

management that he should encourage WINDMILL POET to see her release as a vital step along the way to her eventual return to the UK, and as a sign that diplomatic efforts had been successful. WINDMILL POET should be urged to remain in the UK and await her eventual return. Meanwhile August should refocus WINDMILL POET on his UK work and discuss new tasking around a number of priority SOIs in Manchester. This meeting took place on 15 September at a hotel in Green Park. August's contact note, written the following day, states the following: "WP" – that's WINDMILL POET – "expressed relief at the news of his wife's release and gratitude for whatever behind-the-scenes work HMG had done to bring about this welcome development. He agreed to return to Manchester the following week and showed enthusiasm at the prospect of re-engaging with the important work he had been doing to prevent terrorist attacks in the UK."

DAPHNE: Lawrence, can I just check, is it your suggestion at this point that August has done anything wrong?

LAWRENCE: Another excellent question. Where is the line and when did August cross it? Our view is that his account of that meeting with WINDMILL POET is almost certainly inaccurate. He might have written that WINDMILL POET was grateful, that he agreed to return to work, but what happened next throws the credibility of that story into serious doubt. We believe it was at that meeting in Green Park that August decided to do what he did, which is nothing less than act against the interests, values and ethos of this office and then lie about it, for reasons that remain unclear. An important caveat at this juncture, Daphne, as we roll up our sleeves and prepare to dive into the detail: as is so often the case in matters of intelligence, we do not have a full picture of everything that happened going forward. In fact, we might liken our task here today to that of someone piecing together a puzzle —

BILL: You're joking.

LAWRENCE: Excuse me?

BILL: The members of this panel probably have close to a hundred years of experience between them. You're not really going to use the intelligence-as-a-puzzle analogy on us, are you?

LAWRENCE: I wasn't aware that you were here today to judge my use of the English language, Bill. Perhaps I might be allowed to —

IMOGEN: Lawrence, please continue.

LAWRENCE: Thank you, Imogen. Let me list a few hopefully unarguable facts. Number one: on Thursday evening, exactly one hour after meeting with WINDMILL POET, August made a withdrawal of two thousand pounds from his personal bank account. Number two: the following morning, instead of returning to Manchester as August's contact note suggests was his intention, WINDMILL POET purchased a ticket to Cairo from the Alitalia desk at Heathrow airport. He paid in cash. His own bank account was not accessed and in any case had a balance throughout this whole episode of £172.45.

Number three: WINDMILL POET's mobile phone next appeared at Cairo airport at 1443 on the Friday. Number four: on the same day that WINDMILL POET travelled, August came to the office, wrote the report of their meeting that I have quoted from and requested one week's emergency leave. This was granted despite the extremely short notice, in light of the recent distressing incident involving his wife – an incident that has upset everyone in the office greatly. Number five: the following day, a Saturday, August bought a last-minute ticket online and flew to Sharm El Sheikh in Sinai with Egypt Air.

DAPHNE: So August meets WINDMILL POET, which he admits, which is all above board, and then withdraws two thousand pounds from his personal account. Is there any evidence to suggest that August met WINDMILL POET after making the withdrawal? Because that's what you're suggesting, isn't it, Lawrence? That August gave him the money? Any travel data, CCTV footage, phone calls, text messages, that sort of thing?

LAWRENCE: A very interesting point. Someone of August's experience would certainly know how to avoid leaving any trace of a meeting. He would know, for example, that both parties should avoid using phones and —

BILL: That's a no then, is it?

LAWRENCE: Excuse me?

BILL: You're telling us there is no evidence to suggest that August had a second meeting with WINDMILL POET after withdrawing the money.

LAWRENCE: Things are not that simple, Bill. There are no calls or texts between August and WINDMILL POET, you're right. But there are also no calls or texts on their phones to anyone else. There's a compelling argument to be made that the reason for this is that neither of them were in possession of their phones, that they'd both left their phones somewhere else to avoid leaving a data trail. That's exactly what we'd expect a trained operational officer like August —

BILL: So the absence of any evidence, in your view, is itself evidence that August is guilty.

LAWRENCE: You have to admit, Bill, it would be astonishing if August had taken a phone to a meeting he wanted to keep secret.

BILL: My problem with what you're saying, Lawrence, is that you could use that logic to plug any holes in your theory. Do you follow? Whenever you don't have evidence, you'll turn it round and present it as evidence that August was being clever.

LAWRENCE: It's an assessment rather than a fact, you are quite —

BILL: No, it's not even that. An assessment is when you take facts and use them to build a theory. If you had their phones co-locating after the bank withdrawal, for example, you could assess that August gave WINDMILL POET the money. What you're saying is nothing more than speculation.

LAWRENCE: With all due respect, Bill, the facts are that August withdrew a large sum of cash and then WINDMILL POET made a cash purchase despite not having access to any money himself —

BILL: More speculation.

LAWRENCE: I beg your pardon?

BILL: How do you know what money he had access to? This is shoddy stuff, Lawrence, and I'm not going to sit here and let it pass unchallenged.

IMOGEN: Bill, please – let's keep this civil.

BILL: A career is on the line, Imogen. And no one is challenging this highly partisan version of events.

DESMOND: Bill, calm down. We hear the chap out and at the end we make up our minds.

BILL: It'll be too late by then to separate the facts from everything else.

IMOGEN: What exactly is your objection?

BILL: It's a basic investigative fallacy that you assume the information available to you is all the information there is. If you see that someone doesn't have money in their bank account, you assume that they don't have money. What about cash hidden under a mattress? What about friends and relatives? What about the theory that WINDMILL POET lied to August, made up his mind to go to Egypt and borrowed the funds from a neighbour? What about the theory that seeing WINDMILL POET gave August the idea of travelling to Egypt and that he simply withdrew the cash to pay for his own holiday?

LAWRENCE: There's no evidence that August ever researched Egypt online as a holiday destination, and if you look at the figures, there has been a drop of over 50 per cent in the number of tourists visiting Sinai in recent years because of the security —

BILL: Oh, for Christ's sake. This is threadbare stuff.

DAPHNE: There is a striking coincidence here, Bill, you can't argue with that. They fly to the same country within a day of each other? Lawrence, is there anything to indicate that August went from Sharm El Sheikh to Cairo?

LAWRENCE: Nothing solid. August's phone remained in Sharm for the whole week. Three emails were sent from his account, on the Sunday, Tuesday and Thursday – very neatly spaced, I'm sure you will agree. They went to his parents, contained innocuous descriptions of the hotel, weather, food and so on. All displayed the IP address of the hotel. If I may add a technical footnote, however, it is relatively straightforward to set up a system whereby emails are stored and sent at a time of your choosing.

BILL: I can't believe we're listening to this. Is there something else going on that I'm unaware of, Imogen, something that would explain why we're here today? Are we hanging August out to dry for something completely unrelated? This isn't connected to all that INKWELL stuff, is it? Has someone at the top decided that August has to go and come up with this kangaroo court as a way to force him out?

IMOGEN: You'll have a chance to express your views at the end. Lawrence, please continue.

LAWRENCE: Thank you for the vote of support, Imogen. Let me pick up where I left off. Fact number six: exactly five days after August arrived in Egypt, a British diplomat living in the Cairo district of Zamalek reported his vehicle licence plate stolen. Number seven: according to an official letter of complaint later delivered to our ambassador by the Egyptian Foreign Ministry, on that same day a British official helped WINDMILL POET's wife escape from house arrest.

DESMOND: Now we're getting to the nub of it.

LAWRENCE: The letter states, I'm quoting here, that at approximately 1300 a British embassy official arrived at the building in the suburb of Dokki in which WINDMILL POET's wife was being held under house arrest. The soldiers on duty reported that the individual had a diplomatic passport and drove a vehicle with official embassy plates. Unfortunately they didn't take a note of the number. They hadn't been told that a consular visit was a possibility and so didn't know the standard procedures, something our mysterious diplomat no doubt exploited. In reality such a visit would have been organized in advance between the embassy and the Ministry of Foreign Affairs. Fact number eight: August was issued with an alias diplomatic passport in 2013 for an unrelated operation. Despite that operation coming to an end, the passport was never returned. August claims it has sat unused in his cupboard throughout this time.

BILL: I've got a cupboard full of passports, the oldest probably from twenty years ago. That doesn't mean anything.

LAWRENCE: Let me admit, Bill, before you point it out helpfully for us —

BILL: Excuse me?

LAWRENCE: — that we are standing firmly in the territory of assessment here. I am merely pointing out that August had the means necessary to execute this plan. It is perfectly possible that he made his way to Cairo without his phone, met up with WINDMILL POET, carried out basic surveillance of the house where she was being held —

BILL: Basic surveillance? Lawrence, this is crazy stuff. You're displaying a complete ignorance of operations. I know you're relatively new to the office, and I'm sure there's merit in bringing in bankers and consultants as middle managers to broaden our impossibly narrow perspective on the world, but are you really suggesting that August, operating completely on his own, conducted surveillance of foreign soldiers in a capital city where the counter-intelligence threat is considered to be extremely high?

LAWRENCE: August, possibly, or WINDMILL POET, or one of WINDMILL POET's friends. The opposition is quite sophisti-cated in what they can do – they've learned the hard way. They have access to equipment, people, vehicles, local knowledge. It may well be that August's role was to devise a plan, allocate the roles, coordinate and play the part of the diplomat. He may have had someone else steal the licence plate, for example. Bill, hold on, let me finish. With all due respect... Listen, I'm not denying that this was an exceptionally risky thing to do. A plan like this would never have made it past your desk, or the desk of anyone in this building. But we're not talking about an official operation. We're talking about an individual acting on his own with complete disregard to matters of risk and reputa-tion. We're talking about an individual, and I know this is not within my remit, but we're talking about an individual who has clearly gone off the rails since his wife's terrible accident... All right, I'll stop there, but everybody knows it. And you can't point to any part of this that would have been impossible, can you? Nobody is claiming that August parachuted in at night, scaled a wall and shot the guards. We're claiming that he drove up to a building in the middle of the day, wound down the window, held up an official document and with nothing but brass neck argued his way inside. We're claiming that he built rapport, projected a mixture of authority and deference, told a joke at the right moment, shared a packet of cigarettes around, found a way to hint that they'd get in trouble if they didn't let him in. We're claiming that he planned, improvised and took his chances as they came. Isn't that exactly what you tell your officers to do every day?

DESMOND: You can't deny that we're looking at something fishy here, Bill. The cash, the travel, the licence plate, the appearance of a British official with a diplomatic passport. The bottom line is that if we were looking at a terrorist network and saw a series of coincidences like this we would be all over it. You would too, old chap, with your team, come on – don't pretend otherwise. None of us wants to believe this is true, especially after everything that's happened recently. Another good man careering off the rails. Stop shaking your head. Listen, I know better than anyone else here the impact of that whole episode – I was on the ground in Beirut. But at some point we've got to draw a line in the sand and make it clear to this new generation that the word loyalty means something. You pay a fee when you join this club, and that fee is agreeing to follow the rules and keep your mouth shut. Corvus oculum corvi non eruit and all that. Why don't we get to the end of the story. Lawrence, chop chop, how are you going to tell us he smuggled her out?

LAWRENCE: Number nine: at 1412, approximately ten minutes after the diplomat was finally allowed to enter the building, a small fire was reported in the garden of a villa belonging to a general two hundred metres away. It later turned out to be

173

an old mattress soaked in lighter fluid. A minor incident, but one that caused the general's wife to call the general in a state of panic and an order to go out to all troops in the area to respond immediately. This took at least one of the soldiers away from their duties, maybe more. Number ten: at 1420, shortly before the diplomat attempted to leave in his vehicle, a small group of student activists arrived at the house and demanded to see WINDMILL POET's wife. They got into an argument with the soldiers and one of the female students alleged that she had been struck. Some of her colleagues began to record the altercation on their phones.

BILL: Where's all this from? The Egyptians didn't put all this in their letter, did they?

LAWRENCE: There's some additional sensitive reporting around the incident. I can't say any more than that. Anyway, in the subsequent internal investigation, the Egyptian soldiers claimed that while dealing with the fire in the general's garden and the group of angry students they also carried out a thorough search of the diplomat's vehicle as he left. Make of that what you will. Nevertheless, number eleven: twenty-one hours later WINDMILL POET's phone pinged on the border with Libya. Number twelve: the next day, on Saturday 24 September, WINDMILL POET and his wife appeared on the manifest of a Libyan Wings flight from Tripoli to Tunisia and from there on to Stockholm.

DAPHNE: Well, that's quite an escape. So she came out in the diplomat's car while the soldiers were distracted.

LAWRENCE: That's for you to judge. But there's more, and fact number thirteen might be the most damning of all. A brand-new CIA source with links to the student opposition movement reported last week that what he calls "a foreign expert" was brought in from outside to rescue WINDMILL POET's wife.

BILL: "Brand-new", eh? Well, I guess that settles the matter. I've only got one question, Lawrence. What does "brand-new" mean in this context? All its parts working, under warranty, all shiny and clean?

LAWRENCE: Someone they've recently recruited, I imagine. Isn't it obvious? I don't really see —

BILL: You say "brand-new" as though it is a positive thing. Do you have any experience of agents, Lawrence? Another word for "brand-new" is "untested". "Brand-new" means they have no idea what the source's access is or where he gets his information from. It means they don't know what his motivation is. It means he might be making it up. "Brand-new" – we're not talking about a toaster here, Lawrence, for Christ's sake, we're talking about a person. We might well be talking about some clown who's wandered in off the street hoping to pick up some cash in exchange for rumours. Did the CIA's "brand-new" source say anything about Iraqi WMD while he was at it?

IMOGEN: It's still relevant —

BILL: Speaking of relevant, Lawrence, where's the stuff from Stockholm in this steaming pile of horseshit you've put together?

IMOGEN: Bill, you can't speak to —

BILL: I know you sent someone out to Stockholm to speak to WINDMILL POET last week.

IMOGEN: Bill, however much you might want to defend —

LAWRENCE: It's all right, Imogen, it's no secret he's friends with August. I was surprised to hear that he'd been appointed to this panel, to be honest. Perhaps that's something for us to follow up on at board level after this is over. Here it is. Last week, after multiple requests, WINDMILL POET agreed to be interviewed in Stockholm. He was described by our officer as friendly and courteous but unwilling to discuss the matter in great detail. He claimed to be astonished by the suggestion that August was involved in the rescue of his wife and said he had organized it himself with the help of a few friends.

BILL: Did he offer a version of events?

LAWRENCE: He said that his sister knew the cousin of one of the soldiers on duty and that he was able to pay a bribe so that they'd look the other way. He said this is how things are done in the Middle East. According to him, he simply got a relative to take her out of a side door. He said nobody pretended to be a diplomat or an official of any kind and that this was probably a story made up by the soldiers to cover their backs.

BILL: Anything else?

LAWRENCE: Nothing relevant.

BILL: What did he say, Lawrence?

LAWRENCE: Only that he had never thought August was particularly capable and that pulling off something like this would have been way beyond his abilities. He said he was surprised August could get himself dressed in the morning without help let alone make a plan to rescue a political prisoner from house arrest in a police state. He called him a jackass and an idiot and said he'd never in his life met such a — What's the matter, August? Why are you laughing? Do you think this is funny? Do you really think we can't see through this absurd cover story you've fabricated with WINDMILL POET to hide your involvement? If only Martha was able to see —

[Loud noises and shouting. End of recording.]

20

It wasn't the first time August had been attacked. There had been any number of playground beatings, briskly designed to bring the new boy up to speed (lessons in history, lessons in geography), and the time he'd turned the corner and found himself in the middle of a fight between rival football fans, and plenty of routine skirmishing outside nightclubs during his Cambridge years. A kid on a moped had once lashed at him with a car aerial and snatched his mobile phone. He couldn't complain; he'd been an active participant in violence on other occasions. The only time it had threatened to get out of hand was when two men in Lisbon had followed him to the port, where he was due to meet an agent, and hit him around the back of the head and in the kidneys before taking his wallet and running off. He'd spent just under a week in hospital. Everyone had been alarmed by that. Violence and spying didn't go together. Spying was all about maintaining the appearance of a smooth, untroubled surface, as though nothing untoward had ever taken place, and that was the opposite of physical violence. It was different when it came to psychology. On the psychological level everything was permitted. That was the place where spies brawled, where teeth were knocked loose, where blood was spilled.

Looking back, it should have been obvious that something was about to happen. But his mind was preoccupied with the events in the cemetery the night before, and the urgent need to tell Lawrence the whole story as quickly as possible, to let him take responsibility for finding the vizier. August had messed up, it was as simple as that. There was no way the vizier would contact him again, not after he had arrived late and drunk and fallen asleep underneath a tree. There was no way they would trust him with something as important and sensitive as the Iranian scientist. He pulled his coat around him and hurried through the late-afternoon gloom towards the café where he had arranged to meet Lawrence.

Still, he thought afterwards, the warning signs had been there. But the information came to him in unintelligible stages, like downloads encrypted by darkness, rain, fatigue and alcohol. A recurring figure at the blurred edge of his vision; the wet uneven slap of accelerating footsteps; the sound of laboured breathing; and the sudden application of something cold and metallic to the side of his face as he turned to see what was happening. He stumbled sideways and put his hand up to shield his head from a second blow. It must have hit the wall during its descent because he heard a soft, pained grunt and something hard landed on his shoulder and clattered into the gutter to his right. The skin above his eye screamed with pain. He went down on one knee. A fist came swinging into his back and another skidded across the top of his head. Feet scuffled in search of a better position. It came to him that it was one man, that he had little experience of such things – it was apparent in the hesitancy of his strikes, changing direction even as they fell, in his obvious confusion about what to do next, in the decision to use his hands rather than his knees or his feet. People who knew what they were doing rarely used their hands. There was an awkward pause as though a conversation had run its course. August felt a hand go to his back trouser pocket, which was empty, and come round to paw at the front of his jacket, looking for a way in. To his surprise, a tie swung into view, patterned with *Playboy* bunnies. He took hold of it with both hands and yanked it forward and down while pushing up off his knee, and the man gurgled and rolled into the wall and would have got up and run away if August hadn't taken hold of his ankle.

"Please!" he cried in a strangled voice.

August hit him solidly in the stomach. It was at least a minute before either of them could do anything. Then the man started to fumble at his tie, yanked high and tight and hard like a noose after the drop. August leaned over and rearranged it for him.

"It's twice now that tie has been your undoing," he said.

"I don't like to take it off."

"It's your neck."

They were in an alleyway off a busy shopping street. On one side was a bin and on the other a pile of wooden boxes. A few metres away a cat nuzzled at a half-eaten bowl of food. August touched the wound above his eye and examined his fingers but in the darkness it was hard to tell the difference between blood and rain. Neither of them said anything for a while. The rain sounded like a voice, low and anxious and insistent, in a hurry to get something off its chest.

"I'll be on my way then," August said finally. "Unless there's something else I can help you with, Youssef."

"I don't want your help."

"Is it money you're after?"

"I don't want anything from you."

"That's not how it looks from here."

"It was an accident," said Youssef, getting to his feet. "I was running around a corner at great speed and I lost my balance on the treacherous ground." He smoothed his tie over the dented mound of his belly and winced. "If anyone should be furious, it is me."

"I'm sure that's how the police would see it too." August bent down to pick up the metal bar from the gutter. "Don't forget your weapon."

"The police?" Unsure what else to do with it, he put the bar in his pocket. "Naturally they will take your side."

"They may take into account the fact that your fingerprints and my blood are all over that piece of metal. But I'm no expert. See you around."

There are many ways to draw the line, thought August as he walked away, but that's probably as good as any: on one side, people who assume the police are there to help, on the other, people who know from experience that the opposite is true. He found a coffee-stained napkin in one of his pockets and pressed it to his eye. He stumbled and leaned against a wall. In his state it was hard to tell the difference between the alcohol, the blow to the head and the wet, uneven ground: they were all ranged indivisibly against him like an army. He made it around a corner and a few dozen steps further before someone shouted at him in Turkish and a torch pointed in his direction.

"Everything is all right," he said, holding his hands out to show they were empty. "I fell over. There is no problem here."

The torch bobbed closer.

"English? American?" one of the policemen asked.

"English."

"What happened?"

"I fell over." He gestured weakly. "The rain."

Which might have been the end of it, if Youssef hadn't come around the same corner, stopped abruptly at the sight of the policemen and taken two steps backwards. It was clear from the expression on his face that he thought August had gone looking for them.

"What country?" one of the officers asked him.

"Spain."

"You are Spanish? Come here." When Youssef was close enough one of them reached for the metal bar sticking out of his pocket. He spoke in Turkish to his colleague and then asked, "You know him?"

It wasn't clear who he was talking to, or what answer would make them go away quickest. August wanted this to be over. He wanted to sit on his bed and open a bottle. He didn't want to stand in the rain being questioned while holding the fluttering remains of a bloody napkin to his head like a rosette pinned to a prize-winning vegetable.

He didn't want to feel responsible for what might happen to Youssef.

"Yes, he's my friend," August said reluctantly. Of the two of them he was the professional. Better that he handle it.

"So why you are not walking together?"

A reasonable question. Perhaps he should have said they didn't know each other. Too late now. "We arranged to meet here at" – he glanced at his watch – "nine o'clock."

The one asking the questions frowned. "Here?"

An alleyway with no visible sign, no shops, no other people in sight.

"We were originally going to meet on İstiklal, you see," August said, before remembering it was on the other side of town, "but because of … because of the weather we changed it. It's quieter here, no crowds. My friend doesn't like crowds, do you? He's always been like that, since… Well, it's personal. We're good friends. Very good friends, very old friends. School friends. Not school, more like university. University mates. What was the question again?" He felt dizzy. It dawned on him that this wasn't going well. That blow to the head must have been harder than he thought. He wanted to lie down and close his eyes. If the principles of a good cover story were that it was simple, logical and dull, this one was a failure on all counts. Perhaps the rosette was a consolation prize, he thought – perhaps he wasn't such a champion vegetable after all. He had to find a way to stop talking.

"You are friends," the policeman said, nodding. August realized his awkwardness had led the officer to conclude they were a couple. If you allow them, he thought, people will usually let you know what they are expecting to hear – they will lead you to the right cover story. But Youssef had decided to take a different approach.

"I have never seen this man before in my life," he said. "Can I go?"

"Passport," said the officer.

"I do not have it with me," said Youssef.

"You speak Spanish?"

"Officer, there's no problem here," said August. "My friend and I are just on our way —"

"I am not your friend."

"You're right, you're a lot more than that. It was just a silly argument. Let's have some dinner and get out of this rain."

"What are you talking about? I am not going anywhere with you."

"It's my treat, Youssef —"

"I told you before, I do not want anything from you!"

The second officer slapped Youssef across the face and he rocked backwards against the wall.

"It's okay, it's okay," said August quickly, stepping between them, "you don't have to do that. There's no problem here. We just want to go. I'm feeling dizzy, I might throw up. God, all this blood everywhere. I need my friend to help me. Please." He reached out and took hold of Youssef. "Come on, old friend." He would give it one last try. If Youssef preferred to take his chances with the police that was his choice. He tightened his grip and pretended to stumble in order to jolt Youssef loose from the wall. The first policeman pulled his colleague to one side. August leaned in, once they were a few paces away, and said in a low voice, "They won't do anything as long as we stay together."

The two officers followed at a distance until they reached August's hotel. In the room on the third floor Youssef stood at the window, watching the street below, waiting for them to leave.

"I'll swap you a whisky for a cigarette," said August.

There were aspects of the pain he felt that turned out to be welcome. It made everything else seem unimportant; it pulled down the shutters on the world outside. He set about counting his injuries greedily like a shopkeeper emptying the till after a busy day: an open cut above his eye, a bruise across his shoulder, a stiff neck, a twisted ankle. He had the beginnings of a headache too.

"How are you feeling?" he asked, lighting Youssef's cigarette.

Youssef didn't reply. His attempt at a mugging had resulted in physical defeat and a humiliating encounter with the police. August realized that to get him talking he would have to meet Youssef on his own frequency and slowly dial him down to a manageable level.

"I hope your stomach hurts as much as my head does," August said.

Youssef shifted his feet for a better view of the street.

"I guess I should be grateful you don't know how to fight."

Youssef's head turned one way and then the other, looking for the policemen.

"It's hard to see how you ended up losing," August said, "considering you attacked me from behind with a weapon, like a coward."

Youssef's eyes briefly flicked back.

"Are we even?" August said. "Do I need to watch my back every time I step outside? I'd happily pay for that not to be the case. My wallet's over there. Take what you want."

"I am not a beggar."

"No, you're a thief."

"Then you should have let them take me to prison."

"I wish I had."

"Why didn't you?"

"I felt bad about what happened at the office. The insulting way Beatrice spoke to you while I stood by and did nothing. I'm not surprised you wanted to get your own back. But next time I'll tell them to throw away the keys."

"Next time? You will never see me again. I think the policemen will go very soon, when the rain stops. Then I will go too."

"They're still there? That's impressive. A pair of proper bloodhounds."

"Impressive?" said Youssef. "They did not hit you."

"I know what point you're making, but don't lose sight of the fact that you attacked me with an iron bar."

"They did not know that."

"There were clues."

"Clues?" said Youssef. "You think they hit me because of clues?"

"Well – blood, a weapon."

"Like Sherlock Holmes."

"All right, they might be a little bit racist too."

"What do you think they will do to me if you are not there?"

"Send you back to Spain?" August said.

"You are not funny."

"They would probably have done the same thing that you tried to do to me. Stop feeling sorry for yourself, Youssef. Nobody put you in this position."

"Lots of people put me in this position. The Syrian police, the Mukhabarat, Al Nusra, Daesh, two Turkish policemen, a drunk, greasy-haired English son of a bitch —"

"It's not greasy, you idiot, it's wet from the rain. Because I was standing around making up stories for two police-men instead of —"

"Instead of sitting on your own in a hotel room getting drunk."

"Says the man who tried to sell me cocaine and prostitutes. What would your priest have to say about that?"

"My priest?" said Youssef.

"That scar on your wrist. What is it, were you trying to cover up a cross? That's the only thing I've seen tattooed on the inside of people's wrists here. Throw those cigarettes over and pour yourself some more of that. It must have hurt like hell, looks like you tried to burn it off."

"It is none of your business."

"When I was at school a boy stubbed out a cigarette on my leg. Pass the bottle, would you?"

"Why?"

"No reason. I was the new boy."

"Or maybe he just did not like you. Maybe nobody liked you. This is also possible."

"A lot of people regret a tattoo. You know, the name of an ex-girlfriend. You grow up and it starts to look silly."

"Are you joking?"

"I knew someone who got a tattoo of a band they liked —"

"When Daesh came to my city many people converted to Islam so they would not be killed."

"I'm guessing they weren't fans of the *Playboy* tie either."

"*Playboy*? What are you talking about? They are rabbits. My daughter likes rabbits. She gave it to me for my birthday."

"How old is she?"

"Two years."

"Where is she now?"

"Either Macedonia or Serbia. Or possibly Hungary."

"What do you mean?"

"I do not know where she is. My wife and my daughter sailed from Izmir on a boat seven weeks ago. I only had enough money for them. I promised to follow as soon as I could buy a ticket. The man said they would arrive in Greece in a few hours, it would be slow because the weather was not good, but after they arrived people would look after them. And one week after that they will arrive in Germany. But my wife's phone is not working so I do not know where they are. Her cousin was on the same boat, her phone does not work too – I think this is because telephones work differently in Europe. But if I look at a map and try to decide which way they are travelling and how quickly, I think by now they are in Macedonia, Serbia or Hungary. It is also possible they are in Vienna. My wife will be slow, her health is not always good, but she is very determined. Do you think this is right, the problem is the phone network?"

"Absolutely. It's completely different in Europe."

"And the bad weather, you do not think it is possible —"

"No, not a chance. We're not talking about crossing the Atlantic here."

"You hear many stories."

"You could do it in a bathtub."

"My sister-in-law says they —"

"Did you ever read your daughter the rhyme about the owl and the pussycat going to sea in a pea-green boat?"

"What are you talking about? Are you drunk already?"

"A little bit, maybe. They took some honey and plenty of money, wrapped up in a five-pound note."

"They wrapped money inside money? This is crazy. Better to wrap it in something small and plastic and hide it so nobody can steal it. Give me the bottle."

"Or money and plenty of honey, it might be that way round."

"Who were they running away from?"

"That's a good question. No one, I think. They were in love. The owl proposed to the pussycat and they went looking for a ring. They were at sea for a year and a day and they were completely fine, so a journey of a few hours will have been a walk in the park for your wife and daughter."

"Did they find a ring?"

"Tied to the end of a pig's nose. Where's the lighter?"

"For someone who drinks all the time, you get drunk very quickly."

"I had a head start. Most of the time I have a head start."

"Why do you drink so much?"

"Oh, well. My wife, she…"

"What?"

"It's a long story, Youssef."

"You had an argument?"

"No, it's not that."

"She left you?"

"You could say that."

"You are a difficult man, to be honest I cannot blame her."

"I blame her."

"Don't … it will be all right. Why do you not say sorry to her? Maybe she will come back."

"I say sorry to her all the time."

"And what does she say?"

"She doesn't say anything."

"Stop… Mr August, please, there is no need… I have an idea, climb into the green boat with me and together we will go and find our families."

"Now who sounds drunk?"

"You, me, the dog and the thing, what is it called, the thing."

"The owl."

"I do not want the pig in there."

"What's wrong with the pig?"

"Are you crazy? A pig?"

"If anyone's crazy, it's you."

"Idiot."

"You're the idiot."

At some point that night, according to evidence on display the following morning, they must have decided that they needed a bottle of local spirits and two sandwiches wrapped in greasy paper, that August should sign a contract promising to help Youssef find his wife and daughter, that they should write a joint letter setting out their thoughts on the situation in Syria, that Youssef would sleep in the bed and August would fashion something from pillows on the floor. "Dear Mr President," the letter began, in handwriting that differed enough in style and legibility to suggest they had taken it in turns with the pen over the course of the evening, "you are a fool, a dog, a son of a dog, a dickhead, a father of smells, a pimp, a shoe, a knobhead, an arse-licker, a son of a whore and a donkey." It was signed by them both and illustrated with doodles. Other evidence suggested an attempt to fashion a blowpipe from a piece of bamboo previously seen holding up a plant in the hallway outside, and a target of concentric circles had been drawn vigorously in pen on the wall opposite the bed, with a different score allocated to each circle. Pellets were scattered on the carpet below like a light dusting of snow. There were signs that as the evening had progressed they had ventured further afield. A note from reception circulated the following morning asked guests with children to keep them under control at all times following complaints of someone knocking on doors in the middle of the night, giggling loudly and running away. And the hotel porter was sent up to the rooftop with a new padlock and chain after a report that two grown men had been seen dancing around up there, but the manager was sceptical about this particular complaint because it came from an old lady across the street who could be guaranteed to write to him at least once a week, whether about the noise or the rubbish or the smells from the kitchen or occasionally something more outlandish, as in this case, which the manager put down to the full moon and the way it could make even the sanest of people go slightly crazy.

21

The call from the vizier came late the following day. August hadn't even realized the phone was switched on.

"We have the package," he said. "You must act immediately. Gather your belongings and travel to Gaziantep. There is an overnight bus that leaves in one hour. We will meet you outside the Grand Hotel at noon tomorrow. I will hold a copy of an English newspaper under my arm so that you recognize me. My colleagues are ready to take us to the other side. Any questions?"

"Wait, what are you talking about? You've got the what?"

"I cannot hear you, say it again."

August lifted the blanket off his head and peered into the gloom. He was lying on the floor. His head was pounding and he felt confused. Youssef was snoring underneath the bedcovers.

"What's going on?" he asked, as much to his hotel room as to the voice on the other end of the line.

"The package," said the vizier. He sounded impatient. "The one from the other country, the one you … inspected for us. We need to move it now. It is already badly damaged. There is no time to waste. Take the bus to the border tonight and we will see you there tomorrow."

He hadn't expected this. What should he say? Thoughts fled from the screaming alarm of his headache. He reached for the coat-tails of the obvious ones, the ones that found it difficult to hide from his trembling hands. Number one: he had to stop them taking the Iranian anywhere near the Syrian border. Number two: he had to buy enough time to tell Lawrence and his colleagues what was happening. This was his chance to remedy things.

"Hold on," he said, looking around for a glass of water. "Wait a minute. I can't … I can't just jump on a bus. There are checkpoints, police come on board and ask people where they're going."

"So? They may ask you questions but they will not stop you. Remember what kind of person they have been told to look for: Muslim boys, early twenties, probably Pakistani or Arab or Somali. You are a white man in his thirties. Clean-shaven, well dressed, Christian, with a story about visiting the world-class Roman mosaics preserved in the Zeugma Museum."

"What if I mess up?" August said. "What if I get nervous and say the wrong thing? Can't I travel with you?"

"Stop, take a deep breath. By this time tomorrow you will be in the place you have dreamed about for a long time. Do not make unnecessary problems for yourself, brother, do not hesitate. Put some clothes in a bag, buy a bus ticket, meet me outside the Grand Hotel. It is as simple as that. We have many things to discuss but after tomorrow we can do it face-to-face. Now go."

"I can't, I'm sorry, I wish I could." Quickly, think. *Think.* "I'd never forgive myself if I said the wrong thing and messed this up for you and the brothers." He reached for the excuse that was closest to hand, he reached for the truth. "My head," he said, groaning loudly and turning away to retch. "I can't believe I've done it again, not after what you said to me last time. But I can't lie to you. In this condition I just don't trust myself not to mess everything up."

The vizier was quiet. Youssef's breathing settled into a high-pitched wheeze, as though a bus had changed gear for an uphill climb.

"You have been drinking again," the vizier said. "After everything I told —"

"I can't hide it from you. I don't *want* to hide it from you. I'm weak, that's the truth. I need to have my brothers around me, giving me strength. On my own and the jinn start whispering in my ear, saying that I'm a loser, that I'm no good, that I haven't got what it takes. All that stuff my old man used to say. And then I'm thinking about my mum and her health and how she's on her own —"

"All right, I understand. You are weak – this is my mistake, I should have seen it before now. We need warriors, we need soldiers, not children playing games —"

"No, you don't get it – I want to come more than anything in the world, I swear to you. If you make me stay here, I wouldn't blame you after everything I've done, but I'd probably kill myself. The thought that I've missed my one chance… I've wanted to go there so much, it means more to me than anything. I'm just so scared that without you telling me what to do I'll mess it up. Let me come with you, let me travel there with you. I can hide out of sight, or we can make up some story about who we are and where we're going, maybe you're a tour guide, maybe having a white guy with you will help you get through checkpoints."

"It is too dangerous for you to travel with us because we have the package. Do you understand? We have the package. And if they find it —"

"I don't care. I'll fight to the death to protect you, I'll take a bullet for you. Listen, you told me the first time we met that I was part of this thing, you told me what I did was helping the brothers. So let me be part of this. I don't want to play it safe in some air-conditioned bus, reading a newspaper and pretending to be a kafir tourist. I want to be with you, I want to learn from you, I want to show you that I'm ready to put it all on the line. There's no going back for me. Let me go forward alongside my brothers with my head held high."

August listened to the flush of a distant toilet, an argument on the street outside. He peered into the gloom at what looked like a series of circles drawn on the wall.

Youssef stirred and sat up in bed.

"What is going on?" he whispered.

August signalled that he should be quiet.

"It is too difficult," the vizier was saying. "There is nowhere in the city we can safely meet."

"What about the cemetery?"

"Do not be a fool. We have been there too often. If they know about us, this is one place we can be sure they will be watching."

"Okay, what about somewhere near the bus station? Find a quiet side street, we'll get lost in all those crowds."

"The clock is ticking, my friend, someone will have reported what happened. We had to collect the package from a busy street in daylight. We cannot drive back into the middle of the city, this is madness."

"August," whispered Youssef. "What are you talking about?"

"Hang on – I've got an idea," said August, turning away and cupping the phone. "There's this place, it's a house but nobody lives there, it's in the middle of nowhere. It's right on the Black Sea. There's trees around, nobody will be able to see a thing."

August knew it was still empty. He had signed the contract but the company hadn't started to move in equipment.

"What are you talking about?"

"We can meet there. It's less than an hour's drive from the city. We'll have time to work out a plan before we head for the border together."

"How do you know about this place?"

"I was on a hike in the forests up there, trying to clear my head and get in shape for … for the place we're going to. I needed some water and I went there to see if I could get a drink. Listen, it's the only house around for miles. No one has lived there for years, it's got smashed windows and everything. The key is on the door frame, just run your fingers along the top. And there are plenty of places to hide a vehicle. Seriously, it's perfect for this. Shall we meet there in one hour?"

It would be perfect for Lawrence and the police too. Only one road in and one road out and no bystanders to get in the way. He gave the directions and hung up.

From the back of a taxi he tried repeatedly to call Lawrence. He didn't know if Lawrence was angry with him for missing their last appointment, or how he should explain the situation if he did get through. Outside the city rushed by, one long blur of blameless people leading blameless lives. It was hard to tell whether the nausea he felt was the result of his hangover or the realization, apparently for the first time, of the enormity of what he had done, the scale of his misjudgement that engaging with the vizier was a bold step, even a helpful one, as though he was in his own way contributing to the war against IS, rather than naive, reckless, self-indulgent and monumentally stupid. He opened the window and breathed deeply. "I saw a man on a plane and I pretended to be him," he said aloud, trying on the words for size. The taxi driver glanced in the rear-view mirror and turned up the radio. "I'm in contact with an IS facilitator. An Iranian scientist has been kidnapped." Everything he said sounded nonsensical, as though he had made up a new language and was trying it out in public for the first time. Until that moment it had remained safely trapped inside the echo chamber of his head, where the only reaction to each new proposal – that he should pretend to be 34c, that he should follow the Iranian and search his hotel room, that he should even *consider* turning his back to the vizier – had been one of admiring approval. Yes, he had said to himself, over and over again: now *that's* a good idea.

By the time he was close to the house it was almost dark. The taxi dropped him several hundred metres from the driveway that swung down, cratered and puddled, towards the sea. Other than two cement trucks there was no traffic. He tried Lawrence's number again and stepped off the road to wait among the trees. He didn't have much time – the vizier might decide at any point he couldn't wait any longer and head for the border without him. After that there would be nothing anyone could do about it. August wouldn't be able to tell Lawrence what vehicle they were in or how many of them there were or even what they looked like.

His eyes adjusted slowly to the dusk. Trees dragged their branches across the surface of a puddle-coloured sky. He called Lawrence again and this time left a message. He walked through the trees towards the driveway, his hands held out in front of him. The wind grew louder.

He stepped out onto the driveway. Following its edge, he walked down until the whole house came into view, battered and leaning as though it might fall over at any moment. A dark-blue or black saloon car was parked just beyond it, its nose pointing towards August and the way out. He couldn't see if there was anyone inside. There was no point hiding. If he was being watched from the house, behaviour like that would look more suspicious than standing in plain sight. A faint glow came from the top floor. As he came closer he saw that the car was empty but that the boot was open, its interior light flickering dimly. A dark wet patch that looked like blood stained the edge of its roughly carpeted floor.

The front door was unlocked. He stepped inside and pressed himself against the wall. There were things in his favour. That the vizier hadn't seen the house before today, that he would need to keep the hostage alive until they crossed the border. The sound of a man's voice came from upstairs. If violence was necessary – and he had little doubt that it would be – he would choose his moment and use as much speed and force as possible to take the vizier by surprise.

On the first-floor landing he stopped to listen. A low voice was coming from the top floor. Was the vizier with someone? Or making a phone call? He placed his foot on the next stair and suddenly heard a scraping sound in the room to his left. He pushed the door open and saw a dark figure slumped on a chair. The only light came from the half-shuttered window at his back. Stepping into the room, August eased the door closed.

It was the Iranian. He was dressed in the same grey suit and black shoes he had been in before and his hands were tied behind him. Dirt and oil were smeared down the left side of his face and a blood-soaked bandage had been wrapped loosely around his neck.

He said something in Farsi. When August didn't reply he tried again in heavily accented English.

"Please. Help me."

A pair of pliers lay on the floor in the corner of the room. The voice upstairs rose slightly as though arguing.

"Doctor, please," the Iranian said weakly. "Help me."

He shifted on the chair and the floorboards groaned.

"Who is upstairs?" August said quietly.

"Doctor, doctor. Please."

"Upstairs." August pointed. "How many?"

"What? One. One person. I need doctor." He started to cry. "This man, he is … monster."

"Be quiet," said August. "I'll bring help."

"Who you are?" he asked. "Police?"

"No. Tell me, does he have a weapon?"

"What?"

"The man, does he have a gun or a knife?"

"No, no. You are here alone?"

"Yes. But I'll bring help, don't worry."

"Someone he knows you are here?"

"No, but I'll —"

In an instant it all becomes clear. August smiles. What else can he do? He could take a step backwards, he could reach for the door handle, but he knows it wouldn't make any difference. It is far too late for that. Slices of dying light fall through the shutter and onto the floor between them. How does he know what is happening? Even he can't be sure – an inflection in the man's voice, a smell, one question too many as he tries to find out whether August has come on his own. He smiles again, this time in admiration at the ability on display. To have done all this, to have fooled him so completely, and for so long. The man in the chair smiles back at him.

And stands up. His hands aren't tied any more. He removes the bandage from around his neck and straightens his powerful shoulders. As he steps forward, August sees he is holding a knife.

And he says, with the face of the Iranian, in the voice of the vizier, "My friend, it is nice to meet you properly at last. I only wish the circumstances were different."

PART TWO

Ideology

August wakes folded into a darkness so profound that it is clear what he previously took for darkness was merely the veiling of a distant glow – from a street lamp, headlights, a charging phone. Here there is nothing. Here there is none of that. Beyond the immediate darkness of whatever he is trapped inside is the darkness of a room, the darkness of a house, the endless darkness of night. His knees are jackknifed into his chest. He can't move and the muscles across his shoulders and down his back start to cramp violently. His wrists are bound together in tape. He reaches out with fingertips to touch … plastic. Smooth and then moulded into ridges. If he strains his head upwards he can feel something hard above him. He has lost all sensation in his feet and a wound pulses above his left eye, irregularly, like a code tapped out against a cell wall, the blood running down to the corner of his mouth. It tells him things he didn't know: that he is upright, that the injury is recent, that he is alive. Panic circles him. His fingers spider across the cold plastic until they reach, finally, something that yields. Rubber, a thin ridge of rubber. It comes to him that he is locked inside the fridge on the top floor of the house. At least it isn't switched on. At least he isn't cold. The whole thing is almost enough to make him laugh. But he doesn't. Instead he opens his mouth and screams.

•••

There is no way of knowing how long he sleeps for, but it can't be more than an hour. What wakes him is not pain but noise. A knocking, persistent and steady. It might be a loose shutter. His hands return to the rubber ridge. He has worked it loose enough that he can slide two fingers between rubber and rusted metal. A hundred tiny arrowheads flurry into the soft soil of his skin. He expects the opening he has created to let in sound, and it does – the knocking becomes more urgent – but to his surprise it also lets in light. Someone has switched on a light. He pushes his head forward as far as he can, ignoring the stabbing pains around his neck and across his back, and sees through the gap a number of surfaces that he struggles to understand: peeling wall, rotten door frame, a narrow slice of hallway. The vizier steps in and out of view. When he reappears a few minutes later the transformation is so complete that at first he thinks it must be someone else. Gone are the suit, the glasses, the neatly combed hair. He has lost ten years and acquired a dirty vest and a dressing gown. His hair sticks up in places as though he has just been asleep. August isn't aware of making a noise but the vizier turns to look directly at the fridge. The metallic rattle suggests at least one chain and padlock. It is startling to see the vizier at such proximity. Afterwards August struggles to locate his impressions, as though they are valuables hidden inside a strange house. He turns each detail over repeatedly with trembling hands. Unblinking grey eyes, dirty teeth, a sense of profound calm. A body packed so densely with power that August wonders how he ever managed to conceal it beneath the Iranian's grey suit. The vizier smiles, reaches out and snaps one of August's fingers at the middle knuckle. When he opens his mouth to scream it is filled with a damp choking fist of material and he hears the shriek of tape and feels a tightness clamping around his head. It takes all his concentration to keep the gag from slipping down his throat. But the vizier doesn't know that. And so for good measure he slams an open palm into August's ear with such force that his head cracks the plastic casing at the back of the fridge.

••••

Family is sleep, he hears the vizier say. The windowpane in the room must be broken, the closed shutters a few metres above the front door. No, no, he hears.

He bites down on the gag to muffle the pain in his hand as he works open a gap.

Is this your house?

A familiar voice, one he wants to hear.

Caretaker. What you want?

I'm looking for someone. It's very important.

No here, my friend. You go now —

Well, he told me he was here.

Lawrence sounds tired and irritated.

Here? No, no.

Yes, he definitely said he was here. And I've been here before, so I know this is the place he was talking about.

Family is sleep, baby is sleep. My friend, look time. Very —

Your family is inside?

Yes, my —

I thought this house was empty. I thought it was being rented out. Who did you say you were?

August thinks: what else does he remember? That the house is unfurnished and unheated, that it's the last place anyone would bring a baby, that on the day he came here there was no sign of a caretaker? Lawrence should make his apologies and leave now. It won't take a moment to call the local police from his car and give them the address. Better still, ask the embassy's consular section to make the call, they'll already have the right contacts, it'll conceal his interest in the matter. Either way they'll be at the door within the hour. It won't be pretty, but he can hold on for that long.

Listen, my friend. Not here.

Wait a second, don't shut the door. I know it's bloody early. I've got money. Tell you what, take this. Let me have a quick look around to put my mind at rest and then —

A lorry on the road above the house changes gear to climb the hill. August fumbles against the tape covering his mouth but the pain in his broken finger slows him down. Instead he tries to hook an edge over the broken plastic at the back of the fridge.

— a friend of mine. Look, it's really important. I won't wake your children, I promise. Otherwise I'll have to call the police and report a missing person and I'm sure nobody wants that. They'll wake everyone up. They'll probably have to call the owner too. Out of interest, who is the owner? Maybe I should give him a call myself.

He finds a sharp plastic edge but it slips off the tape and tears open his cheek.

This man, your friend, how he look?

He's very tall, with dark hair. He was here a few hours ago.

Very tall, very...

What, his build? He's pretty skinny.

Skinny?

You know, thin. Like ... like this door.

He is English?

Yes.

Okay, no, no.

No one like that?

There was Turkish man here yesterday but no English man.

He tries again and the plastic hooks into the cut and rips it open further.

Let's talk about him. What time was that?

No, this man Turkish, he is, I don't know word in English.

Describe it to me.

He is not like you, he is drink alcohol, his...

Clothes.

They are dirty.

What time was this?

Maybe, six, maybe seven. But he is Turkish —

Why, because he's dark? I don't think you could tell at a distance. What was he doing here?

I do not know. He has bottle, maybe telephone, he is talking.

And then, in case at a later date it all looks to Lawrence just a little too convenient, the vizier provides a random detail.

I think there is man with car also.

What, a second man?

Yes, but I don't see him.

And what, he leaves with this other man?

Yes.

Christ, okay.

He finally catches the tape on the plastic edge and jerks his head down sharply to pull it free of his mouth. He is desperate. *Christ, okay.* In those two words he hears Lawrence's train of thought swerve into a ditch. He hears him think: August is probably sleeping off a heavy night in his hotel room. This whole thing might have been a joke, or worse, some sort of trap. It's a good reminder that he'll need careful handling. Far better to do one's due diligence before involving the police. Send someone round to his hotel, check the hospitals, trace his name against flight manifests. *That's* the point to start thinking about the police. Set hares running now and you'll end up looking like a fool when he turns up with a hangover in a few hours.

You don't happen to know where they went, do you?

He tries to pull the gag out of his mouth but it catches on the tape and when he tries to shout the sound is muffled.

What's that noise?

Children. My friend, look, the time is —

All right, all right. You don't know where they went, do you?

He tries to pull the gag free from his mouth but it's long like a sock and even to him his shouts still sound muffled. He bangs his head against the fridge door.

No, no.

Okay, I'm sorry to have bothered you. Take this for your trouble. No, I insist, it sounds as though I've woken the whole place up. Got lots of children, have you? Buy them all a nice lunch tomorrow to make up for it.

Okay, okay.

This is your house, then, is it?

What? No, owner he live Ankara.

Got it. Well, thanks for your help … what's your name?

Mehmet.

I won't bother you again, Mehmet.

The gag comes loose. He pushes all his weight against the door and tears at the rubber with his fingers, even the broken finger, and shouts as loudly as he can. He tries Lawrence's name, he tries his own name. The vizier's footsteps rattle like gunfire in the stairwell. He opens the fridge door and stuffs the gag back into August's mouth and winds fresh tape around his head so tightly that he struggles to breathe. A single blow is enough to knock all the air from his body. Somewhere he hears the sound of a tap running. He doesn't know what is happening. The door opens again and the vizier throws a bucket of cold water over him and then re-padlocks the fridge. The water washes the blood from his face and feels refreshing. An odd punishment, he thinks. But then he hears the quiet hum of a motor and he realizes he's in trouble. The vizier has switched the fridge on.

••••

He examines his situation, looking for a way out. Within minutes he is trembling like a tuning fork. It is difficult to bring his mind to bear on anything other than his immediate circumstances. He concedes an admiration for the ruthless efficiency of the vizier. Here is a man who understands the economics of suffering, the balancing of input and output in his favour. Why waste time and energy on an unnecessary demonstration of force? Far better to weaken the prisoner. That way he won't have the will to struggle, to shout, to escape. Already he is exhausted, fighting the cold, fighting to keep the gag from slipping down his throat, and so he looks again with his cheek for a sharp edge. He rattles against the sides of the fridge like a nut inside its shell. The plastic finally catches on the tape and he pulls it loose from his mouth. He spits out the gag and breathes deeply and the air, like electricity, makes him glow brightly with pain. He feels within himself the possibility of surrender. He cannot let that happen. There is work to do.

••••

There are some things that must be true. Number one: there is no Iranian, there was never any Iranian. There was only ever the vizier, playing a role. The Iranian was a fiction designed to keep him engaged and busy until ... what? He realizes it was probably his own impatience to get things moving at the start that made the vizier come up with the idea of the Iranian. Number two: the vizier doesn't intend to kill him, at least not yet. If that had been his plan he'd have done it hours ago. August's value is as a commodity of some kind. Number three: it's inexplicable that the vizier hasn't moved him by now. It would have made sense to move him immediately, rather than lock him up inside the house. But it is beyond crazy to keep him here after someone has come to the front door asking for him and talking about going to the police. The only possible reason for staying here is that the vizier has nowhere else to go. But IS have extensive facilitation networks in Turkey: they have access to people and properties and money. August knows this as a matter of fact. Is it possible, therefore, that the vizier isn't connected to them? Or that he doesn't have access to their resources? How could that be the case?

••••

His mind is a crowded washing line that lifts and tugs and settles and whips in the cold wind. Facts – phone numbers, postcodes, street names – are the pegs that keep him from blowing away. He spends at least half an hour traipsing corridors until he can picture the face of the headmaster who suspended him for filling the pipes of the chapel organ with ping-pong balls. He is desperate to get away. He is desperate to get away from himself. His mind has no loyalty to his broken body; it's prepared to do whatever it takes to escape. Facts patrol the perimeter of his sanity like guards. The code name of every agent he handled. The paintings on the walls of his father's offices in London, Cairo, Geneva and Hong Kong. He swims in icy darkness to an old Star Ferry at anchor a hundred metres from shore and clambers on board to sit in the captain's chair and operate the dials and levers and switches before descending into the black glistening engine room like the belly of a sea monster. Sucking on a damp corner of his shirt to draw out moisture, he twists his wrists apart to loosen the tape and with trembling fingers fashions a weapon from shards of broken plastic. He asks himself the questions put to him by the police in the week he was fired. Have you ever had unauthorized contact with a foreign government? Who instructed you to leak intelligence? How much were you paid? What role did your wife play in this? How many times did you carry material out of the building without permission? At the time it came as a shock to realize they suspected he had been acting on behalf of another country, instructed not just to steal secrets – although they clearly assumed he had done that too – but to act as an agent of influence, to make mischief, to sow the seeds of a subtle chaos, to create the impression that British intelligence was vulnerable and to demonstrate to its foot soldiers that disobedience was not just possible but would go unpunished, in the hope that in time others might be persuaded to follow suit. If he'd made any comment at all it would have been to tell them what a ridiculous idea this was. Any government with an agent in such a position would have instructed them to be unimaginably careful. But it seemed his accusers actually *wanted* him to be working for another country – it would have been easier to understand, it would have fit neatly into the imprint of history. Lawrence wanted his Philby, his Maclean. In his desperation August is prepared to entertain every idea lavishly and so he questions whether he was too quick to dismiss their theory. Do they know something he doesn't? Something about Martha? What if *she* had been working for another country? What if *she* had been the agent of influence? What if she had been provoking, suggesting, steering him in the direction of another country's objectives? He knows this is false. He knows it is false as a matter of factual and emotional certainty. But he cannot help pursuing the idea with outstretched hands because he sees that it might lead him to a place where she isn't dead, where the accident was a carefully staged piece of theatre, where she was spirited across the border by her handlers, where she is right now cycling along a country lane in bright foreign sunshine. The thought is too much to bear. The sound of a bicycle bell, the way the wind lifts her hair. It is all too much. Finally untethered by fact, in imaginative free fall, the washing line whips loose and fills the sky with bright clothing like birds of paradise, and the only thing that saves him is that the vizier chooses this moment to open the fridge, and August tumbles out in a shivering heap onto the floor.

••••

Five minutes, he says, cutting the tape from his wrists with a knife. Use the bucket in the corner. Eat some food.

August unfolds on the floor like a piece of violently crumpled paper – a blackmail demand, a Dear John letter, a terminal diagnosis. He is dazzled by the weak dawn light through the window. Five minutes? Five minutes might just be long enough to stretch out an arm, he thinks. A leg would take at least ten. He can't begin to imagine standing up, or walking, or swinging the tiny plastic blade in his pocket towards the throat of the vizier. To his surprise he misses the fridge and the way it held him as tightly as a splint in one single agony, rather than this, which evolves every time he —

Four minutes, says the vizier.

It hurts when he laughs.

You're joking, says August.

The vizier reaches down and places the pad of his thumb on August's eye. He presses it quickly like the doorbell of someone he is reluctant to disturb. The pain is sudden and vast. August twists away and puts his hands up to protect his face but the vizier has already lost interest and is looking out of the window. He has the air of a man who has been involved in violence on an industrial scale, thinks August, once the worst of the pain has gone. The vizier seems utterly bored by it, as though he has once spent days, weeks, months doing little but this – hurting people. Debriefs of Daesh prisoners suggest a gleeful, adolescent approach to torture. This is different. This has an institutional feel to it. Which probably means someone with power in a police state: a prison guard, a militiaman, an intelligence officer. Plenty of them defected from Saddam or Assad, if this has anything to do with IS, which he is no longer sure of. In any case, August has met their kind before. He remembers one man, an Iraqi, with a scar that —

Three minutes.

Wait. I can't … can you bring the food closer?

A piece of stale bread hits the floor next to him.

What's this about? he says. What do you want with me?

He eats the bread.

He thinks about survival. He has to stay alive.

Can I have some water? he says.

He wonders if this is the first time he has seen the vizier as himself, as he really is, without a disguise. The metallic grey hair lies flat and lifeless against a curiously small, round skull, shaped at the back like a question mark. His cheeks are covered with a day's worth of white stubble. The shirt he wears is pale blue and loose-fitting, but when he turns and crosses the room to fill a cup of water it is plain to see the power rolling across his shoulders.

Two minutes.

His eyes are the colour of rain.

A small black rucksack sits in the hallway at the top of the stairs. He understands that it is wrong to think of the vizier *as himself*, that everything the vizier does will be calibrated towards a certain purpose, that even *the vizier* has just been a role temporarily inhabited by a man on the run, for this is what he has decided he is looking at. A man on the run who is being forced to stand still. Which makes him even more dangerous.

He drinks from the water being offered to him. It tastes dirty.

217

Which is why the five-minute limit is important, because he is staying elsewhere and only coming to the house to check on August. He decides —

One minute.

— that the vizier must have lured 34c here under the black flag of IS but the truth is that he's cut loose from them somehow. IS is part of what is happening. He just doesn't know what part.

You know you're going to kill me if this goes on much longer.

August feels terror at the thought of another hour in the fridge. He groans and rolls over to hide a movement towards his pocket.

I've got a fever. I need a doctor.

He thinks: how can I change what is happening here? Shall I tell him I'm not 34c, shall I tell him what I did, shall I tell him that Lawrence is on his way with the police? Anything that might force a change of direction.

The vizier opens the fridge door and turns around.

Wait, don't do this, I need to tell you something. Something about —

He lifts August in his arms in one smooth and effortless movement. The only sign of physical exertion is the appearance of a vein in his neck. August grips the tiny blade between his fingers and lunges but the abrupt movement forces his muscles into a cramp and he stiffens and cries out in pain. The vizier waits patiently for it to pass and then places August in the fridge. All he has to do, when August resists, is raise a single finger as though about to press on a doorbell.

August tries to prepare himself for what is coming next: a beating, a dousing with water, the gag that slips down his throat. He knows something is coming.

But when he sees what it is, he thinks: that's genius. Forget about everything else. *That's* the last thing I need.

The vizier reaches into the fridge, places a bottle of spirits in his hands and closes the door.

••••

August understands this is just another way of controlling him, that the vizier knows a sick *and* drunk prisoner will struggle to think clearly, let alone try to escape. For this reason he waits ten minutes before taking his first warming sip, fifteen before his second, seventeen before... After all, he doesn't want to make it too easy. But with nothing in his stomach other than a piece of stale bread and a few mouthfuls of water, he is well on his way to being drunk within the hour.

In this state of inebriation and extreme fatigue, not to mention terror and tedium, or the discomfort caused by any number of cuts, bruises and broken bones, his mind – a skittish and fragile thing – alights once again on the theory that Martha was a foreign agent. The idea that she is alive is so powerful as to have an almost analgesic effect. Little wonder, then, that he indulges in it so comprehensively, that he dismisses out of hand all rational objections that the idea is clearly nonsense. Let's hear the evidence, he says, gripping the bottle like a gavel. And so he finds himself preparing to entertain the case for the prosecution in the courtroom of his battered and bleeding head.

The alcohol has the rough sweet taste of cheap raki.

He takes another sip from the bottle and sees her sitting in the dock, her pea-green coat buttoned up to the neck, her eyes downcast. He looks at her. He looks at her again. But she won't look at him. Not yet.

He hears the vizier walking around.

Is he supposed to say something to start the proceedings? Something about the importance of due process or the rule of law? Is that what judges say?

The sea makes a noise like murmurings from a restless public gallery.

The Russians, Your Honour.

The bottle almost slips through his fingers.

Lawrence steps out of the gloom. August wasn't expecting to see him, but it makes sense now that he thinks about it. Lawrence is wearing his best grey wool suit and twirling a pair of expensive spectacles.

There can be no doubt they were behind this. Her Majesty's experts are agreed that this whole thing *smells* of Russia: painstaking and patient, mischievous, unspeakably cruel.

He doesn't sound like Lawrence, this lawyer. He looks like Lawrence, but he sounds … he sounds as though he has been *drinking*.

Let us pin the tail where it belongs, Your Honour, squarely on the hindquarters of the Russian donkey. In fact, let us go further and take a moment to close our eyes and imagine the defendant's handlers sitting around in their Yasenevo headquarters, shirtsleeves rolled up, laughing with delight at news of their latest success and toasting each other's brilliance.

August toasts their brilliance too. It'd be churlish not to. He's enjoying this more than he expected, now that Lawrence is getting into the swing of things.

Then there's the matter of the German lorry driver. Or the *East* German lorry driver, to be exact. This was careless. If they needed to stage an accident in order to exfiltrate the defendant they should have used an agent from France or India or South Africa. Or even one from Bonn or Munich. But one from *East* Germany? Come on. Your Honour, this really gives the game away. Think how mortified they must have been when a vengeful August tracked their agent down, lured him to a meeting in a hotel lobby and then followed him home through the park. How close he came to uncovering the whole plot! If only he had gone through with it and given that man the thrashing of his life, he might have spilled the beans, he might have confessed to everything! One can only imagine the panic around the table when they heard of *that*, and the resulting scramble to recall their agent to Moscow for a routine meeting in the deepest, darkest corner of the Lubyanka, one of those meetings from which no one ever emerges...

What is she doing, just *sitting* there? Why won't she look up? Why won't she look at him? Doesn't she know how *bad* this is looking for her?

It was amateurish, Your Honour, the whole operation – that is, once you begin to unpick what happened. The evidence presented today should explode once and for all the myth of Russian competence. In fact, I'm a little embarrassed for them. No wonder they chose not to turn up. One implausibility after another, the coincidences and unlikelihoods stacked precariously high. Take the defendant's first encounter with August, for example. That she was seated next to him, an uncommonly beautiful woman of the same age engaged in an activity that positively invited collaboration. Who spends long-haul flights doing crosswords? And the way she studiously avoided fourteen across, the answer to which just happened to be the name of a writer he admired!

Is that … was that a shake of her head? It must be difficult to hear her deceit and treachery exposed in this ruthless fashion.

Now, I grant you this: she was wearing headphones and adopted a stand-offish manner, as though to deter him from conversation. This is what the defence will claim, Your Honour. They may even offer up the "male friend" she was travelling to visit, a male friend who suddenly and conveniently stopped being important to her once she had ensnared August, almost as though he had never existed. But we can all see what's going on here, can't we? It doesn't require any particular expertise to understand that such crude obstacles as a pair of headphones, a frosty demeanour and a fictional boyfriend are little more than red rags to the bullish psychopathy of your typical case officer, selected and trained to exploit, manipulate and disregard social niceties in the service of their country. The truth is that the defendant might as well have jumped into his lap and thrown her arms around his neck.

She looks up, visibly distressed. She shakes her head and looks around for someone who might be on her side. But she still won't look at him. She knows that *he's* not on her side, not after what she did.

Let's drag it all out into the light of day, Your Honour. While we're at it. Look at the defendant and then look at August. Even putting to one side his dishevelled appearance today, it must be clear to everyone in this court that she is too good for him. Even *he* wouldn't argue with that. In fact, his own statement indicates as much, that in his view she is funnier, cleverer, kinder … where's that piece of paper? Ah, here we are. She laughs more and worries less. She gives better presents. I'm sorry, I really am, ladies and gentlemen – there's some maudlin nonsense here. Something about enriching and enlarging his life. Solipsistic nonsense, if you ask me. I don't know how the warning lights didn't flash. She'll be a wonderful mother. She is passionate about – oh yes, oh yes, ladies and gentlemen of the jury, look at this. We have a treat for you today. Lift your eyes to the dock. What a performance. As though anyone here is going to be fooled by a few crocodile tears after everything we've heard. And there is more, Your Honour – much more. Clerk, play the tape.

There is a pause as the clerk finds the recording and then a dusty crackle as the loudspeakers are switched on. The sound of breathing, the rustle of a page. Then her voice, saying:

— Gus, you still awake?

— Mmm. Not really.

— Listen to this. "Reading such a file you see how an informer is gradually played in, like a fish on a line, starting from the initial resolve to talk only of 'professional concerns' and ending up with the most private betrayal." Is that what you do?

— Well, I suppose so, in a way. Sometimes. It's not always like that. What are you reading?

Clerk, press pause. Your Honour, this is from a bug we planted in their bedroom. We acknowledge the privacy issues involved in playing this in open court but believe that it exposes the insidious way in which the defendant carefully dripped Russian propaganda into August's ear over a period of time. Clerk, please continue.

— What about this? Don't go to sleep, you big lump, this is interesting. I'll change the names. Ready? "Here, in part 1 of the file, is August Drummond's proposal to make contact with him, using a 'legend'. Drummond will ring up, pretending to be from the city council. When they meet, Drummond will introduce himself as 'John Smith' from the Ministry for State Security and will say that the other man's name has appeared on the books of a foreign intelligence service. It looks bad, and they need his cooperation to clear this up. In effect: prove your innocence!"

— The Ministry for State Security? Is that —

— Sssh. Answer the question.

— Is the man's name actually on the books of a foreign intelligence service? If it is, then it's perfectly legitimate to go and talk to him.

— In this case it's not. Officer Drummond has fabricated that detail.

— I wouldn't do that.

— Would others?

— I don't know.

— What about the principle? Would you ever take an association or connection or friendship that you believed to be harmless and present it to one of the people involved as a thing they needed to clear up? As a way of getting them on the hook as an informer?

— Um, I don't know. Possibly. What's the book about?

— The Stasi.

— The Stasi? Hang on, you're not saying —

— Of course I'm not. But it's interesting, don't you think? The overlap in technique.

Ladies and gentlemen of the jury, more thoughtful, more resilient, more imaginative, according to August. More *treacherous*, I would suggest to you. More treacherous, more deceitful, more underhand, more cowardly. And this is one conversation among dozens that we might have used. What they all have in common — would the defendant please sit down and stop making a scene? What they all have in common is the way that this woman sought to undermine the integrity of the British establishment by suggesting that the way we carry out our intelligence activities is somehow unethical. The irony of such an accusation coming from a Russian agent is beyond — if you don't settle down I'll have no choice but to request that the bailiff remove you from this courtroom. Do you hear me? No one here is interested in your sentimental nonsense. Now where was I? We might conclude, ladies and gentlemen, that her tactics worked, judging by August's subsequent behaviour, by his willingness to break the rules in order to prove that he remained *his own man, independent in spirit, no mere servant of the deep state* – or whatever adolescent words they whispered to each other in the darkness of night. Unfortunately our bugs failed to pick up everything they said. But this is not how the world works. All of the adults in this room understand that. We need obedience, we need discipline, we need order, we need people with a grown-up understanding that the world is a complex and dangerous —

— for the last time, will you stop making such a —

— Bailiff, please remove the defendant from the court-room —

— August, sit down, this is nothing to —

— if ever you needed further proof, ladies and gentlemen, see how our enemies seek to disrupt our venerable institutions with their —

— if she won't go quietly, you fool, then use necessary force —

— August, what are you doing, stay in your —

— August, where did you get that bottle from, August, August, put that bottle down —

— Bailiff —

••••

Come on, let's get this done. This place is creepy. So what's going on? You said you'd get him to the border.

There were difficulties.

That's your problem. What use is he to us here? This city is full of kafir tourists we could help ourselves to if we wanted. You've got one locked in a fridge. So what?

If you kidnapped a tourist from here the whole country would be shut down before you got halfway to the border. Checkpoints, searches. They would close all the holes in the fence. The difference is that no one is looking for this one. You can confirm that yourselves easily enough – no one has reported him missing, his picture hasn't been on the television. The police do not even know he exists.

How'd you manage that then?

That is my business. Do you want to see him?

Wait, if he's so incognito, this guy, why don't you take him to the border yourself? Stick to the agreement.

You know how it works. You need the right vehicle with a reason to be travelling, you need a Turkish driver with papers, you need to know where the checkpoints are. This is easy for you. Not so easy for me.

But you said you'd do it.

The circumstances were different. I thought it might be possible to have him … delivered there.

Delivered? I like that. A delivery service. End of the day it's a lot of risk for us though. Lot of army to get past. If we said yes, you're suggesting what, that we knock the – what shall we call it? – the delivery charge off the price? What is it, about six hundred miles? That's a lot of delivery charge. Not sure it'd be worth it for you any more.

We can discuss the price.

I bet we can. Look, don't get me wrong. You've done well. This is impressive. Last we heard you had literally nothing, now here you are with something to sell. What would you do with the money?

This is also my business.

Not many places to run, is there. Afghanistan, Pakistan – your name's dirt there too. Back to London? Won't be cushy like it was last time, with your fancy house in – where was it again?

When can I get the money?

When you called us we were amazed. Never thought we'd hear from you again. To be honest I've come mainly for the curiosity value. This isn't realistic, what you're selling. You must know that. There's all sorts of politics to think about. Doesn't matter that the local police aren't looking for this guy *now*, once they realize he came from here they'll go fucking nuts. They can make things really difficult for us around the border. End of the day it's not my call but I don't think it's worth it.

I am not interested in what you think. Talk to —

What?

Talk to Abu Mustafa.

I talked to him already, man.

What did he say?

What did he say? He said you're a lying scumbag piece of shit is what he said. You don't get it, your brothers aren't your brothers any more. Not after what you did. Abu Mustafa's not pulling strings for you, nobody is.

I am not asking for an act of kindness. This is a business deal. I am giving you more than you are giving me. And we both know that the brothers are in trouble. They need this.

No, you're calling us up and saying, hello, there's a package but you've got to come and pick it up from the depot. And by the way it's a big package so you need to hire a truck. What's the point, we're doing all the work here but you're supposed to be the fucking delivery boy.

Watch your mouth.

Watch my mouth? Watch *your* fucking mouth, bro. You're not my emir any more. You're not anyone's emir after what you did. You should hear the brothers talk about you now. Like you're something on the bottom of their shoe. Don't even think about it, don't you even... There's two of us, take one more step and we'll stick you in the fridge with this cunt and throw the pair of you in the fucking sea.

So we have a deal?

Funny. Look, we're done here.

There is not much time. I need to know your decision very soon.

Is he even in one piece? I've seen your handiwork before.

Have a look.

Fucking hell, you've done a number there. At least he's got all his fingers attached. You're going soft in your old age. Let me take a picture, send it back. Where did he get the bottle from?

It does not matter.

What's he saying? Fucking hell, he's drunk – I can't make out a word. Hello mate, enjoying your holiday? What's your —

That is enough.

Who is he anyway?

It does not matter. What matters is who knows that he is here. And the answer is nobody.

•••

There is sleep, or something like it. Afterwards he tries to measure its duration by considering how he feels, the precise proportion of drunk to hung-over. He has recent experience of hangovers, plenty of it, so he has a degree of confidence in his judgement. Four hours, he thinks.

He doesn't know how much time has passed, but he knows how much time he's got.

Five minutes, the vizier says. He's standing by the window. A lorry strains up a faraway hill. The sunlight has a washed-out, late-afternoon quality.

August is lying on the floor. He moves his arms and legs to force the blood back into his extremities.

Who were those guys? he says. If it's about money, I can get you money.

He doesn't expect a response. He just wants to hear his own voice, which is more slurred than he expected. Maybe it's closer to three hours.

Water. Can I have some water?

He has to do two things. Firstly, accept as a fact that the vizier will always be a step ahead of him. He thought the bottle of raki was about keeping him quiet. It turns out that was only part of its purpose. Even more than that, it was intended to make it impossible for him to claim – as 34c might have been expected to do – that he was a Muslim, a willing volunteer to the IS cause, cruelly tricked into this position by the vizier. It was intended to make sure that anything coming out of his mouth would be laughable.

Four minutes.

Secondly, August has to disregard the fact that the vizier will always be a step ahead of him, because it will lead to surrender, and he has to do something. If IS decide they want him, what will follow is a tranquillizer and twenty-four hours in the back of a lorry. Bored soldiers aren't going to search through boxes of rotting foodstuffs when nobody's even been reported missing. And after that, once he's across the border...

He drinks some water. When the vizier's back is turned he touches his pocket, looking for the sharp edge of the plastic blade hidden there.

If IS don't want him, in an instant he'll become worthless, pure risk, and he'll be dead within minutes. This is why he keeps on returning to the question of how much time has passed since their visit. Because if they don't want him, they'll just ditch the phone they were using with the vizier and move on. There won't be a courtesy call to explain their reasons. And so the vizier might decide at any moment that the deal is off.

But for now he seems intent on keeping August alive.

I need to use the toilet.

There is a bucket in the corner.

Can you help me?

He has no chance in a fight. It has to be sudden and brief. It has to be the eye or the throat.

Please can you help me? If you don't...

They won't want to have to wash him and change his clothes before taking him away.

The vizier takes a last look out of the window and lifts August to his feet as though he is weightless. With one powerful arm the vizier supports August as he tries to walk across the room. He fights the urge to be sick. He slowly twists, leans his back against the far wall and puts his open left hand on the vizier's shoulder as though to steady himself.

Thank you, August says. He is breathing heavily.

The vizier's eyes are pale grey and bloodshot. Too much hard bone. Any sudden movement in that direction will only be understood one way.

I've been thinking about it, August says. He steadies himself. Thirty-one, he says, maybe thirty-two. No more than that.

What —

With his right hand he pushes the tiny plastic blade deep into the vizier's neck and twists and drags it downwards and across. The blood is sudden and violent. He pulls it out and jabs upwards towards his left eye but already he is ducking his head like a boxer to protect his neck and the plastic point misses by a centimetre and blunts itself against his temple. With one hand at his neck the vizier makes a slow short precise turn and plants his shoulder where August's chest and stomach meet. He presses him backwards against the wall. In an instant the air is driven from August's lungs. He has never felt force like it. He grabs at the vizier's hair and tries to turn his head while with the broken blade he stabs desperately into his exposed face. He can't breathe. He hears a cracking sound that might be his ribs or something in the wall behind him. The vizier makes a small, precise adjustment and presses harder. August is close to blacking out. The plaster slowly crumbles at his back and falls in soft sugary clouds onto the puddled blood around their feet. Still he pushes.

When he regains consciousness he is slumped on the floor. The vizier stands above him, his chest heaving, the skin around his right eye punctured with tiny holes.

From inside the fridge August listens to him breaking apart the room with his bare hands.

••••

Shaving cut, was it? That'll teach you to get rid of your beard.

Have you got the money?

Calm down, we've got it. How's our boy? Let's get him out, shall we.

First the money, says the vizier.

Just need to check you haven't chopped him up into little bits. I wouldn't put it past you… You got the key for this?

Let me do it.

The door swings open. The man who stands there is in his late twenties, slender, of mixed race. He is dressed in black trousers and a black hooded tracksuit top.

Fucking hell, he says. He scratches a straggly beard.

He is alive, says the vizier. You will not have any problems with him.

I've always been a big fan of your work. Hello, mate. Tour bus is here, going to take you on a little ride, visit a few sites. Is he still drunk? Not a bad idea that, keeps him quiet.

The money.

It's all there. Abu Mustafa wanted to halve it because … well, because he thinks you're a cunt, basically, but I talked him round. Told him you're looking pretty desperate. What you doing? You actually counting it? I don't know whether we should be offended, Ahmed.

He turns to another man, who fills the entire doorway with his bulk. He hasn't said anything.

Come on, we've got to go —

Be quiet.

Doesn't this seem odd to you?

They look at August. Even the vizier looks up from the money.

Whoa, he can speak! Thought you might have chopped his tongue off. You all right, mate, how's your hangover? You just sit tight, we'll have you on your way in no time. They serve cold beer on the bus so you'll be right as rain.

Can I…

You're a free man. You can do what you like.

August tries to climb out of the fridge but stumbles and falls to the floor. He pulls himself into a sitting position and clears his throat.

Doesn't it seem weird that just a few hours ago they didn't want me and now they can't wait to get going?

It's called negotiating tactics, mate. Blowing hot and cold.

And how did they work out for you, August says, those tactics, what with that discount you've just negotiated?

What's that? How about you just —

He swings a vague kick in the direction of August. The vizier looks up again.

If you hurt him it is your responsibility. Be quiet and let me finish counting this. Then you can do what you want.

Yeah, be quiet like the boss says.

Shut up, man.

I'm just saying, as a neutral observer, it's clear who's in charge in this situation. And it's definitely not —

Yeah, whatever, let the old man count his money.

Seriously though, August says, am I the only one who thinks this is odd? You basically said a couple of hours ago that you'd give them a discount and now they can't wait to pay you the full amount.

The man's got a bag of cash, what does he care?

He'd care if he knew you're trying to cheat him.

What? How are we trying to cheat him? We've just paid him his money. Every last penny.

You should be paying him ten times that much.

What are you talking about? Ten times for some string-bean kafir drunk cunt? This is how much he asked for, this is how much he's getting. What is this, *The Apprentice*, you're having a go at my negotiating skills? Shut up, man. Are you done counting that fucking money, bro? We need to go.

The man filling the doorway shifts his feet and looks at his watch.

The vizier is halfway through his count. There's no sign that he's listening. August allows the silence to settle and then tries to laugh. The pain in his ribs makes him gasp.

What's so funny?

How you're getting worked up. If only you could see your face. You're worried that he's going to realize what's happening and call you out. You're worried that you're going to have to crawl back to Abu Mustafa with your tail between your legs and explain how you messed up a simple task.

What are you even talking about?

The vizier pauses.

Why do you think you are worth ten times this amount?

Bro, don't even waste your breath on him, just count your money. We need to get out of here like now.

Why do you think you are worth ten times this amount?

Do you remember last time they were here? They took a picture of me and sent it back. It's obvious. Someone recognized me.

The man in the tracksuit laughs.

Someone recognized you? What, you think you're David Beckham or something?

Someone I've met before recognized me, says August. One of the brothers. I worked for British intelligence for a long time so it could have been any one of them. The number of people I stopped at the airport or bumped on the street... The point is, they saw my picture, realized who I am and understand that I'm worth a lot more than some random guy. Both in terms of what I know and publicity value. That's why I've no doubt they'd give you ten bags of cash in exchange for me, and if this is your one chance to set yourself up properly before you disappear forever, it'd be a shame —

What, you're a spy, are you? Course you are. That's why you're locked up here with no one coming to rescue you.

I was. I'm not any more. The reason there's no one coming to rescue me is because he persuaded the only person who knows I'm here that he's a caretaker and that I'm off getting drunk somewhere. The truth is … well, I don't expect you to believe this. But I'm here because my wife died, and then I lost my job, and I saw a young man acting weirdly on a plane, and then I went to a cemetery and met you. This has all been a mistake. I was just looking for… I don't know what I was looking for. Something to do, I suppose.

This makes no sense at all. Come on, we've got a van downstairs, we can't hang around —

The vizier closes the bag and stands up.

Can you prove any of this?

What? Are you seriously —

Do I need to? You know that I'm telling the truth, says August. You can see that this guy doesn't even want to engage with the idea, he doesn't want to ask me a single question about it. He wants to get out of here as quickly as he can. If he genuinely didn't know who I was he'd be jumping with joy right now at the thought of what he had in front of him. Instead he can't wait for this to end. It's written all over his dumb face.

I don't want to ask you any questions because it's all bullshit and you're trying to waste time. Ahmed, grab his arm.

I don't know if you'd call it proof, but if your boss is Abu Mustafa, then his boss is a Saudi guy who uses the kunya Hajj Mohammed and sleeps in a farmhouse fifteen miles outside Raqqa. His second wife lives there too, but her in-laws are from a small town on the other side of the border called Wardiya, so every two weeks she takes the children and travels —

Enough of this. You've got your money so now he's ours.

He steps forward and hits August hard in the mouth.

Don't touch him, says the vizier. He unbuckles his belt and pulls it loose, wrapping the leather end around his fist twice.

You've got your money, exactly what you asked for, says the man in the black tracksuit. Don't be an idiot – there's two of us. Take the bag and fuck off. Ahmed, grab his arm —

Step back.

Don't tell me —

The vizier swings the buckle in an arc through the air.

I said step back.

Ahmed continues forward and the buckle catches him across the face and tears his forehead open. He raises a hand to wipe away the blood that is pouring into his eyes. From somewhere behind his back he takes a knife and steps towards the vizier, who shuffles backwards and then lunges forward so quickly that nobody is prepared. With his right hand he grips Ahmed's outstretched wrist, twisting it sharply down and towards him so that the knife clatters to the floor, while with his open left hand he hits Ahmed hard on the side of his neck. He slumps to the floor. His wrist sticks out at a funny angle.

What the fuck you doing? You want to fight with us? We've just given you exactly what you asked for. You telling me you believe this bullshit about him being James Bond? Man, are you crazy? We had a deal, you gave us your word. You can't do something like this and just walk away.

Nobody is walking away, says the vizier. He is your prisoner. And this money is your deposit. Come back before dawn with the same amount again and you can take him. I give you my word. You are still getting him cheap and we both know it. Now pick up your friend and go.

••••

Each minute is packed so densely with fear that time bulges and swells and distends out of all recognition. Later on he hears the front door open and close. He waits to hear the creak of the floorboards. There are possibilities, none of them good. They've come back with the money, they've come back with a weapon, they're not coming back at all...

The footsteps climb the stairs, pad once around the room and then leave.

He has been given another bottle of raki but instead of drinking it he fashions a blade from its metal cap. He tests its sharpness against his throat. If there was a hard edge and room to swing the bottle he'd smash it into pieces. He pours some of it over his clothing. His best idea so far – his only idea – is to pretend to be unconscious. The vizier might expect something like that, after what happened last time, and IS will come in numbers. But if they think he's passed out they may just place him in their vehicle as he is, and his priority must be to get out of this house alive. He can worry about the rest later.

The footsteps return. It occurs to him that whoever it is, their tread is hesitant, cautious, as though uncertain of their surroundings. It might be IS. They might be hesitant because they don't know where the vizier is. But would one of them come here on their own?

He taps on the side of the fridge. A pause, and then two steps in his direction. He taps again and there is a soft tap by way of reply.

Hello?

Someone pulls hesitantly at the door.

Who's that?

Who is that?

He doesn't recognize the voice. He prises open a gap in the rubber seal, but it is completely dark in the room.

Can you help me?

Who is that?

August.

What … are you inside a fridge?

Youssef? Is that Youssef?

What are you doing in there?

What? I…

He doesn't know how to answer.

You gave me your word, says Youssef. You said you would help me find my wife and daughter. I know you were drunk but you signed a piece of paper.

It occurs to him that in his confusion Youssef might think sitting in a padlocked fridge is something he has chosen to do. He doesn't know what to say.

Are you angry with me, August? I heard you talking on the phone about this house —

Get me out.

What? Okay. Do you have the key?

Keep your voice down. Can you see the key anywhere? On the floor? Okay, forget that. Slide the chain up and over the top of the fridge. As quietly as you can.

There is a loud scraping noise.

Jesus. Quietly, I said.

It will not go.

What do you mean?

Well, it is very heavy.

Seriously? Try again. Quickly.

It is stuck. Wait, I will go and get help.

What? Where will you get help from?

I saw an old guy outside. I think he is the caretaker. Wait, is there a light in here? I cannot see what —

What? What did you say?

The light, is there —

No, no – don't switch the light on. Did you say you saw a caretaker outside?

Yes, he is doing something down by the water.

Did he see you?

What?

Did he see you?

I do not think so. I walked down from the road —

He's not a caretaker, Youssef. He's the man who's done this to me. You can do it on your own. Just push the chain up a few centimetres at a time and work your way around.

August tracks the noise of the chain as it climbs higher up the fridge.

What's happening? Why have you stopped?

My hands are tired. Just a minute.

For Christ's sake. Keep going, Youssef. Come on, faster.

All right, I think that is —

The fridge door swings open and he falls out.

The bottle falls out after him. August empties it onto the floor and smashes it as quietly as he can against the edge of a wall. They fumble their way towards the stairwell. He waves the broken bottle into the darkness ahead of them as they begin to descend. A blue midnight glow presses against the unshuttered windows.

They stop on the first floor, at the back of the house.

Can you jump from here, Youssef?

What?

Can you jump down from here?

Youssef pushes the shutters open.

Are you mad? It is completely black, I cannot see —

We're on the first floor. It's about three metres down, no more than that. The ground is soft. Run straight through the trees up to the road. Don't use the driveway, don't let anyone see you. Especially the caretaker. Got that? Have you got a mobile phone? When you get to the road, stop the first vehicle that goes past. I know it's the middle of the night, but I've heard traffic at all hours. Get them to come down into the driveway with their lights on and sounding their horn. Get them to make as much noise as possible. And call the police.

Youssef lands with a dull thud and a loud curse. August listens to his angry progress through the trees towards the road. He has no idea what he's going to do. He should run, he should run as far away as he can from this place. But amid the wreckage of his broken mind, amid the horror and bewilderment and grief, is a refusal to accept that this man should be allowed to cause such destruction and simply walk away on his own terms. He can barely take a step without help. Each breath stabs at him. He's covered in blood and his broken finger is black and stiffly swollen. But he doesn't want to climb through a window and disappear among the trees. He wants to walk out on his own. He wants to look this man in the eye and show him that he hasn't won.

Gripping the banister, he makes his way down the final flight of stairs and pulls open the front door. The night sky is the colour of bruised flesh. He stands there for several minutes, revived by the cold air, long enough to see the driveway and the scrubby grass, the way the trees lean together conspiratorially, the moonlight and the rustling water and the bag on the passenger seat of the parked car. He walks down to the car and slowly circles it. He holds the broken bottle lightly in his right hand. There is no sign of the vizier. He reaches in through the window and opens the bag and sees bundles of money wrapped in plastic. He stops and straightens and listens for any sound of a vehicle passing on the road above the house, but there is only silence. He wonders if Youssef has gone. The plastic rustles when he touches it. A figure kneeling in the distance hears the noise. When he stands it is as though he is emerging out of the black water. He turns and the light catches his pale unblinking eyes. He starts to walk towards the house, towards August, who tightens his hold on the bottle and steps forward.

They are twenty paces apart when they hear it. An engine, a clamour of voices and a horn, sounded repeatedly, followed by a scattering of loose earth. A lorry swings into sight and comes to a stop. Youssef is shouting something from the open window, but no one can hear what he's saying.

The vizier looks at August for a long time. And then he turns and walks down to the water and begins to wade through the shallows until it is deep enough to swim. Only when he has almost disappeared from sight does August see a rowing boat bobbing fifty metres from shore, and he watches as in one powerful motion the vizier pulls himself on board, and then he is gone, finally swallowed by the darkness.

PART THREE

Coercion

You might have ruined everything. Jesus Christ, Youssef. What on earth were you thinking?

What do you mean? Actually it went very well. As we agreed, I told him —

This is what I mean. Listen to this bit again. *Perhaps you will not be able to help me, my friend. But I remember meeting you at the office of Miss Beatrice and I understood immediately that you are a kind and helpful man. I also know that you are a senior diplomat and would not dirty your hands with the business of spying. But I do not know who to speak to about this very sensitive matter.* You're not trying to sell him a car, Youssef. If you flatter him this crudely, he's going to realize you've got an ulterior motive. There's no way anyone in their right mind would call Lawrence "kind and helpful", let alone a "senior diplomat". And don't say "my friend" to him – he's an Englishman, we don't even say things like that to people we've known our whole lives. And what's this about *him* helping *you*? It's the other way around, we discussed this, you're the one who's going —

August, I think you should rest. Have you slept at all? It is not good for you to become so excited, so soon after what happened in that house. Remember that we do not have to do it this way. There are other ways to find out where my wife is. Perhaps they will take longer —

My way will work, Youssef, but you've got to do exactly what I tell you to do.

I am telling you, the meeting was a success. Mr Lawrence was very happy indeed when we finished talking. He asked for my phone number and said that he will call me —

What you've got to understand is that he's one of those spies who's in love with the idea of spying. I knew someone in London who took him along to an agent meeting, and on the way back to the office Lawrence insisted on ducking into an alleyway to burn his handwritten notes. It made no sense. In fact, it probably drew attention to him. But bending over the papers, striking a match, watching the words crumble into ash and disappear – I suspect he'd never felt more alive than he did at that moment. He's the sort of person who checks every night that he isn't being followed home. Do you know what I mean? In his conversations with you, he wants to think that he's acting as puppet master, that he's manoeuvring you from a place of mistrust to one in which you see him as your closest confidant. He wants to think that he's practising a mysterious and ancient craft, like a Druid. Trust me, that's the key to this: allow him to think he's a druid and you'll be able to lead him wherever you —

August, you need to calm down. I really do not know what you are talking about. Can I open a window in here? I do not think this is good for you. I told you, he was very interested in our story —

Are you sure this phone was hidden from sight?

What? It was in my jacket —

You didn't wear that tie, did you?

What is wrong with this tie?

I told you not to wear it, Youssef. Those aren't ordinary rabbits. It makes you look dishonest —

My daughter gave this —

I'm telling you, they're not ordinary rabbits.

August, you are speaking very loudly. You really must rest. Look, I brought you food. Please eat something.

Did you bring anything to drink?

Shall I change these bandages? Can I open a window in here?

Let's get back to work.

When can I ask Mr Lawrence about my wife and daughter?

Not yet. We've got to convince him that you've got access to real intelligence of value, plant the idea that the most important thing to you is your family and let him come up with the idea himself. Now let's go through the recording again. What exactly was the expression on his face when you first mentioned Daesh and the emir?

• • • •

VESTIBULE/001

TOP SECRET

FOIA EXEMPT

FROM: ATY4
TO: C14B1

Freddy —

Brace yourself: I'm about to fire both barrels of the intelligence blunderbuss in your general direction to ensure that I get everything down in one blast. Let's have a chat first thing tomorrow morning, pick out the choice pieces of birdshot from your flabby arse and agree a way forward. I'm keen that my report lands on the desks of seniors in London a) quickly b) with either (i) a red flag waving atop it or (ii) an accompanying fanfare c) in an appropriately lean form (we know how they hate fat – poor you) and d) with my name front and centre. I make no apologies for d). If you even think of sharing this with Sally Barber and her four thieves at this early stage I'll be firing both barrels of a real blunderbuss in your very specific direction.

We had a walk-in this afternoon. It was someone I'd met briefly before, a Syrian national called Youssef HADDAD (p/d.o.b. Homs, 17/9/1980) who happened to be interviewing for a job with Beatrice at Endgame Consulting when I was there recently. We exchanged a few words on that occasion. He didn't make a hugely positive impression, to be honest with you. He came across as a trifle slippery, desperate for work, falling over himself to be friendly. You know the sort. Sports a rather bizarre tie festooned with *Playboy* bunnies. Plenty of red flags, in terms of his character – if it wasn't for the fact that he was clearly so hesitant this afternoon about passing high-grade intelligence to a British official. But I'm getting ahead of myself.

In line with protocol we would have put someone unimportant in front of him, but he asked for me by name. Said that he knows I am a "senior diplomat" and not involved in "the great game of espionage" but that he places a lot of weight on "the personal touch" and was able to tell during our short encounter that I possess "enormous integrity, understanding and compassion" (his words). He asked that I pass the information he was about to provide to a colleague who works in intelligence but to omit any mention of him as the source, as he considered this a one-off and was not prepared to attend further meetings with British officials under any circumstances.

For a neophyte, he gave an admirably succinct, to-the-point and waffle-free account of the facts. In brief, he has a childhood Syrian friend (name withheld) in Turkey who is involved in low-level criminality: people-smuggling, theft, procurement of false documents, etc. HADDAD himself disapproves of much of what his friend does but accepts the imperative to provide for one's family. In the past, he told me, this friend has performed services on behalf of IS in return for payment. When pressed for an example, he said that he had once procured a piece of medical equipment for a high-ranking member of the group with a kidney condition.

Anyway, this friend has heard rumours that a "significant" IS emir has been expelled from the group and forced into hiding in Turkey. So far, routine scuttlebutt. Nothing at all to get excited about – in your position you'll no doubt hear a dozen such rumours in any given week. Two "facts" set this apart. Firstly, that this emir was until his expulsion in charge of the foreign-fighter battalion, which means – if true – he would be aware of a) the identities and whereabouts of all Europeans fighting with IS and b) any extant attack plans focused on the UK. Secondly, that this individual is described as being Iraqi, in his mid-fifties, a former member of Saddam's secret police and – are you sitting down? – a *one-time resident of London.* I'm pretty sure I know which name has just popped into your head. American reporting suggested he had gone the other way, towards Baluchistan – but what if he's here? I don't need to tell you what a coup it'd be to get our hands on him first.

Next steps, Freddy: take a deep breath, walk around the room, eat a chocolate biscuit – whatever it is you do to relax. Don't call William. Talk to Nigel or Meredith to get a sensible view on this – and make sure you tell them I'm involved. That'll reassure them.

HADDAD was adamant that he didn't want to discuss this matter further and under no circumstances would countenance doing a little spadework to find out more, but I persuaded him to give me a contact number. It's apparent that he holds me in high regard and so I would strongly suggest that I remain in pole position on this case and either a) declare as an intelligence officer or b) offer to act as an honest broker on his behalf with the intelligence community. I'll leave it up to you to decide which is better. I'm confident I can manoeuvre him into an active role in order to provide us with more intelligence but, if needed, we have leverage aplenty: he is, after all, an undocumented migrant in a hostile country, and we can always fall back on his wife and daughter if necessary. He seems pretty desperate to find them.

Cheerio,
Lawrence

PS. I'll send details of HADDAD's selectors separately. Can you find a competent analyst to pull together a summary of the LEG IRON files, and get GCHQ to have a quick-and-dirty peek at HADDAD's recent phone usage?

••••

VESTIBULE/002

TOP SECRET
FOIA EXEMPT

SUBJECT: LEG IRON file summary
DATE: 18 December 2016

1. Our understanding of the background and career of Ahmed Naji Al Hadithi (also known as Abu Laith Al Dulaimi and Abu Laith Al Iraqi but hereafter referred to as LEG IRON) is marked by significant gaps. Defector reporting suggests that he was born between 1960 and 1963 to a relatively poor family in the town of Haditha in Iraq's western Al Anbar province, and that his father worked in a local bakery. LEG IRON himself was the youngest of five siblings.

2. A former general in the Iraqi Air Force (POLARITON) told his US debriefer in 1992 that he had been LEG IRON's commanding officer in the mid-1980s, and that LEG IRON had graduated from military academy with a reputation for ambition, discipline (he had taught himself at least four languages) and ruthlessness, and for having briefly been part of the Iraqi national wrestling team, a

position he gave up in order to concentrate on his military career. At some point in the late 1980s he requested a transfer to Air Force intelligence and served with distinction during the latter years of the Iran–Iraq War. Liaison reporting indicates that during this period he was part of a small team responsible for tracking down deserters who had fled the extremely arduous conditions on the front line, and for enforcing discipline among rank and file Iraqi conscripts. This was achieved through beatings, torture and public executions, as well as the practice of cutting off deserters' hands or ears and branding a horizontal line across their foreheads (the latter following complaints from veterans with genuine war injuries that they had been mistaken for deserters).

3. LEG IRON reappears in our files in the aftermath of Iraq's invasion of Kuwait. Following the Allied rout of the Iraqi army, uprisings began to appear across the south of the country, fuelled by the expectation that Western powers would support them in their attempt to overthrow Saddam Hussein. When this support did not materialize, Saddam mounted a series of brutal counter-attacks to suppress internal opposition. In a notorious film clip from March 1991, Ali Hassan Abd Al Majid Al Tikriti, known more widely as Chemical Ali for his use of mustard gas and sarin in the genocidal Anfal campaign against the Kurds, can be seen hunting down and personally executing rebels in the marsh-lands around Rumaytha, and defector reporting from both POLARITON and HEPTAHEDRON (a former head of security at the presidential palace) indicates

that LEG IRON can be seen in the footage on at least two occasions.

4. Once the rebels in the south had been defeated, Iraqi forces were redirected north to deal with the Kurdish uprising. POLARITON credits LEG IRON with the idea of throwing ordinary baking flour from helicopters onto crowds of Kurdish civilians in order to create the impression they were being attacked with chemical weapons, which led to widespread panic and hastened the mass flight of refugees into Iran and Turkey. This was viewed in Baghdad as a masterstroke, and HEPTAHEDRON reporting (in addition to multiple SIGINT strands) indicates that LEG IRON was among those presented with a medal by Saddam Hussein in a ceremony at the presidential palace in early 1992. In what quickly became a part of the folklore surrounding LEG IRON, a junior officer present at the event is reported to have jokingly described him in passing as "the baker of Baghdad", in a reference to his use of flour against the Kurds, his father's humble profession and to the widespread description of Saddam Hussein in Western media as "the butcher of Baghdad" – a description in which Saddam himself apparently took some pleasure. The "baker of Baghdad" epithet circulated widely in military and intelligence circles until the junior officer was beaten to death several weeks later during the routine search of what was believed to be an abandoned property in a Shia neighbourhood of Mosul.

5. An internal investigation into the incident exonerated LEG IRON, but the episode – heightened by the bereaved family's demand for retribution – is likely to have been

behind LEG IRON's sudden posting in May 1992 to the Iraqi Cultural Centre in London to take up the unlikely position of Assistant Administrator.

6. MI5 was unaware at the time of LEG IRON's military background and so did not designate him as a person of interest until six months after his arrival. Subsequent coverage (it appears from the files that investigators relied upon sporadic surveillance, telephone and postal intercept and a handful of agents within the Iraqi diaspora) indicated that LEG IRON lived with his wife and young child in a house in St John's Wood, drove a brown Vauxhall Astra, attended monthly classical concerts in his local church hall and carried out his administrative duties in a quietly professional manner.

7. He is also assessed to have been responsible for an increase in the number of killings (attempted and otherwise) of Iraqi dissidents in London. These included the murder of a Kurdish poet whose mutilated body was found floating in the Thames near Chelsea Bridge; the apparent suicides – both by hanging, both in the month of March – of two journalists writing for an opposition publication; a third suicide, this time by overdose, in which the coroner noted unexplained bruising around the deceased's neck and mouth; and the stabbing of an Iraqi defector in Highgate Cemetery. On that occasion the attacker was disturbed by a dog walker and fled the scene before completing his task. The victim later provided a statement to police in which he described seeing a blind man with a cane shortly before the attack; a white stick was later found discarded and wiped clean of fingerprints in a nearby flower bed.

8. During this period there were also seven assaults on Iraqi dissidents, for which a resident of the Isle of Dogs was later convicted. Given the accused's membership of a gym within a hundred metres of the Iraqi Cultural Centre, a psychiatric assessment indicating he was profoundly impressionable and eyewitness reporting suggesting he had been seen in public with LEG IRON, detectives pressed him to implicate LEG IRON in the assaults, but the man maintained to the end that he had acted alone and went on to receive the maximum sentence possible.

9. LEG IRON fled the UK in October of 1994 after becoming involved in a pub fight in which a man lost an eye.

10. Coverage of LEG IRON in the years following his return to Iraq is patchy, but records indicate that he was a casualty of the disastrous de-Baathification process insisted upon by the Coalition Provisional Authority in the aftermath of the 2003 invasion, in which thousands of military and intelligence officials were stripped of their positions, salaries and pensions. Despite the fierce competition during this period for stretched resources, we retained some coverage of LEG IRON because of his activities while in the UK, and CX reporting suggests a certain drift: a brief and unsuccessful stint running a haulage company, some fuel smuggling and extortion, a month or two in prison for kidnapping. His eldest brother, a former infantry colonel, was linked to Abu Musab Al Zarqawi's al-Qaeda in Iraq and later detained by the US in Abu Ghraib, which may have provided LEG IRON with a route into the armed Islamist insurgency. Even if there was no connection, however, this was a transition undertaken over the following years by

many hundreds of former Iraqi military and intelligence officials who had suddenly found themselves without work and excluded from the now Shia-dominated state, and welcomed by the likes of Abu Bakr Al Baghdadi, who recognized with considerable foresight the contribution their skills could make on the battlefield and in the building of the fledgling IS state.

11. Things went quiet until the autumn of 2012, when GCHQ voice analysis confirmed that an IS commander using the kunya Abu Laith was in fact LEG IRON. Reliable reporting on him during this time is scarce. Like many former professionals who had moved across, LEG IRON exhibited extremely high levels of operational security, changing his location every day, avoiding mobile phones, using multiple aliases and only trusting long-standing associates. He surfaced in 2014 as an adviser to a member of the Military Council, and again in 2015 in a senior role within the Amniyat, responsible for identifying and executing spies within IS (including a number of British and American agents who had been deployed upstream). Things then went quiet again until last month, when a flurry of CIA reporting indicated that he had been acting as emir of the foreign fighter battalion, following the killing by US drone of the previous incumbent, and that a dispute had led to his removal from the post and his departure from Syrian territory. The same reporting suggested (with a low to medium degree of confidence) that he had been sighted in Baluchistan.

12. The only coverage we have of LEG IRON at present comes from SIGINT of long and angry telephone conversations

between his wife and her parents in which they complain that his flight from IS has placed them at significant personal risk.

NNNN

••••

VESTIBULE/003

TOP SECRET

FOIA EXEMPT

FROM: ATY4
TO: C14B1
SUBJECT: Re: New intelligence lead in Istanbul
DATE: 19 December 2016

Freddy —

It was an enormous pleasure to talk to you this morning, and to have Meredith call just a few minutes later to convey the same message all over again with characteristic charm and diplomacy. (I do hope for her own sake that she finds a way to deal with her bitterness at missing out on the top spot.) I note your wise words of counsel and can assure you that I will a) exercise "due caution" b) keep a "proper written record of decisions and judgements" and c) most definitely not "rush headlong into something that will take time, expertise and patience to understand fully". As I noted in my last message, I am fully aware that "rumours" of this kind surface from time to time and must be treated carefully. There really is nothing for you to worry about. The last thing I want is to be the cause of your inevitable heart attack. Credit for that should go to the mountain of Turkish delight I intend to deposit on your desk when I'm next in town.

I also note your observation that GCHQ traces on Youssef HADDAD's phone indicate that he made a call to 112 (the Turkish equivalent of 999) four days ago, and your suggestion that this MIGHT mean he has already tried to volunteer the information about the IS emir to the Turks. This is a plausible hypothesis and should be factored into our thinking. HADDAD's credibility will certainly be damaged if it transpires that he has attempted to offload this intelligence elsewhere. This possibility should not, however, act as a handbrake on the excellent forward momentum I have engineered. Your recommendation that we discuss this matter with MIT and ask them for details of the call between HADDAD and 112 is a sensible one, but would you mind if we parked it for now? Talking to them will complicate and slow the case down to the point that we might lose access to HADDAD. MIT is obviously a competent intelligence agency and our natural partner in Turkey for a conversation of this kind, but once we go to them with this there is no turning back, as they will insist on being involved. I've already had a few run-ins on other matters with one of their deputy chiefs, a woman called Elif, and once she gets her painted nails into something there's no shaking her loose.

Freddy, a broader point, if I may. There is a potentially UNIQUE opportunity in front of us. Can you see that, with your focus on risk and liaison equities? Noisy teeth-sucking in London is only going to distract those of us toiling in the field.

Please allow me the leeway to develop this further. There is skill and artistry involved in cultivating this relationship, and what I need more than endless words of caution is a brief moment of hush from the cheap seats to see whether I can pull this off. Would that be all right? Would you be able to do that for me?

In anticipation of securing your agreement, I met HADDAD for a second time this morning. (Calm down – when you hear how well it went you'll be telling everyone it was your idea all along.) It took several attempts to reach him on the number he had provided, and even then he protested that he had nothing further to say, but after some persuasion he finally agreed to meet. I intercepted him at the metro station, fed him a story about the interview room being redecorated and took him instead to a quiet corner of a local restaurant, where I proceeded to order a mountain of food (enough to keep even you happy). He repeated early on that he didn't want to become an "informant" and had simply felt it was his duty as a proud Syrian to pass on information that might weaken IS. I told him I understood and respected his position, and that the meal was simply a way of thanking him for his important contribution.

I moved the conversation along briskly, putting him at his ease with topics such as the weekend's football results, favourite Syrian dishes, the importance of family and future career aspirations. Once things were humming along nicely, it didn't take more than a couple of sly verbal pivots to get us back onto the subject of his friend, and he soon disclosed that he had bumped into him by chance the previous evening at a Syrian café they both frequented. With my interest in the matter in the back of his mind, HADDAD said he had raised in hushed tones the subject of the exiled IS emir, and over the course of the evening had been able to elicit the following information from his friend: that the man is in his mid-fifties; that he has the physique of a weightlifter; that he previously worked under an IS figure called Abu Mustafa; and that he has access to a small boat.

You are known for your common sense, Freddy, and so I was confident you would agree that these details have lifted us clear of the foothills of mere rumour and speculation. In light of this, I told HADDAD that he clearly had all the natural abilities British intelligence would want in an agent, and that I knew this for a fact because I was among their ranks. He was in equal measures astonished, impressed and flattered (which is exactly the effect I wanted).

If the thought flitting across your mind is that I've moved too quickly, that this might all be a hoax, and that we really must get MIT on board, then let me put you at ease. When I said that he should consider becoming an agent, HADDAD became quite emotional and said the one thing that might change his mind was if we were able to tell him where his wife and infant daughter were located. He explained they had crossed by boat to Greece several weeks ago but that by now he expected they might be in Bulgaria, Hungary or even Austria. If we could find out this information for him, he said with tears brimming in his eyes, with a fierce grip on my arm, with his voice wavering, he would be in our debt forever. At this point, he looked around the restaurant and whispered that he was confident he would be able to find out from his friend exactly where in Istanbul the IS emir was staying.

That tingling feeling you're experiencing isn't a heart attack, Freddy – it's excitement. HADDAD doesn't want money or a passport or any of those things hoaxers typically ask for. He wants one single piece of information, and in return he'll give us the intelligence prize of the century. You and I will go down in history as the intrepid hunters who netted one of the biggest beasts in the jungle. And HADDAD's request is the easiest thing in the world for us to deliver. We won't even have to get Meredith's agreement. Let's fire off a message to the European network with his wife's details and see where she's registered. Of course, it's possible nothing will come back. A lot of people don't survive the crossing, and not everyone registers with local authorities. But as she's travelling with an infant there's a reasonable chance that she's been forced to access healthcare and in the process provided her details.

Let me know the second you get this information back.

Cheerio,
Lawrence

•••

VESTIBULE/004

TOP SECRET
FOIA EXEMPT

FROM: ATY4
TO: C14B1
SUBJECT: Re: New intelligence lead in Istanbul
DATE: 21 December 2016

Freddy —

There was really no need to go over my head and inform MIT of this case via their London rep. You and I have always been on the same page – different paragraphs, perhaps, but most definitely the same page. If you refer back to my first message on this subject, you will see that I described HADDAD as "slippery, desperate for work, falling over himself to be friendly" and highlighted the presence of "plenty of red flags". That we are now getting confirmation of that assessment – of *my* assessment – as a result of our dialogue with MIT is sound evidence that my operational antennae are bristling, pointed in the right direction and highly sensitive.

(By the way, I see that Meredith has tried to call me a number of times. Can you please make sure that she understands the above? In return I will loudly sing your praises as having been a source of wise counsel throughout.)

We've had a flurry of correspondence from MIT following our meeting with them. They have confirmed that Youssef HADDAD made a call from his mobile phone at 0122 on 15/12/16 to the police emergency number. In the recording a breathless and flustered HADDAD can be heard saying the following (in English):

— Hello? Can you speak Arabic or English? Hello? I need the police to come very quickly, there is a man who is a prisoner in a house. He has escaped now but he said I should call you. He is injured, maybe send a doctor also. I do not know who the other man is, the man who did this. Hello? (HADDAD then switches to Arabic and repeats

the same message, adding the location of the property
and claiming that the prisoner was being held inside a
refrigerator.)

The police responded to the call by sending a patrol car to
the address within the hour. According to MIT, the police
logs show that upon their arrival the officers found an empty
house with no sign of any injured prisoners and concluded it
had been a hoax call. Follow-up attempts to reach HADDAD
on his mobile phone were unsuccessful.

In light of our reporting, MIT sent two of their own officers to the house to conduct a more thorough investigation.
They describe it as a remote four-storey residential property
in a dilapidated state that is located fewer than fifty metres
from the Black Sea shoreline. They note the presence of a
stolen car parked outside the house, but their report focuses
on a room on the top floor which contained an old refrigerator. Various items were found in the room, including a
chain and padlock, an empty bucket and fragments of a
glass bottle. The plastic interior of the fridge was cracked
and broken in places and smeared with what appeared to
be dried blood. The wooden floorboards were also stained
with blood in a number of places, and the officers noted that
someone had partially destroyed one of the interior walls
with a hammer.

Given that the room is clearly a possible crime scene, MIT
will work with the police to carry out a full forensic examination. In the meantime they have requested that we arrange
to see HADDAD as soon as possible in order to allow them
to carry out surveillance on him following the meeting, as a

means of establishing where he lives and who his associates might be.

So we are in a good place, Freddy. Your very reasonable concern that HADDAD might have tried to sell the information about the IS emir to the Turks appears to be unfounded, but I wholeheartedly agree that this incident (whatever it relates to) is very worrying – as is the fact that HADDAD has made no mention of it in his conversations with me. This is exactly the sort of thing I had in mind when I (presciently?) described the red flags fluttering all around this case.

Speak soon, old friend.

Lawrence

••••

VESTIBULE/005

TOP SECRET

FOIA EXEMPT

FROM:	ATY7
TO:	C14B1
SUBJECT:	MIT surveillance report on Youssef HADDAD
DATE:	22 December 2016

We received the below from the MIT liaison officer this morning. Translation is our own. Original available on request, along with their surveillance photographs.

BEGINS

1143: Subject X observed entering Kadem Café Taksim near British Consulate and joining Male 1 at rear of premises.

Comment: Subject X is dressed in dark-grey trousers, thick blue sweater, red patterned tie and loose-fitting black suit jacket with a visible tear on lower right sleeve. He is of Arab appearance, 35–40 years old, slim, 1.75–1.80 m, with short black hair and a thin black beard. He is smoking Anadolu cigarette brand with his left hand. Subject X does not appear observant of his surroundings.

1207: Subject X seen shaking hands with Male 1 before departing the café alone.

1209: Subject X turns left on İstiklal Cd. and walks in northeast direction towards Taksim Square, stopping twice to enter shops (men's clothing and a small grocery). Subject X does not make a purchase in either shop.

1223: Walking at a brisk pace, Subject X goes directly to Taksim Square. He consults his watch repeatedly, finds a bench and waits five minutes. From there he walks to Sultan Ahmed metro station and using a pre-purchased ticket takes the T1 line 2 stops to Sirkeci station, from where he walks to the Mısır Çarşısı (Egyptian Bazaar).

Comment: Subject X waits until last minute before boarding the metro.

1240: Subject X spends approx. 26 minutes walking around the bazaar with no apparent purpose. He inspects items in several shops and stalls. In final shop (large fashion outlet on Âşir Efendi Cd.) he enters via main entrance and after 4 minutes departs via rear entrance.

Comment: at approx. 1255 an officer observes a foreign male (Male 2) seated at a café in the bazaar. Although Male 2 is reading a newspaper and does not appear to be looking around, the officer believes he also saw Male 2 on İstiklal Cd. at approx. 1215 after Subject X departed initial meeting, but cannot be sure because Male 2 is dressed differently on this occasion. However, Male 2 has distinctive wound above left eye and fresh scarring across right cheek that is consistent on both occasions. Male 2 is Caucasian, 35–40 years old, thin, approx. 1.90 m, with medium-length dark hair and a beard. At second sighting he is dressed in blue baseball cap, grey sweatshirt and scarf and dark-green trousers. Covert photograph obtained. Following instructions from team leader, 3 officers redeployed to surveil Male 2. Male 2 leaves café shortly afterwards but within 5 minutes officers lose control of him. Male 2 not observed at any further point during the shift.

1306: Subject X walks at brisk pace from bazaar to Haliç metro station, where he boards bus number 74A and travels directly in direction of Simal Sk. Subject X disembarks and walks to the Museum of Modern Art on Meşrutiyet Cd.

1327: Subject X asks for a glass of water in the museum café and takes a seat. After waiting 25 minutes, Subject X leaves the café, walks out onto the street and looks around. He smokes

2 cigarettes. He then returns to the café but after 5 minutes is asked to leave as he has not purchased anything.

Comment: during this time Subject X checks his watch and looks around frequently.

1415: Subject X walks directly to Şişhane metro station and takes 76D bus to the Fatih neighbourhood. He disembarks next to Sarachane Park, walks to a residential building on Sofular Cd. and takes the lift to the fourth floor. Team takes up positions around the address.

Comment: checks indicate that the apartment on Sofular Cd. is occupied by a number of Syrian nationals resident in Istanbul.

1910: Shift ends. No further sightings.

ENDS

••••

Hello?

Hello?

Is that Youssef?

Why did you not come to meet me? Did I go to the wrong place? You said the Museum of Modern Art, didn't you?

Youssef, listen to me. There's a problem. You were followed away from your meeting with Lawrence.

What do you mean? I did not see anything. Who would want to follow me?

It was a professional team – almost certainly local.

Local? You mean Turkish? What are you talking about? Why are the Turkish authorities involved? August, how do they know about me?

I don't know. They might have been carrying out routine surveillance of Lawrence as a diplomat and out of curiosity decided to see who he was meeting. But that's unlikely, based on the way they behaved. I think you were their main target.

What? I do not understand.

They were waiting for you outside the café where you met Lawrence.

But this means … this means he told them he was meeting me. Why would he do this?

I thought he'd want to keep you to himself a bit longer. But for some reason he must have decided that he needs their help to validate what you're telling him. What's that noise?

It is one of my flatmates – he is always losing his key. August, if Lawrence has told the Turkish police that I have information about Daesh, this is a very big problem.

I know —

I cannot get into trouble with the authorities here. I cannot, August. If a Syrian gets into trouble here, they put him in prison immediately. I cannot stay here, I have to go and find my wife and daughter. It is her third birthday next month, I said —

I know, Youssef, that's why we're doing this. I made you a promise that I would help, and I'll keep that promise.

I could have left Turkey already, I would have found Syrians in other countries very quickly. They will know people in other places, they can ask them about my family. But you said this would be a quick and safe way to find out where they are, August. You said we can trick Lawrence into getting the information for us. You said he would not tell anyone about this until —

That's what I thought would happen.

We did not need to play this stupid game with him.

Let's stay calm. We don't know what's going on yet.

Okay, okay – yes, we need to be calm. Maybe there is not a problem. So the Turkish know that I gave information about Daesh to the British. This is not a problem, this is not a crime.

I'm afraid there's something else, Youssef. I'm pretty sure the surveillance team saw me, too.

What? How did they see you?

They must have spotted me more than once in the same area and drawn the obvious conclusion. I'm sorry. I'm not feeling very well and it's obviously affected —

But what does this mean, that they saw you also?

It's not good. I have a complicated history with Lawrence. He doesn't trust me. If he thinks I'm connected to this, if he thinks I've been helping you behind the scenes and that he's been tricked, he's going to be very angry. He's going to —

Wait, let me open the door for my friend. I will call you back in five minutes.

● ● ● ●

VESTIBULE/006

TOP SECRET

FOIA EXEMPT

FROM: ATY7
TO: C14B1
SUBJECT: Transcript of meeting with MIT and August
          DRUMMOND
DATE: 24 December 2016

BEGINS

ELIF: Okay, introductions. August, may I call you this? Good. My name is Elif, I am the deputy in charge of anti-terrorism investigations in Turkey's National Intelligence Organization. You know Lawrence already. Can I get you anything? It looks like you are in some discomfort.

AUGUST: I'm all right, thank you.

ELIF: There is a serious-looking injury above your eye, some other bruising and scarring on your face, your finger is wrapped in a bandage. Anything else? You are moving in a strange way. Your ribs?

AUGUST: I might have cracked one of them.

ELIF: Have you seen a doctor? Have you had an X-ray? You look very pale.

LAWRENCE: No gestures, August. You'll need to say your answers aloud for the tape recorder.

AUGUST: I'm okay. A bit of a chest infection, perhaps. It's wiped me out.

LAWRENCE: Louder, please. No whispering in here. You're not on a secret mission any more. You're not running around playing cowboys —

ELIF: Okay, okay. Take it easy, gentlemen. August, I am hearing you say that you are well enough to continue with this interview. If that changes, please let me know. Now, I can start by asking you some questions, which is what I would normally do, but I hear from Lawrence that you used to do this for a living, so why don't you save us all some time and just tell me what the hell is going on.

AUGUST: I wouldn't know where to begin. Could you ask a question, just to start me off in the right direction?

ELIF: Okay, fine. Good idea. In fact, I've got a better idea: I'll give you a selection of questions and you can pick which one you want to begin with. Since you're not feeling well. Does that sound fair? Excellent. Let's see. Which laws have you broken since you arrived in Turkey? No, not that one? Okay, okay. What is the prison sentence for engaging in activities in support of a terrorist group? Not that one either? How about this one? On balance, do you think Youssef Haddad is in a better or worse position than you right now? Do you think Youssef

Haddad had a representative of his government sitting in the room to make sure that he was all right when we interviewed him? Do you think Youssef Haddad is happy with his current situation? Do you think — Is something the matter, August? Shall I continue?

AUGUST: Youssef hasn't done anything wrong, Elif. He hasn't broken any laws, he hasn't done anything to harm Turkey's national security. [Sound of coughing.] When he was told about a crime being committed he called the police to report it immediately. He doesn't deserve to be in trouble.

LAWRENCE: Come on, give him some credit, August. You might have been the director, but he was your leading man. It's just a shame that we saw through your little charade straightaway.

AUGUST: You mean his meetings with you? That's a different matter. He might have embarrassed you, Lawrence, but he didn't break any laws.

LAWRENCE: He didn't embarrass me, as I said —

ELIF: Wait, wait, wait. This is my interview. You are here as a courtesy. August, let's have the full story, please.

AUGUST: Where shall I start? I used to work for British intelligence, but you know that already. In fact, Lawrence was there the day I left, weren't you? Can you remember the date? No, my memory's a bit foggy too. Anyway, after a few months I got a job here. And on the flight I saw a young British man behaving strangely. [Sound of coughing.] Something about him reminded me of other Daesh converts I've met. It was obvious he was on edge, pretending to be something he wasn't. When we landed he was immediately detained by your colleagues, Elif, but before they took him away he was able to discard a piece of paper with directions to a meeting place.

LAWRENCE: Wait, this guy was British?

ELIF: William Lewis Evans, 31 years old. Prefers to be called Billy. Or Abu Ahmed Al Biritani, if you look at his Twitter account. He's a bit of a joke, this one. It was his third attempt to get into Turkey. Each time we stop him and send him back. We keep asking your colleagues to do something about him, Lawrence, but they tell us they don't have enough evidence to arrest him. So what next, August? He throws away the piece of paper and...

AUGUST: It had directions on it.

ELIF: And you went there.

AUGUST: I went there. It was a —

LAWRENCE: Hold on, why did you do that? Why didn't you just hand the piece of paper to the authorities at the airport?

AUGUST: It seemed like a good idea at the time.

LAWRENCE: What? Speak up – I can barely hear you.

ELIF: Come on, August. Tell the story, please.

AUGUST: I thought there might be a message waiting for Billy. Or some money, or directions to a meeting place. I really don't know. I was curious. It was only when I got there that I found that someone was waiting for him. An Iraqi man – a Daesh facilitator, or at least that's what I assumed. He seemed to have some sort of arrangement with Billy that he'd get him across the border into Syria. I was in a difficult position. [Sound of coughing.] Billy and I don't look too unlike, give or take ten years. We both have dark hair, we're both tall. So I went along with it. The man gave me a phone, said he'd be in touch. My plan at this point, Elif, was to wait until I had something solid to pass on and then get in touch with you through Lawrence and his colleagues.

ELIF: But you knew this was a stupid idea, right?

AUGUST: Can I have some water?

ELIF: Help yourself. I mean, it's about the stupidest idea I've ever heard. You had no idea who this man was, you had no idea if he was dangerous, you had no idea if we were already following him around.

AUGUST: I was looking for distraction. I guess that blinded me to how stupid it was. Anyway, as I said, I went along with it. He tried to delay things, and when I got impatient he told me there was another thing I could help out with while I was waiting. He said there was an Iranian scientist in Istanbul, and he asked me to follow him around.

ELIF: Okay. So Daesh asks you to follow an Iranian scientist around a foreign city and you say yes. Why not? As long as it keeps you from getting bored.

AUGUST: Then he told me that I should travel to the border area —

ELIF: Wait, wait – the Iranian. What did you do? I assume you understood that they probably would want to kill him.

AUGUST: I followed him to a warehouse. Another time I searched his hotel room. That was it. But he doesn't exist, Elif – there is no Iranian. It was just the Daesh guy pretending to be an Iranian scientist to keep me busy. I'd told him I was in such a hurry to get across the border that he must have come up with this whole Iranian scientist scenario just to make me think I was doing something worthwhile here. I know it sounds… Then the whole border thing happened. He called one morning and told me to go to Gaziantep immediately. I stalled and eventually talked him into meeting me just outside Istanbul at this empty house I'd been to for work. I guess you know the place I mean. But when I got there he pulled a knife on me and locked me inside a fridge. [Sound of coughing.]

LAWRENCE: For God's sake drink some more water.

AUGUST: He tried to sell me to Daesh as a hostage. But it's clear that he's not with them any more. They've had some sort of falling-out. You know who he is, right?

LAWRENCE: Let us worry about that. Can you explain why he would be kidnapping hostages for them if they've fallen out?

AUGUST: My best guess? He finds himself on the run in Turkey with nothing – no money, no friends, no papers, no way out of the country. So he goes online, creates an Instagram account, pretends to be a facilitator or radicalizer and starts fishing for a gullible white convert in Europe who wants to get into Syria. He knows that as far as IS are concerned, any white British hostage would be hugely valuable – the person doesn't have to be famous or important. All that matters is that he can pass them off as a non-Muslim. And he finds Billy. He tells him to fly here, shave his beard, dress like a tourist and lie low while he negotiates the money with his former friends in Daesh. It's a clever plan, when you think about it. Using a social media account to net a valuable asset. It's not perfect, but he was working with nothing. And it worked, two Daesh guys came to the house to do the deal. The beauty of it is that Billy does all the hard work – if things had gone to plan he would even have transported himself to the border to be sold. The only reason it didn't work was Youssef. He got me out of the house.

ELIF: And the Daesh guy?

AUGUST: He left in a hurry. He had a small boat moored fifty metres from the shore. Listen, Youssef has done both of you a big favour. If it wasn't for him, Lawrence, you'd be dealing with another hostage in Syria, and the Turkish government would be trying to explain how all this had happened under their noses.

LAWRENCE: If you'd left it there, maybe. But then you told him to approach me with a fabricated story about a friend of his who runs errands for IS.

AUGUST: Everything Youssef told you is true. Every fact he gave you about the emir is true – his appearance, his age, his links to the UK. None of that was fabricated. I wanted you to have that information so you could work with Elif to catch him.

LAWRENCE: If he's even in Turkey. There's nothing to say that you didn't just take a handful of facts you remember from when you worked for us and make the whole story up.

AUGUST: I made up the context, that's all. I'm admitting that. The facts are all true.

ELIF: Why did you do that?

AUGUST: Make up the context? Youssef is trying to find his wife and daughter. [Sound of coughing.] I thought that if I gave him this information and created a way for him to use it, he could find out in return from Lawrence where his family are. I owed him that, especially after what he did for me. Look, I can see that I've made some huge mistakes, Elif. The only thing I ask is that you don't punish Youssef for things that I've done.

LAWRENCE: It's a bit late for that.

AUGUST: Did you find out where his wife is?

LAWRENCE: I'm not going to answer that. To be frank with you, August, I find it very hard to believe anything you say. It would take more time than we have today to untangle this ridiculous story. And I imagine Elif feels the same. There's absolutely no evidence that —

AUGUST: It's not as though you didn't know any of this before today, Lawrence.

LAWRENCE: What do you mean?

AUGUST: I called you the night I was going to the house to meet him. [Sound of coughing.] There'll be a record of that call. And then you came to the house to look for me. You spoke to the Daesh guy.

ELIF: You went to the house? You didn't —

LAWRENCE: I was going to mention this. August left a long and frankly incomprehensible voicemail about needing to see me. I went out of my way to go and check he was okay, but I didn't find him. End of story. Listen —

AUGUST: That was the second time you went there. I assume you've told Elif about the first time.

ELIF: There was a first time?

AUGUST: He had a … proposal for me. Is that what you'd call it, Lawrence? He wanted me to look into a sensitive matter for —

LAWRENCE: It was nothing, just old acquaintances catching up.

ELIF: You haven't been running round doing secret things without telling us, have you, Lawrence?

LAWRENCE: Of course not.

AUGUST: We've gone off-track a bit. We were talking about Youssef's wife, weren't we? Where she is now?

LAWRENCE: In a town called Altenburg. Not far from Leipzig. Not that he'll be able to do much with that information from a prison cell.

ELIF: What are you two doing?

LAWRENCE: What do you mean?

ELIF: Do not treat me like an idiot, Lawrence.

LAWRENCE: I wouldn't dream of it. I went to the house and spoke to a caretaker and didn't see or hear anything that raised my suspicions. That's the extent of my involvement in this.

AUGUST: He's right, Elif, that's the whole story.

ELIF: Bullshit. And the money?

AUGUST: What money?

ELIF: What money? You said that two Daesh guys came to the house to do the deal. Those are your words. I assume they brought money with them. But we didn't find any in the house, and you said your captor left in a hurry.

AUGUST: I imagine he took it with him.

ELIF: That's what you imagine, is it?

AUGUST: Look, can we talk about Youssef and what's going to happen to him? He really hasn't done anything wrong. He wasn't involved in any of the stupid things I did. Please, Elif. He shouldn't be punished for something he had absolutely no responsibility for or involvement —

LAWRENCE: Nonsense, you're both up to your necks in this —

ELIF: Enough. Stop talking, everyone. I am reaching the conclusion that we could sit here all day and things would not become clearer than they are right now. And August, I'm not sure you're going to be able to sit upright for much longer. So let me summarize. Firstly, we have a handful of alleged facts about a former Daesh emir who may or may not be in Turkey. We file this information, August, and we wait to see what happens. What else can we do? If he is here, thanks to you we have no idea where he is or what he is doing. Secondly, we have a Syrian national who was aware of some of this and chose not to make a full statement to the police. Instead he played this game of yours, August, and went to Lawrence with a made-up story. Okay, a partly made-up story. But that changes nothing. You should have done this differently. I am afraid that he is currently in detention and he will remain in detention. We do not want people like this running around free in Turkey.

AUGUST: But —

ELIF: Thirdly, we have a former British spy who has admitted here today to breaking the law many times. In ordinary circumstances we would arrest you, August. But the British ambassador has already been on the phone to the minister to say that he would be grateful if this matter could be cleared up quietly, and we have enough problems without creating a diplomatic incident. So, your visa will expire in seven days. Before that date you will leave the country. If you remain here after that date, you will be here illegally and you will be arrested, whatever the British ambassador says. My suggestion is that you eat a big Turkish meal, have a good night of sleep, go to the airport in the morning and never come back. You will need to see a doctor, this is obvious. You may need to see someone else, after the things you have experienced. Do you know that your hands are shaking? I have some sympathy for you. I am angry with you, but I have some sympathy for you. But you need to leave Turkey quickly. And if, God forbid, you see someone behaving strangely on the plane home? My advice is that you ignore it. Is that clear?

LAWRENCE: Hear, hear. Can I say, Elif, you have handled this whole thing magnificently, both in terms —

ELIF: This meeting is over.

ENDS

••••

VESTIBULE/007

TOP SECRET
FOIA EXEMPT

FROM:	C14B1
TO:	ATY4
SUBJECT:	Closure of VESTIBULE
DATE:	24 December 2016

Lawrence,

We have taken the decision to close Operation VESTIBULE. This is clearly the right thing to do given recent events. If additional, more credible intelligence about the alleged former IS emir comes to light, we will consider in Head Office the best way to proceed and notify those who need to be involved. It is unlikely you will be among them.

VESTIBULE will go down as one of our shorter operations, and it is one that we would all like to forget as quickly as possible. A few brief points, if I may.

Firstly, the transcript of your meeting with DRUMMOND

and MIT this morning does not show you in your best light. You must already know that you did not represent us in the manner we would expect. For this reason, you are formally restricted to Station duties until further notice.

Secondly, we are puzzled by the reference in the transcript to your first visit to the house under discussion, during which it is stated that you asked DRUMMOND to "look into a sensitive matter" on your behalf. Is this a reference to your recent proposal that DRUMMOND should be recruited as an agent to collect intelligence about Beatrice's alleged embezzlement of government funds? You may recall that when you raised this with Head Office we firmly rejected the idea. There was no good reason to engage with DRUMMOND, given his recent behaviour. It is unthinkable that the relatively trivial matter of Endgame Consulting's finances would be justification enough for us to engage with a former officer who stands accused of such serious misconduct. Furthermore, it is clear that your unauthorized contact with DRUMMOND has complicated the relationship with MIT. Please forward us your written record of this meeting at the first opportunity.

Thirdly, on this subject, it is clear that DRUMMOND is unwell and in need of medical and most likely psychiatric help following recent events. Our interest in this is twofold: that he is a former officer to whom we maintain a duty of care; and that in his present condition he clearly continues to pose a threat to British intelligence. For both these reasons we would like him to return to the UK as soon as possible. Obviously we cannot force him to do anything against his will, but if you have any further contact with him we would like you to encourage him to leave Turkey immediately.

Finally, Meredith has repeatedly tried to call you, without success. She has asked me to tell you that she considers it a matter of regret, given your excellent work in the Gatekeeping team, that in recent weeks your behaviour has fallen short of the high ethical standards we demand of our officers. When you are next in London she will want to discuss VESTIBULE with you in some detail. She may well also have views on your next posting.

Warmest regards, and with best wishes from us all for a merry Christmas.

Frederick

PART FOUR

Ego

DAY 1

This is no way to spend Christmas Day. I am lying on a bed in a room on the third floor of the two-star Hotel Turkish Delight in the Galata neighbourhood of Istanbul. I am forty-one years old and six foot three in my socks but I am wearing my shoes because it is my intention to leave the hotel at the first opportunity, but on five separate occasions over the past three hours I have stood up, walked to the door and failed to open it, as though it was locked, but I know it's not locked, and so I am lying here trying to understand what is happening. At first I thought the door was locked. I assumed that the tremor in my hand and this quickness of breath were signs of exertion, of the physical effort of trying to force open a door inexplicably locked overnight by Elif or Lawrence or… After all, I have been unwell recently, so it's not unreasonable to expect that I might struggle with everyday tasks. But I've since learned that the door is not the problem. I know this because ten minutes ago the cleaner stepped into the room, a bin bag gripped tightly in her murderous fist, took one look at the tearful figure on the bed and hurried out. So the door is not the problem, we can all agree on that. Which means I am the problem. I am the thing that is locked.

DAY 2

It's no long-term solution but it might just be enough to get me out the door. After spending a long night tangled in the wreckage of a calamitous four-way pile-up of grief, addiction, trauma and guilt, I need to consider all options, however dramatic they appear, otherwise I might never walk free. Look at it this way. There is information it is safe to release into the public domain and information that should remain classified because of its potential to cause harm. This is common sense. In the same way, there are some thoughts it is safe for me to have and there are other thoughts that cause me huge distress. There are things I just can't afford to look at right now, because they tip me into a downward spiral that can take hours to recover from. For example, it would be acceptable – uncomfortable, perhaps, but acceptable – to admit I am experiencing a craving that makes my hands shake, that makes me vomit, but there is nothing to be gained from going further than this and stating that above all else what I want is a tall cold glass of straight ▮▮. Saying that word would help no one. Likewise, it would be fine to say that certain physical injuries are causing me discomfort, but there is simply no need to catalogue every ▮▮▮, ▮▮

and ▮▮▮▮▮▮▮. And while it might be a statement of the obvious to say that I can't close my eyes without seeing the face of the ▮▮▮, what good can possibly come of saying his name out loud?

If this is censorship, it is censorship of the most benign and necessary sort – akin to blacking out details of troop movements in letters home from the front. There will be time to relax into a Scandinavian-style liberal democracy in which anything can be said – all grievances aired, all wounds healed – once this particular existential crisis has passed. Until then, I am on a war footing. Until then, I will not permit any mention of ▮▮▮, of the guilt I feel towards ▮▮▮, of the ▮▮▮, of the appalling ▮▮▮▮▮▮▮▮▮▮▮▮▮▮▮▮▮▮▮▮▮▮ in that house. It doesn't matter how harmless the thought might at first appear. A harmless thought might just be the thin end of the wedge, and it should come as no surprise to anyone that the thin end of the wedge, positioned correctly and with the right amount of pressure applied, can very quickly be turned into an instrument of ▮▮▮ as lethal as any ▮▮▮ or ▮▮▮.

Having said that, I don't want to rush into anything. I don't know how long I'll be able to keep this going. This morning I made it onto the landing, this afternoon I got as far as the lobby. And I was contemplating a stroll (neither word quite right) down the street this evening when Lawrence came to visit. He stood outside and knocked at my door – intermittently, apologetically – for over ten minutes. In between he talked.

"August, are you all right? Is there anything I can get

you? Fancy a ▮▮▮? Just say the word – I can easily call down and have them bring us a couple of cold ▮▮▮. Listen, I can imagine the meeting with MIT must have been horrendous. I'm really sorry we didn't get a chance to speak properly afterwards. Elif's a tough nut, don't you think? Anyway, having had the opportunity to reflect on things, I can see that they've treated your friend ▮▮▮ very harshly, and I wanted to reassure you that we will be working night and day behind the scenes to persuade them to show leniency."

He's got one of those sonorous musical voices that somehow retains the shape of the instrument it emerges from, like a trombone. As I listened to him, I knew with certainty that he was leaning against the wall, that his brow was furrowed, that he was checking his phone or his fingernails.

"We're here to help you back onto your feet. In practical terms that means a plane ticket to London and a cottage in the countryside for as long as you need it. We'll lay on the best doctors, and if you decide you want to speak to someone about the horrible things you've been through – and who can blame you, after your experience in that ▮▮▮▮▮▮▮▮▮▮, as well as what happened to ▮▮▮ – we'll find the right person and give the two of you the space and time needed to work through it all."

Space and time. Like a god he plucks them loose from the universe and offers them as his gift. I really do admire his self-belief. No matter how badly he behaves one day, he wakes up the next with unshakeable confidence in his ability to persuade you that he is on your side. I don't know whether this makes him a psychopath or just good agent-handler material.

"And in case you're worried about your safety with that ████ on the loose, you can be reassured by the fact that Elif has put a few of her guys around the hotel. They're trying their best to be discreet, but with the kind of training you and I have had it isn't difficult to spot them. There's a young guy in the lobby getting bored of his newspaper, and a couple of goons with leather jackets and moustaches making eyes at each other from opposite sides of the street outside, and then a fourth chap hanging a bit further back. I suspect he's the one in charge – better at his job, a bit older, but tough-looking with it. No doubt Elif's got someone at the front desk reporting to her too. Anyway, the point is that there's a friendly shield wrapped around you, August, and it'll stay there until you board the plane. There's absolutely no prospect of anyone getting through, however skilful they might believe themselves to be. In fact, the best thing for all concerned would be if you let me drive you to the airport right now. That way Elif's guys can go back to hunting down the ████, and we can go back to persuading her to release your friend ████. It'd put her in a much better mood if we were able to report back that you'd followed her instructions and left the country. After all, *that's* how we're going to get leniency, *that's* how we're going to get ████ released – by playing ball. Really, August, with only six days left on your visa, there's nothing you can do other than leave. What do you say?"

Lawrence is replaced by dusk, like a changing of the guard. Later comes the night shift. In packs of two or three they roam abandoned corridors – unshaven, dead-eyed, looking for new ways to be cruel.

DAY 3

Dawn arrives in its gleaming uniform, and with it the certainty that I can't survive another night like that, and the knowledge that censorship can only ever take you so far. It might work (to develop the military analogy) if what you want to conceal is something minor and specific, such as the rank of an officer or the location of a landing point. But it's wholly insufficient to the task if what you want to hide is the fact that *there's a war going on out there.* I leave the hotel at a trot and find what I am looking for three streets away.

The bell above the door jangles nervously.

He doesn't appear surprised to hear such an urgent request at that hour of the morning.

"Calm down," he says. "I need to ask a few questions first. What exactly is the problem?"

"I want something to help me relax."

"Please." He holds up a hand to slow things down. "In what way?"

"I need to … flatten things out. In my head."

"I do not understand."

"It's like a room full of sharp edges. I keep on bumping into things."

His eyes go to the bruises and cuts, to the bandaged finger, to the way I grip my side.

"It certainly looks as though you have been bumping into things."

"I don't mind this so much. I can deal with the physical pain."

"You are talking about psychological pain."

"Yes."

"Are you sleeping?"

"No."

"Eating?"

"I'm not hungry."

"Alcohol? Drugs?"

"I'm clean."

"Why is your hand shaking?"

"I don't know. I'm pretty tired. Look, please, I just need something to help me find my balance. The world's gone a bit wobbly."

The bell above the door rings again. A young man who just a few moments ago was seated in the corner of the hotel lobby has rushed in and is now breathlessly examining a shelf filled with bottles of sun lotion.

"Of course there are things I can give you," says the pharmacist, eyeing his new customer with suspicion. "But I am not sure this is what you need. It will be better if you speak to a doctor before thinking about medication, given the nature of your problem. Do you have family or friends with you?"

"I only have four days left."

"What do you mean? What happens in four days?"

"I have four days to make things right. I need something that will allow me to be normal for four days."

"What will you do in these four days?"

"Find someone."

"And after that?"

"I can be as crazy as I like."

He shakes his head and starts to say something.

"I'm joking," I tell him quickly. "I'm only joking. Crazy people don't make jokes, do they? Look, after four days I'll speak to a doctor. I give you my word."

He considers the situation for a full minute before disappearing among his shelves.

"This affects people in different ways," he says, placing a small white box on the counter. "It may take several attempts to find the right dosage. Start with half a tablet at mealtimes, no more. If it does not allow you to do what you want, try a smaller or larger amount by one quarter of a tablet. But be careful – this is a temporary solution, do you understand? If you have ever had any problems with addiction —"

"I'm very grateful. More than I can say."

"There is enough here for four days. Come back after that. I cannot give you more of this, but there may be other things that will help."

"Thank you for listening to me."

"Have you eaten breakfast yet? I have some —"

Even the bell above the door sounds relieved.

At the time I didn't know how much I meant it when I thanked him for listening to me, but it turns out that he *really* listened to me, because within minutes of getting back to the hotel and swallowing a tablet I feel completely flat, exactly as I requested, but not in a bad way, and softened to the extent that the things causing me such distress just an hour ago have suddenly lost their ability to hurt me, despite retaining their sharpness, by which I mean that I can still see every edge and line and point with astonishing clarity. The vizier, the abandoned house, the puddles of plum-red blood; Youssef locked in a detention centre many hundreds of miles away from his wife and daughter; the craving for a drink – these things might all be features of someone else's story for all the significance they possess.

Just as surprising is that Lawrence's inevitable return doesn't prompt any irritation.

"Hello? August? Hello?" He coos at me through the door as if I am a baby. "I've brought you a coffee. I'll leave it outside your door, unless you feel ready for a chat. Your call, mate."

Even the memory of Martha's death evokes no particular feeling. I take another step forward, curious to test the boundaries of the medication, curious to see how far I can go before hearing the click of a landmine underfoot.

"Elif's goons are still in place, you'll be pleased to hear," Lawrence is saying. "The guy in the lobby looks a bit hot and bothered, as though he's been for a run around the block. You haven't left the hotel this morning, have you, August? I couldn't see the older man, but it might still be a bit early for him."

It really does appear that an entire emotional landscape has been declared safe: the coroner's photographs,

Martha's diaries, the birthday present I found hidden among her clothes.

"Any thoughts on when you want to leave? You can't be comfortable here. It's a funny old hotel, don't you think? There was a blind man checking in downstairs. I imagine he's their ideal guest – no complaints from *him* about cobwebs and peeling walls. But you could really do a lot better than this."

The terrain quickly becomes hostile – ravines, a cliff face, an impassable river – but it feels as though I am floating above it all. And it isn't long before I stumble upon a conversation with Martha just a month before she died. She is asking me to help her plan a protest against a visit to London by the Egyptian Minister of Justice. She is giddy with excitement at the thought of what we can achieve together. Not just the usual ineffectual placard-waving, she explains, but something that will take political protest to a new level: a personal note pushed under the door of the minister's hotel room, loudspeakers concealed in the embassy gardens that interrupt a reception to broadcast the names of imprisoned journalists, an impassioned speech delivered from a neighbouring table in his favourite Mayfair restaurant. She has dozens more ideas. Her favourite involves someone – she suggests with a giggle that I should do this, that the costume will allow me to remain incognito – dressed as a clown who appears mysteriously wherever the minister goes. She's even bought a wig for me to try on. There is a real possibility, she says, that the media spotlight will compel the regime to release one or two of their more high-profile prisoners. And all that's needed is an advance copy of his itinerary. But before she has even finished speaking I am shaking my head. There's simply no way I can help. The Egyptians will complain, and her involvement will mean that the leak is traced back to me immediately. The only resistance she offers is to suggest in a quiet voice that this might be a suitable parting gesture to a job I've come to hate, but I interrupt to explain why this isn't the right time, and she leans forward and kisses me and says that she understands.

Then I find myself sitting in the back row of the coroner's inquest watching CCTV footage of a woman on a bicycle stopping at a traffic light alongside a black Mercedes with a diplomatic number plate. She reaches into the basket in front of her for an A4-sized piece of paper and carefully places it on the rear of the car. The driver and his passengers aren't expecting this; she is able to place a second, third and fourth piece of paper onto the car by the time someone gets out and approaches her to see what is happening. He reaches for a piece of paper but discovers it is stuck on, and by this time the lights have changed and the cars around them are beginning to sound their horns, so he makes a half-hearted attempt to wave her away before getting back in and driving away quickly as the lights turn red.

But rush hour is against them, and minutes later she comes into view again, on a different camera, this time scattering a crowd of pedestrians on the pavement as she races towards the car. She has a piece of paper ready in her hand, but the driver sees her coming and begins to nose forward, so she has to weave between the traffic and lean forward with one arm outstretched to get close enough to slap a piece of paper onto the rear left window in the seconds before they pull away.

It takes her another ten minutes to find them, or to catch up. By now the passenger has opened his window and is trying to remove the piece of paper stuck there, but when he sees her coming and tries to close the window the paper jams the mechanism and keeps the window open. The woman leans down and speaks to him. She appears animated. His hand comes out and grabs her hair and pulls her roughly towards the car so that her head slams into the door, but she takes hold of his wrist with both hands and gives it a sharp twist in a move I remember teaching her, and the man quickly lets go.

There is a sixth piece of paper and a seventh piece of paper. By now the back of the car is beginning to look more white than black. She is clearly tiring. By the time they approach King's Cross she is weaving recklessly through the traffic and shaking her fist and shouting at the car when it gets away from her. A stream of obscenities filthy enough to turn the air blue, claims one eyewitness, but a second says it was simply a list of Arabic names. One thing they agree on is that there was no suggestion of wrongdoing on the part of the minister's driver. The car is at least five metres clear when she is pulled underneath the lorry. And the remaining papers in the basket fall out onto the street, and for a while pictures of imprisoned and murdered journalists swirl around in the breeze before attaching themselves to the surface of the road, to a lamp post, to a puddle of blood, even to the blanket covering a homeless man asleep in a nearby doorway.

Lawrence has gone. The only noise I can hear is the steady ticking of a cane on the stairs outside.

And the last coherent thought that occurs to me before I fall asleep, and the first coherent thought I've had in three days, is that it seems odd they would give a blind man a room on the third floor.

DAY 4

It's dark outside by the time I wake up, a full thirty-seven hours later. I feel calm, clear-headed, hollow with hunger. The only thing I take with me is a rucksack. In the hotel lobby the young man half-asleep on the sofa tosses aside his newspaper and scrambles to his feet but then doesn't know what to do with himself when I stop at the front desk to tell them I'll be leaving in the morning. The checklist of questions would do credit to a five-star hotel: what time will I be checking out, will I have any bags, where will I be going, do I have a flight booked, have I fully recovered from my illness, can they expect to see me again?

The night is cold and cloudless and the narrow cobbled street is quiet. My first objective is to let the team fall into a routine and get used to me as a surveillance target – to my height, build, clothing, silhouette and gait. After three long days sitting around with very little to do, it's essential they quickly feel they have the situation under control. The last thing I want is to alarm them into calling in reinforcements – that is, until it's too late. And I need it for myself, too, this chance to stretch my legs and swing my arms and fill my lungs with air and walk off any last trace of the drug in my bloodstream. It takes about half an hour to reach the restaurant, and before ordering food I take a seat near the window in order to be easily observed from any number of vantage points on the street.

By the time the meal arrives I am confident that in addition to the young man from the lobby there are at least four others: a dark, lean man in a tracksuit who follows me into the restaurant and takes a seat at the back beside the toilets; two men in their early forties, both running to fat, bored by the assignment and clearly of the opinion that it won't require any particular expertise; and a fourth man on a moped who parks opposite the restaurant and begins to play a game on his phone. The decision to keep the young man out of my line of sight suggests that their intention is to be covert, rather than to intimidate me into staying in the hotel. This must be why Elif gave me seven days rather than ordering me to leave immediately – she must have concluded she'd been lied to in our meeting and hoped that surveillance would shed some light on what I'd really been doing. After forty minutes I signal my imminent departure with some elaborate waving for the bill and a long pause on the steps outside to take my bearings.

It takes another hour to confirm that there are two others: one behind the wheel of a black Toyota Corolla – a short taxi ride draws him into the open – and the other a man in his early fifties who appears to be coordinating the team and staying in contact with his superiors via a collection of mobile phones so large that when someone calls him he frequently reaches for the wrong pocket. This man interests me – at various points in the evening I am able to engineer sightings of him in the Toyota, on the back of the moped and on foot; he takes his turn behind me just like everyone else. He is often engaged in angry conversation. I don't know how many officers Elif will have assigned to this task. Even if it's just the seven I've identified this is going to be difficult. They know the ground intimately, and if they get the vaguest of hints that I'm going to do something unexpected they'll draw the net around me so tightly that it'll never work. I have one chance to get this right.

In my favour is the fact that this team is unusually consistent in its use of tradecraft. Over the course of the evening I lead them through all types of urban environment, from busy markets to the metro to quiet residential streets, and they stick rigidly to certain rules – about formation, about use of cover, about distance. Also in my favour is the fact that the team – like every other surveillance team – is a living thing with a character all its own. It might follow a set of rules, but within those rules it expresses its uniqueness in hundreds of small decisions about risk: how long to leave an officer in a static position, whether to send someone into an unknown premises behind a target, how often to alter physical appearance over the course of a shift. Two teams following the same SOPs can behave in markedly different ways, and the single biggest factor in determining this is the personality and judgement of the leader.

By midnight I have learned all sorts of things about this team, but only three of them are going to be of any use: that the officer behind me rotates every fifteen minutes precisely, regardless of what is happening at that moment; that when operating on foot in a quiet area they leave an air gap of between twelve and eighteen seconds between the first two officers; and that the team leader is a proud, officious and unpopular man.

They are also susceptible to incorrect assumptions. And so just before the open-air market closes I buy a box of baklava and an alarm clock in the shape of the Blue Mosque and begin to walk back in the direction of the hotel. The closer we get, the more convinced they will be that they know exactly where I am going and that soon afterwards their shift will come to a welcome end. The quickest route back would take less than twenty minutes, but I build in a diversion to ensure that the team leader is in pole position at the right moment.

The road ahead is quiet and wide and brightly lit, and there is an obvious right turn towards the hotel a hundred metres ahead. But I take an earlier turning into a narrow street lined with restaurants that even at this late hour are open and busy. As soon as I have turned out of sight I take several long steps – people would turn to look at someone running – into the open doorway of a building and press myself into the shadows. Exactly on time the team leader comes around the corner, his back and neck stretched upwards for a better view and his head lighthousing to re-establish my whereabouts. His pace quickens as he skirts small clusters of diners saying their goodbyes on the street. He is only ten metres past my position and still in clear sight when – counting down the seconds on my watch – I step out and walk across the street and into an alleyway. This is only the first part of my escape: as soon as they realize they've lost me I have to anticipate they will call in reinforcements, and vehicles will begin to sweep the neighbouring streets, and cameras will be checked. What the team leader should have done as soon as he rounded the corner was alert his team to my possible disappearance, which would have allowed them all to close in. But my gamble is that because of his status and character he will be more reluctant than any of his colleagues to call in the loss of control, and that this will give me valuable extra minutes to get clear of the area.

I zigzag away, keeping to a steady pace. After a certain period of time the only way they'll be able to find me is by examining camera footage, and it's incredibly hard to find one person when it's dark and busy and everyone is walking at the same speed. If my judgement is correct, at this minute the team leader will be hurrying towards the front desk to ask whether I've gone up to my room, and ordering them to send someone upstairs to confirm this, and considering the best way to frame this unfortunate sequence of events to his subordinates and to Elif. I cut away into a residential area, changing direction frequently and pausing every ten minutes to confirm I'm not being followed. The ground-floor windows on both sides of the narrow street are protected by metal bars, and it feels as though I am walking down a long prison corridor. But there's no need to rush at this point. I have a strangely calm feeling that the events of this night have already been set in motion and will follow in the necessary order whatever I might wish to do, like the opening moves of a chess game before the confusion and sacrifice that must inevitably follow.

By the time I reach the cemetery it's after one o'clock. The black metal gate groans and scrapes as I slip through into a kind of liquid darkness in which the only discernible movement is of trees, of grass, of clouds scudding across the night sky. I follow the path in a slow arc in the direction of the north-eastern corner until a small clearing near the middle. The earth is damp from yesterday's rain and comes up easily in my hands.

The hole is half a metre deep before I hear anything.

"I am surprised you buried it here."

He sounds unhurried, as though he has been considering the situation for a while.

"It makes little sense," he says, stepping out of the shadows. In the last ten days he has lost weight. I can smell the sweat on him from fifteen paces. "To come back to the place we used to meet."

It comes as a shock, after everything that has happened, to recall my first impression of this man, that the most dangerous thing about him, beyond the physical power, beyond the total indifference to what another person is experiencing, beyond even the metal object glittering at this moment between the closed fingers of his left hand – the most dangerous thing about him is his mind. It wastes no time in stepping into your space.

"There is no one else here," he says. "You made sure of that."

It forces you into a corner, it leans into you, it presses the air from your lungs.

"Is this a trap?" he asks.

"Not in the way you think."

He considers the possibilities.

"What do *you* think?" he asks.

"I think you're in the right place."

"That doesn't sound good."

"What do you mean?"

"If you think I am in the right place then almost certainly I am in the wrong place."

He takes a step towards me. There's something to be admired about a person whose response to the realization they're in the wrong place is to step forward.

"I think you would have enjoyed it, at the end, watching their surveillance team run in circles," he says. "You left it very late. By that point I was also certain that you were returning to the hotel."

"Were you getting your white cane ready? Would you have come knocking at my door tonight?"

"I searched your room yesterday. I know it is not in there."

"Yesterday? You didn't think of waking me up to ask?"

"You do not remember? I tried to wake you up. I was … ready. But perhaps it is fortunate that you were sleeping. It would have been noisy, certainly, and we both know they had a man in the lobby downstairs. All it would have taken was another guest walking past the room at the wrong moment."

"I'm not sure sleeping is the right word."

"I understand why you would not keep it in your hotel room. But I find it difficult to believe that it is here."

"Yet you've come."

"When I saw them running around I thought it was finished. That you had disappeared, that you would head for the border immediately. This is the last place I thought you would be. But it was the only possible place in the whole city I could look. You knew that. You knew that I would come here." He takes another step forward. "What about them? Do they know about this place?"

"I didn't tell them."

"Good."

"I know that if you'd seen any sign of them around here you'd have disappeared forever."

"So we do not have to hurry. Where is it?"

"The money?"

He smiles. "Yes, the money."

"It's not here."

"I can see that. But you know where it is?"

"You're not having it."

"That was not my question."

"I'm just trying to save you time."

"Ah, you English," he says, stepping forward again. "Always so considerate."

He relaxes the fingers of his left hand and from inside his sleeve a metal spike slides down until the point is level with his knee.

"Can you imagine how many times someone has refused to tell me what I want to know? For a while this was everything I did. You have no idea what is possible."

"I have some idea."

"What?" He smiles. "Oh, in the house? That was nothing."

"Do you think the money is in, I don't know, let's say locker number 36 in the train station, waiting for someone to come along and help themselves to it? Or do you think it might be somewhere completely inaccessible?"

"Shall we find out?"

"I've got this, just to complicate things." I lift a kitchen knife from the rucksack at my feet.

"This is not the complication you think it is."

"You might be right."

"I know what British spies are like. I have met plenty of them over the years. You are gentlemen. You like talking, you like a glass of whisky by the fireside, you like creating and solving puzzles, like everything is a crossword in a newspaper. You never had to fight to survive. But to grow up in a poor family in Iraq under Saddam Hussein? Every day you have to fight. Every day until I was eighteen either someone beat me or I beat them. It is like breathing. My father put out his cigarettes on me if I disobeyed him. In school the teachers hit me with their belts to make me behave, in the military they beat me with sticks to make me disciplined, in prison they tortured me because they were bored. None of this is unusual. It is the same with everyone I know. I was fifteen when I killed a man for the first time. You think you have put me in a difficult situation. But this man had a knife, just like you. He was trying to steal bread from my father's bakery. So you must understand that I have been in a position worse than this a hundred times."

"You've misunderstood. You're not in a bad position."

"Where is the money?"

"You're in the best possible position given your circumstances."

"And you are in the worst possible position. It is unthinkable for a sane person to have chosen this. But here we are. I will ask you one more time."

"Haven't you worked it out yet? What this is about?"

"I can see only one possibility. But it does not make sense. You said you no longer worked for them."

"I don't. I'm … freelancing."

"It makes no difference. I am giving you an opportunity to realize that this is a mistake, and to understand that you can still give me what I want and walk away. So let me tell you something that you need to know. The last time an Englishman asked me to work for him I stabbed him in the eye with a beer bottle."

"Well, times change."

He throws back his head and laughs soundlessly.

For a while he doesn't move. Then he looks around. He is working something out.

"The first time I saw him he wanted to talk about football," he says, taking half a step to one side. "Then it was horses, then it was cricket, then it was politics. What was the name of the pub? The Duke of York, something like this. St Ann's Terrace, not far from Regent's Park. It was a long time ago, perhaps the autumn of 1994. We were both young men. His name was Charles. It did not matter that I wouldn't talk to him. Every Sunday evening he was there, trying to buy me a drink. He always wore the same elegant brown suit. Sometimes he would unfold his newspaper on the bar and talk about which horse was going to come second at Cheltenham or the massacre in Rwanda or arguments between the Iraqi government and the UN. And at some point in the evening, after I had finished my drink, I would leave the pub and walk home – even if he was still in the middle of a sentence. Of course, I knew who he was. I had been told that this would happen at some point, as it happened to everyone, and the important thing was to be polite, listen to him, deny any knowledge of secret matters and refuse to cooperate. The most I should do, if he was extremely persistent, was threaten to lodge a formal complaint with the Foreign Office. But I was not about to complain – there is something enjoyable about meeting your adversary, hearing him talk. And Charles was good at talking. He had been on holiday to Jordan with his wife the year before and spoke a few words of Arabic. I remember he was reading a book by T. E. Lawrence. Until then my experience of British intelligence had been limited to trying to identify their surveillance teams, who were very skilful, far better than anything we had in Iraq."

He takes a step forward. Red tape has been lovingly wrapped around one end of the metal spike to fashion a handle, while the other end taps against his knee.

"Then one evening he said that he had a question about my superior, a fat, venal man from Mosul who had only been posted to London because his brother-in-law was senior in the ministry. I expect that he knew I hated him and thought the betrayal would be easier as a result. All he wanted to know was where this man was planning to go on holiday that Christmas – something unimportant, something that he could have found out a hundred different ways. He pushed his newspaper across the bar towards me and said with a smile that there was an article I would enjoy on page eight. I could see a bulge in the paper, like an envelope was hidden there. It was the *Racing Post*, I think. He was proud of this detail. He said, if you ever get asked, if they ever squeeze you, tell them the money is your winnings. Tell them you have developed an interest in the horses. He said that he would be waiting for me the following Sunday at eight o'clock, and that from now onwards he would buy the drinks."

By now he is five paces away. At no point do his eyes leave me. His skin is pale in the moonlight and rainwater from the trees speckles his black shirt.

"What could I do?" He shrugs and smiles. "In a way I regretted that it was coming to an end. I warned him that I was a proud Iraqi and that as a people we have a reputation for being hostile towards outsiders who try to control us. Do you know what he did then? I remember it like yesterday. He leaned across the bar and tapped my empty glass of beer and said, let me top this up. It can be another one of our secrets, he said, that you enjoy the occasional drink. Something else we keep from your masters.

"I am not sure what happened after that. In those days I had a real temper. But whatever it was, it caused me lots of problems. To evade the police and get out of the country I had to use an escape route built for our most important agent. In Baghdad they were angry with me. I knew they would not understand the truth, so I didn't tell them that the man was an intelligence officer trying to recruit me. Instead I said that he was a drunk who had tried to attack me and that I had been forced to defend myself. But the truth was that I felt a sense of outrage that he could possibly believe *this* was power, that he could tell my corrupt boss who slept with prostitutes and beat his wife that I drank a glass of beer on Sunday nights, and that *this* gave *him* power over *me*. I could not believe it. I still cannot believe it. The night before that, I had followed a man into an abandoned railway tunnel and pressed my fingers around his throat until his neck snapped like a piece of dead wood, and here was this elegant man in his brown suit and his cufflinks and his silk handkerchief demonstrating what he thought was power. And in that moment I simply thought, no: let me show you what the world is *really* like."

Before he's finished speaking he takes a step forward and lifts his left arm out to the side. He's still too far away to do any harm. But as he begins to swing the metal spike through the air towards me I can see that momentum is sliding it down from his sleeve between his fingers, and it's much longer than I realized, looped at the end with a piece of rope. I am still turning away when it hits the back of my head and tears open a long hot cut under my hair.

"Where is the money?" he says.

He puts his hand through the loop to secure it. My one advantage was height and reach but he's neutralized that with the spike. When it hangs from his hand the point is long enough to draw a line in the earth. He takes hold of the end and steps forward and jabs it like a spear at the top half of my left leg. It misses but he pulls it back and moves forward for another attempt. I circle away from him. He's not trying to kill me, not yet. He's just trying to stop me getting away.

This time it rips open my trouser leg, but the wound is superficial.

"Where is the money?" he says.

I swing at him with the knife and try to back away but the length of the metal spike allows him to keep a safe distance. He jabs it again and again at my legs, trying to bring me down. This can't continue. Each time, the rope tugs at his wrist like a dog at the end of its chain. That's his mistake, if he's made one. That it's tied to his wrist. If anything happens to that arm it'll be useless as a weapon. He rushes forward again. And this time I don't back away but instead step forward and switch the knife to my other hand, hoping that the spike doesn't hit an artery in my leg, as I slash downwards across his outstretched forearm as hard as I can.

I know the vizier is close because I can hear him. Even above the wind he struggles to move quietly. His breathing is laboured and his blood gleams like metal on leaves, on the bark of a tree, marking the route he has taken. I cut a strap free from the rucksack and tie it around my leg to slow the bleeding. Everything else can wait – the flesh wound down my back, the bite mark in my ear, two broken hands. "You always surprise me," I call out. "I never know what to expect. I didn't think it would be this difficult." Something moves to my left. I rush towards the noise, stabbing at the undergrowth with the metal spike. He scrambles away noisily into the darkness. "It doesn't matter now, so I can tell you what I really thought." I stop to let the pounding of blood in my ears settle. I feel dangerously light-headed. "Here's a man who's already betrayed his country by joining Daesh," I call out, "and now he's betrayed them as well. There's nothing harder than recruiting someone who actually *believes* in their country. But Daesh have broken him in like a horse and from now on he'll accept anyone's saddle. They've cured him of any nationalistic bullshit. I thought the last thing I'd hear from you is talk of loyalty or pride. In fact, it's hard to imagine anyone more suited to what I was going to propose." There's a scuffling noise, followed by silence. "You're the embodiment of self-interest. You're the perfect traitor – the perfect agent." A shadow moves between the gravestones, less than three metres away. I hold out the knife and rush in his direction and a rock comes hurtling through the darkness. It barely misses my head. "I never even got the chance to list the advantages of changing sides: that you'd be allowed to live, that people would pay you lots of money, that they'd get you out of Turkey, that in time you'd be allowed enough freedom to rebuild your life." I pick up the rock and throw it back in his direction. "It makes me look like a sentimental fool, but when you were telling your story about the man in the brown suit, I even thought, why don't we arrange to meet in another twenty-five years to see how things have panned out? The Duke of York, was it? A Sunday evening at eight? We'd both have been old men by then, so I'd carry a copy of the *Racing Post* under one arm to help you recognize me. You could have told me whether you'd made the right decision, and I was so confident you'd think it had been that I was going to promise you could stick a beer bottle in my eye if you regretted it." He's trapped – I'm on one side, the cemetery wall is on the other. The only way out is a patch of open ground, but he knows I'll bring him down before he gets halfway across. I take a step towards him and suddenly I can see his shape in the darkness. There's no longer any need to raise my voice. "But none of that's going to happen, is it? Even if I let you out of here alive, you'd be in prison within the week. There's no way you could survive on the run with no money and no one to help you. Look at you – you're already starving. And now you've got injuries that need to be treated. It was one thing when nobody knew you were here and you could wander around as you pleased. But the Turks know about you, the Americans know about you, the British know about you. You won't be able to get into Europe. And if you go in the other direction your friends in Daesh will want to know why you stole their money." I reach out the metal spike. His flesh is soft to the touch. He's breathing heavily and the smell of his sweat is overpowering. He raises his head to speak.

DAY 5

"It's pretty around here."

"I can never tell when you're joking, August."

"What's that one called?"

"I suppose you didn't come here as a tourist."

"I've lost count of the number of people who've told me which sights to see. Is it the Blue Mosque?"

Elif sighs. "He's late," she says. "Do you think he'll turn up?"

It turns out a shrug engages significantly with bruised muscle, with torn skin, with a headache. By the end I'm not even sure it's recognizable as a shrug.

"I don't know."

We're sitting on a bench near Sultan Ahmed Square. The light rain is keeping most people away.

Elif glances across at me. "I hope you're going to see a doctor. Either here or in London. I won't ask what happened to your hands."

I hide them in the pockets of my raincoat. "Are you keeping him yourself to ask a few questions first, or handing him straight to Lawrence?"

"To be honest with you," she says, "I'm not sure Lawrence

is allowed to speak to me any more. There are rumours he's been reassigned."

"Probably a good thing. They'll want the heavy hitters to deal with this, and he's been out of his depth for a while. Who's been sent in his place?"

"Why do you ask?"

"I was wondering what to expect."

"Nothing very much. We sit and wait. If he turns up, they take him away. If he doesn't, we take you away. That's about it."

"Who did you speak to, Elif?"

She shrugs. She's better at it than I am.

"Oh, I see."

She's better than me at most things, it turns out. I'm surprised it took me so long to get there.

"What?" she says. But she's smiling.

"You've pulled a last-minute switcheroo, as your new friends would say. It's very diplomatic of you to keep quiet about it. Honestly, though, it's fine with me."

"Do you remember what you said on the phone, August? You said, imagine his value if he agrees to cooperate. Imagine his value if he spills chapter and verse about the internal workings of IS. Imagine all the secrets he could tell. You told me to think big. Those were your words. Well, that's what I did. The Americans simply have a lot more to offer than you British."

"Listen, I'm sure it makes sense. As long as our deal stands."

"Your friend will be released tomorrow morning. You have my word."

"Is he okay?"

She shrugs again. "These are not … comfortable places."

"As long as Youssef is alive and can walk," I tell her, "you can hand the other guy to the Iranians with my blessing."

"There may not be that much difference. The Americans made it clear to me that they're not going to go easy on him. I mean, they're not planning to throw him in Guantánamo. But he's going to have to work very hard to convince them he's sincere and not just looking for a way out of a tight spot. He's going to have to answer every one of their questions and confess every last secret. Then they'll start with the lie detector tests."

"Good. It'd stick in my throat if he landed in clover."

"The CIA man they've sent doesn't seem to mess around."

"He'll have his hands full."

"If your guy wants the Virginia farmhouse and white picket fence he's going to be giving lectures to the new intake at Langley for the next twenty-five years."

"Twenty-five years? Imagine that, if he turns up in a baseball cap, speaking with an American accent."

"Turns up where?"

"Nothing."

"Do you think he'll be willing to cooperate with them?" she asks.

"You know what? To be completely honest with you, I wouldn't have thought so. But then again, take a look at that."

The figure limping towards us through the light rain is dressed in a jacket and tie. The right side of his face is badly bruised. Elif gets to her feet and holds up a hand to keep him at a distance. He doesn't acknowledge my presence. Three men get out of a large black Suburban parked thirty metres away. Two of them approach the vizier and perform an impressively quick, thorough and discreet search. The third, a short Chinese-American man, leans against the car with his arms folded, watching events and smiling broadly. As the vizier is led towards the car, I can hear him say to the man waiting for him, "There's nothing like an American car for power and..." but the end of the sentence is lost in the noise of traffic. Whatever he says makes the man leaning against the car laugh. He opens a reinforced rear door. Before they disappear from sight I see the vizier laughing, his teeth bared, and for a brief moment he looks directly at me.

Elif turns and buttons up her coat. "The thing about seven days hasn't changed," she says. "That wasn't part of our deal. You have to leave by midnight the day after tomorrow or you'll be arrested."

"Can I ask you a question? Off the record?"

"What?"

"You'd like us all gone and out of your hair for good, right?"

"What do you think?"

"Now that the Americans have taken the Daesh emir, and that by all accounts Lawrence is going to be recalled to London before long, that just leaves me and Youssef."

"What's your point?" she asks.

"I can go to the airport and get on a flight to London."

"I wish you would."

"It's not so easy for Youssef."

"Where's this going, August?"

"In theory, if you wanted to find someone reliable with a boat who could do a run to Greece, where would you look?"

"Are you really asking me that question?"

"Yes."

She shakes her head. "In theory? And strictly between us? There is a man called Ibrahim who runs a salvage yard on the Asian side of the Bosphorus Bridge. He's mostly retired, but if you can pay enough then he's the person I'd trust. Why? What are you going to do?"

DAY 6

We meet at a ferry terminal late in the afternoon. He's lost weight and the tremor in his hand has got worse.

"They let you keep the tie," I say.

"I had to hide it in my shoe."

"It seems that everyone's wearing one these days. I'm beginning to feel seriously underdressed."

"You always look terrible," says Youssef. "A tie is not going to change that."

"Here, take this." I press the rucksack on him.

"What happened to your hands?" he asks.

"Take it."

"What is it?"

He opens the rucksack and takes out a waterproof plastic container.

"Put it away," I tell him. "You'll know best, but it might be sensible to divide it up and hide it in several places. It's in different currencies."

"This is a lot of money." He looks at me. "How much is there? I'll pay you back."

"It's not my money. Believe me, it's much better off with you than with its original owners." He starts to speak, but I hold up a hand to stop him. "We haven't got long and there are things to discuss. This is the name of the guy taking you to Greece tonight."

"What?"

"It's all arranged and paid for. He's meeting you at ten – don't be late. And don't annoy him. He seemed like a good guy, I think he'll get you there in one piece, but I don't want him to throw you overboard because you get on his nerves."

"If he has met you and he is still willing —"

"There are a few other things in here you may need," I tell him. "Maps, a first-aid kit, cigarettes, sea-sickness pills, three phone handsets, an emergency space blanket —"

"Like an astronaut —"

"— and I've made a list of lawyers and NGOs who help asylum seekers in the countries along the way."

"It is like my mother has packed a bag. Why are there so many maps of Germany?"

"Why do you think? Your wife and daughter are in a town called Altenburg, near Leipzig. The quickest way to get there —"

"What? They are alive?" He starts to cry.

"There's no time for that, Youssef. Come on, pull yourself together. The authorities have let you go, but I can't guarantee they won't change their minds. And you've got a ferry to catch."

He starts to put everything back into the rucksack.

"What's this?" he asks.

"Oh, just a bad joke. You remember, 'They took some honey, and plenty of money —'"

"'— wrapped up in a five-pound note.' You have put a jar of honey in the bag for me?"

"I don't know what I was thinking, it'll just weigh you down. Better leave that with me."

"No chance, dickhead. Get your own honey."

The ferry horn sounds.

"Okay, Youssef. Time to go."

"What about you? What are you going to do?"

DAY 7

It's not that I don't want to leave. There's certainly nothing to keep me in Istanbul any longer – no job, no vizier, no Youssef. And I have no illusions about the desirability of even a single night spent in a Turkish prison. I'm almost at the bottom of this particular rabbit hole, and although I don't expect to emerge into bright midday sunshine, I have sensed a slight shift in the intensity of the darkness around me that allows for the possibility, no more than that, of warmth and light. That's all I want – to feel warmth and light again. On the bedside table are four bottles of beer, no doubt a gift from Lawrence, and the small box of pills from the neighbourhood pharmacy. But I know that the light they provide will be fluorescent and the warmth will be temporary and the truth is that I feel just about well enough without their help for this last thing I have to do.

It's going to be difficult to slip away from the hotel unnoticed, though, despite the crowds of people on the streets celebrating New Year's Eve. Elif might have said she'd give me until midnight, but by eight o'clock I've had two calls from reception to ask whether I need any help with my bags. By ten it's turning into a quasi-military operation out there. The black Corolla is parked in plain sight opposite, and when its tracksuited driver emerges – first for cigarettes, then for coffee – he glares at my third-floor window with no attempt to conceal his hostility. Every thirty minutes the team leader patrols the street to check everyone is in place. There can be no mistakes this time. I can't begin to imagine how crowded the lobby must be.

Everything is laid out on the bed. But in view of what's happening outside I'm going to have to adapt the plan, and so instead of hiding it all away in the rucksack I put it on now, in the hope it'll act as a crude disguise of sorts, except for the shoes, which I'll carry under my arm until I get there. It'd be hard to walk in the shoes. The door hinges squeak but to my relief there's no one on the landing. Two voices – male, authoritative, bored – float upwards from the floor below. I climb the stairs in my socks to the padlocked metal door at the top of the hotel. It takes less than a minute to open, and then I'm out under a startlingly clear night sky. To be honest, I'm surprised it's been this easy – I'm surprised they didn't anticipate that I might try to escape over the rooftops. The only person who seems to have been expecting this is the old lady standing at the window of her apartment across the street, whose reaction to the sight of a grown man dressed in red spotted trousers, braces, a bow tie and a multicoloured wig is to wave, as though she's seen far stranger things up here than a clown.

The first thing I have to do is find a way down. After that I'll have to trust my sense of direction and hope that I can lose myself in the crowds, just another partygoer in fancy dress. I've studied the maps and I have a fair idea how to get to the prison. As for what exactly to do once I'm there, well, I assume the one thing every prison will have is walls, and in one pocket I've got a bundle of rolled-up photographs of detained journalists that I printed this afternoon, and in the other a pot of glue, so I'm hoping that events will take care of themselves once I get there. It's not the most painstaking plan ever devised, but then I wouldn't claim that I'm thinking particularly clearly today. I know I won't have it all my own way. I remember Martha telling me in our first conversation about a protest she helped organize outside the Bakırköy women's prison in the south of the city, and so I imagine they'll be used to this kind of thing – there'll be cameras, there'll be police. It is a prison after all. If only it wasn't so hard to run in these shoes. The clown suit was her idea, though, and if I'm going to do this then it feels only right that I do it the way she wanted.

But it turns out my escape from the hotel hasn't been as neatly executed as I thought. The metal door clatters open and suddenly three men are standing less than ten paces away, including the surveillance team leader, with an expression on his face that turns from anger to confusion as he sees how I'm dressed. We all stand there, unsure what to do next. One of my socks has a hole in the big toe, and the trousers barely reach my shins, and the bow tie has slid around to the back of my neck. I straighten the wig. A mobile phone starts ringing. He searches his pockets for the culprit, puts it to his ear and in the silence I can hear Elif shouting at him down the line. He tries to explain what is happening and she shouts even louder. I sympathize with him, that's the truth. What can he do? Should I offer to speak to her? I want to tell her that I'm sorry, that everything is all right, that Youssef is on his way to find his daughter, that the world can be a surprisingly beautiful place, that I'm willing to accept this might be the beginning of a long-overdue nervous breakdown. Church bells peal at the approach of midnight and a faraway ship's horn sounds on the water. The sky fills with swirling snow. The old woman watching from her window breaks the impasse for us. Drawing her pea-green dressing gown around her, she launches into an angry tirade in Turkish at the three men and then turns to me. "What are *you* waiting for?" she says, and since I don't have a good answer I start to run. I don't know if this is what she meant. But for the first time in a very long while I feel that I am doing something straightforwardly good, that this is something I won't regret, that in some new and unexpected way this is me. The men are shouting. There are another ten metres to the edge. In the darkness it's hard to see how far it is beyond that to the next rooftop, or how long the drop is to the street below, but just when I start to feel afraid and think of slowing down I remember Martha, pedalling fearlessly on her bicycle, and as I finally come to the edge I tighten my grip on the clown shoes, and with my other hand I reach out for her, and together we jump.